THE KNOCK-KNOCK MAN

Also by Russell Mardell

Cold Calling
Darkshines Seven
Bleeker Hill
Stone Bleeding
Silent Bombs Falling on Green Grass

RUSSELL MARDELL

THE KNOCK-KNOCK MAN

IF YOU HEAR HIM
IT MAY ALREADY BE
TOO LATE

Red Door

Published by RedDoor
www.reddoorpress.co.uk

ISBN 978-1-915194-01-5

A CIP catalogue record for this book is available from the British Library

Cover design: Patrick Knowles

Typesetting: Jen Parker, Fuzzy Flamingo
www.fuzzyflamingo.co.uk

For Dad

Knock! Knock!
Don't look him in the eye
Run! Hide!
Or you may die
Knock! Knock!
Don't take his hand
He will lead you to hell
This is the devil's land

(Children's rhyme, circa 1970s.
Orig. Chillman Grove)

Prologue

The problem was, the boy had said that he had seen a ghost. Where do you go from there? That was the question that Ernie kept returning to as his life slowly ebbed away.

Perhaps if the boy hadn't told Ali about The Knock-Knock Man, and had Ali not then told Ernie, then the face they had seen that night in the woods could have been put down to a vivid imagination. Maybe the whole sorry mess could have ended at the Deveraux estate with the zip of body bags.

Maybe.

But the boy, Jake, months dead himself now, had said what he had said, and then Ali and Ernie had seen what they had seen. There was no going back after that. That moment wasn't an ending to the awful events at Lord Deveraux's estate; it was the start of a whole new story, and now that Ernie had the truth of that night, it seemed it was time for him to bow out, bent and broken on a dirty linoleum floor.

He barely gave his own demise any thought at all. His life hadn't flashed before his eyes as he fell, and even now, as he lay prone on the floor, it all felt slightly ridiculous to him. He could sense his right leg jutting out to the side at an impossible angle, as shattered as his back, but he couldn't turn his head to look. He was sure the wetness seeping from his left ear was blood, but he couldn't move a hand to wipe it away. The tip of the index finger on his right hand was motionless against the cracked screen of his mobile phone. He wondered if the call had connected before the phone broke. He wondered if Ali could hear him breathing his last.

His vision was blurring now, images seemed overlaid and distorted. The blackness of the building rising above him held back a myriad of shapes, but occasionally they drifted and bloomed out of the shadows, and if he looked long enough, hard enough, those shapes would be figures, and those figures would all become the same person.

He thought of two more things before he died. He thought of his dear friend, Ali, and his guilt at not telling her the truth of that night when he had the chance. More than anything, he wished he had done that. Not to give her closure, at least not anymore, but to give her a warning. Then, before darkness drew down, and Ernie finally let go, another thought came to him as soft as a whisper. It was the same thought he'd had every day for the last fifteen months.

I don't believe in ghosts.

It seemed a little stupid now.

Chapter 1

The past is sneaky; it tries to creep back in through the gaps we leave in our present.

Ali Davenport's counsellor had said a lot of things like that to her over the eight sessions they'd had together and, bargain basement philosophy though it may have been, that particular piece of wisdom had hit a little close. That she had spent the whole hour being pushed back to that terrible night fifteen months ago hadn't helped; being reminded of those awful mistakes she had made that had stripped her of everything she had always wanted to be, sending the bones of her life tumbling away, only to end up here. London.

You're a fugitive from your own life, Ali.

He'd said that too, and on that he was probably right as well. Having escaped from a town that seemed to know your every move, a place where your history was etched into every expression you wore, and your secrets were never buried deep enough, London was the perfect place to run away to. London made it easier to be invisible.

Usually.

Ali had felt the little girl's eyes on her from the moment

she and her mother had got on the tube at Tottenham Court Road. Ali had returned the look, fleetingly, and had found the little girl a smile from an old and dusty place. The girl didn't return it.

Ali looked away, feigning interest in the shoes of the lady opposite her, and then at the dried chewing gum on the floor, her left hand now at her face, index finger rubbing at her eyebrow as the palm shielded the ugly semicircular scar around her left eye. She turned her attention to the adverts just above the window then, as the girl continued to stare, a smiling man was making an irresistible offer, a very pretty woman was telling you how she did it. Slogans were shouting, faces were cartoon and empty, dead behind the eyes. Someone had put a sticker across one poster, which read: *The World is Upside Down. Please shake after use.* Euston came and went, and then as Camden Town became Kentish Town the girl and her mother gathered their bags and left the carriage.

Ali settled back in her seat and became invisible again.

Leaves danced around her boots, the sharp November wind setting a frantic tempo as Ali walked the tree-lined residential streets of Highgate. Evening stole in all around her, curtains were drawn and streetlights flickered on. She pulled her coat more tightly around her body and quickened her pace. An old poppy seller was still diligently standing his spot on Muswell Hill Broadway and Ali fed some coins into his tin and took a poppy, pinning it to the lapel of her coat. The man offered his thanks and said she was a kind young lady. Ali informed him that she was forty and then carried on walking, head down.

The raggedy, battle-scarred ginger tomcat that had been

visiting Ali for the past month was sitting on the windowsill of her ground floor flat, cleaning itself. It sprang to life at the sound of her boots on the pathway and slinked up to greet her with a cat's casual coolness. The man who had been perched on the windowsill next to it followed a moment later.

'Hello, Ali.'

DC Frank Gage was a man whose every word seemed to be delivered on the end of a laugh. It was a trait that had annoyed Ali since the first day Gage had transferred to New Salstone. Gage went in for a half-hug and they ended up bumping shoulders. She gently pushed him away.

'Ernie?' Ali asked.

'You've heard?'

'Two weeks, Frank. Two weeks! No one thinks to tell me?'

'It was your decision to fall off the grid.'

'You could have found me. You could have tried.' Ali stared back at her old colleague for the first time in months; Gage's impeccable beard and hair, his short, compact frame bound up in the famous white linen suit jacket that he always seemed to wear, whatever the weather, were all still in place. Yet Frank Gage looked different somehow, like a caricature, an approximation of the man she used to know. 'Thanks for the personal touch, Frank. But a phone call would have done. Sorry you've had a wasted journey.'

'That's not why I'm here. I need your help.'

'Things must be bad.'

Gage gave a weak smile and nodded towards the house. 'Could use a cup of tea as well.'

The smell of weed was thick in the communal hall; Steph in the first flat was clearly home. Across the hall, Archie was playing his old 78s again, big band stuff usually, but today something a little jazzier, a little filthier. The cat took them across the hall, and then under the small archway next to the stairs, down the narrow corridor at the back of the house that had necessitated Ali bringing her meagre furniture in through the window, and then they were at the door to her flat.

Every time Ali walked into her poky one-bedroom flat it felt smaller. Jen, who had helped Ali find it, had called it a flat – a garden flat, no less – but really it was little more than a bedsit hiding in some creative wording. It didn't help the sense of creeping claustrophobia that Ali rarely cleaned, that her belongings were piled high on three shelves and the dining table, and that she never put her fold-out bed back against the wall, but still that room – her pathetic world – was one small place. And now it stank of cat.

'How have you been?' Gage moved a couple of dirty T-shirts from Ali's bed and gingerly took a seat on the edge. His sad gaze around the room gave more of an answer than her non-committal grunt.

A sun-bleached and creased photo of a much younger Ali was Blu-Tacked to the wall next to the bed. She was standing on a beach, smiling wide and bright for the camera, a fake plastic police helmet at a slant on her head, a crudely mocked-up warrant card in her hand, held up in front of her. Her father knelt at her side, flashing his own smile, and his much more real warrant card.

Gage leaned in for a better look. 'The legendary DCI Davenport, I assume? You look like him there.'

Ali turned away and flicked out a dismissive hand. 'Yeah.'

'Didn't expect to see a photo of him on your wall.'

'Why not? He's my Dad. I love him.'

'You've finally forgiven him then?'

Ali shrugged. 'I said I love him. Didn't say I liked him.'

The cat began weaving around the dining table; its erect tail feathering the edge of the tablecloth. The purr was loud and demanding and as it pushed itself between Ali's legs she felt claws through her trousers. She opened the cupboard above the two-ring stove and retrieved one of the cans of tuna she had in there, ran a tin opener around it and then upended the contents onto the plastic welcome mat that had once been a gift from her landlord, and now served as the cat's dinner plate. It made a certain sense – until today, the cat was the only visitor she'd ever had.

As the kettle boiled, Ali crossed to the table next to the bed that she jokingly thought of as her office desk. The business cards she'd had made were still scattered where she had left them in a rage after finding that the printers had misspelled the word *investigator.* **A. Davenport – Invetigator** they now read. 'Investigator of what?' the printer had asked. 'Anything,' had been her honest reply. She swept them under a pile of paper, out of Gage's sight, and took a seat on the table.

'How did you find out?' Gage asked.

'I still check the *Salstone Gazette* website from time to time. When I can't sleep. How did he do it?'

Gage stared at Ali for a moment. He seemed to be scrutinising her, looking for something. Eventually he nodded to himself and then gave a long, overly dramatic sigh. 'He took a jump. He'd been working night security in an old office building in New Salstone. Fourth floor. He…well, you don't need a picture.'

Something in Ali's gut seemed to fold in on itself and her breath caught in her chest. A memory dislodged somewhere inside of her, an image trying to assemble itself in a clumsy mind that didn't want to hold it. She shook it away and rose slowly from the table, turning her back on Gage before catching her reflection in a small, oval mirror hanging at a slant on the wall. As always, the scar was the only thing she saw, it was the only thing anyone ever saw.

Ali lowered her head and let her fringe flop down and cover it. Tears threatened, pricking the corners of her eyes. She took a hand to her mouth and closed her eyes, battling the tears and a sudden wave of nausea.

'He called me,' she mumbled through her hand. 'I had a missed call from him in the middle of the night. The night he did it.'

'I know.'

Ali pulled her hand from her mouth and thumped the table.

'Don't do that to yourself.'

Ali suddenly spun around, her face flushed with grief and a rising anger. 'What are you doing here, Frank? I'm not going back there. That's not it, is it?'

'Funeral is next week. I would have thought you'd want to go?'

'I don't need to be there to grieve for him.'

Gage calmly stood and crossed to the kettle, setting about filling the cleanest mugs he could find with teabags and milk. Ali was instantly reminded of Ernie's swift judgement of Frank Gage, delivered on Gage's first day at the station: 'He puts the milk in first, Ali. We will never truly be friends.' On any other day, she would have smiled at the recollection.

'Everyone knows Ernie wasn't the same since that night at the Deveraux estate,' Gage said. 'Neither of you were. I know what it took from you both. You kept in touch, didn't you?

After you left New Salstone? Guess you must have known him better than most. He struggled being away from the job. You know he was on some pretty heavy antidepressants?'

Ali did, but she didn't say so. They had both spent time curled up with the black dog during the past fifteen months. Gage didn't need to know.

'Why does it feel like you're interviewing me, Frank?'

Gage held up a placating hand. 'Not at all, Ali. Not at all.'

'You don't think it was suicide.'

'It was. Of that I'm sure.'

'Someone isn't. Right?'

Gage fell silent as he filled the mugs from the kettle. When he spoke again, the light bounce had completely fallen away from his words. 'Ernie told you about Maggie? His lady friend?'

'Didn't give details, but he seemed happy. Why? She's questioning what happened? Is that it?'

'She is.'

'She thinks it wasn't suicide?'

'She thinks he was killed. But he wasn't, Ali. He wasn't.' Gage handed her a mug of tea and then returned to sit on the bed. 'I know Maggie, a little anyway. She's an old friend of my wife. They were at college together. I know her and I like her, but I also think she's a bit of a crackpot. I think she's so befuddled with grief that she can't allow herself to accept that Ernie would do what he did. Finding something, anything, that can move the blame somewhere else, would always be preferable. It was suicide, Ali. No evidence of foul play, no evidence of anyone else. The building was all locked up from the inside.'

'Couldn't have been an accident?'

'Could have been, but unlikely. He went over the railings on the fourth floor, forensics is suggesting. No real reason why Ernie needed to be up there at all.'

'Who does Maggie think killed him?'

'He killed himself. There was no one else.'

'That's not what I asked.'

Gage cupped his hands around his mug and gazed at the carpet. 'Friend of mine, Nate Dalton, owns the building where Ernie worked. Going to be flats one day, probably. If he can sell it. He's already had two possibles pull out this week.'

'Because of what happened?'

'Because of Maggie. Because of her crazy talk. She's been getting right up Dalton's nose, turning up at his office at all hours, shouting and screaming at him, phoning the interested buyers, spinning her fairy tales and freaking them out. She's talked to the press as well, she used to be a journo, and she's still got connections that will indulge her. She's got no shame, doesn't care if people laugh at her and call her nuts. It's got to stop. Dalton needs her to accept the truth. My wife needs her to accept the truth too, and therefore, so do I. I need you to help me do that.'

'I don't understand where you're going with this. What does Maggie think happened? And what the hell has it got to do with me?'

To Ali, Gage looked like a chided little boy in that moment, his compact frame seeming to shrivel into his white linen jacket, his head tilting forward as if he were about to bow, his eyes looking anywhere, everywhere, except at her. He took several delicate sips of tea before speaking again, and when he did the words fell out of his mouth in a gabble.

'That night. You and Ernie. What you both saw at the

Deveraux estate. What the kid saw. The man. The ghost. Whatever. What the boy called The Knock-Knock Man. Maggie's convinced that he's come back.' Gage finally dragged his gaze from the floor and met Ali's eyes. 'She thinks he killed Ernie.'

Ali felt a familiar tightness in her body, as if something was falling through her, dragging her back on to the table, and then further, carrying her through the varnished wood and wrestling her to the floor. She didn't know how to respond to Gage, whether to scream, or cry or laugh.

'Sounds like she needs a copper, Frank, and I'm not one any more.' Ali rested her mug on the table and crossed to the door to her flat, opening it wide. 'You seem to forget that I resigned because everyone thought I was mad.'

'You resigned through stress.'

'Stress? If you like, they give it a different name depending on the audience. I don't believe in ghosts, Frank. And I'm not going back there. You're talking to the wrong person. Good to see you and all that, but goodbye.'

'Dalton will pay. Good money. Two grand, he says.'

'Pay me for what?'

'Work Ernie's night shifts until the end of the week. Debunk Maggie's story. Tell her she's mistaken. Tell her there's nothing in that building. No ghosts, no ghouls, no bogeyman. Make her understand that Ernie jumped.'

Ali's breath caught in her chest again as a stubborn memory shook itself loose and started to come into focus.

'Do you realise how absurd this all sounds? You do, right?'

'Please, Ali.'

'Why don't you do it?'

'Because she's only going to believe you, isn't she?

Because of Ernie, because of what you meant to him, because of what you went through. What you saw.'

'What did we see?'

'A ghost, you said.'

'A fifteen-year-old boy said it was a ghost. Jake. A child. Not me. Not Ernie. And I'm done having this conversation. I'm not going back there, Frank.'

'You can't outrun it, Ali. What happened.' Gage stood and finished his tea in two big gulps. 'No matter how long you keep running away.' Gage drew level with her in the doorway and passed her the mug. 'A few days, that's all I'm asking. Maybe a week. Think about it.'

Ali closed the door behind him and stared at the well-fed ginger tomcat that had now taken Gage's place on her bed. Old memories screamed inside her mind, fully formed and impossible to ignore, like a missing reel of film that had just been waiting for a light to go on in her eyes so it could be seen: Reverend McGregor calling Ali and Ernie out to a fight between two workmen on the scaffolding around St Francis' bell tower, and Ernie stopping halfway up, unable to move, his face as white as a sheet; then the time part of a bridge collapsed after heavy flooding, and they had gone to secure the road and stop anyone from going across it, yet Ernie wouldn't go anywhere near the gaping hole, hanging back by the squad car; now she was laughing with her old team as her dear friend, tasked with putting the star on top of the Christmas tree at the front of the station, was so unstable on the ladder that he ended up falling into the tree.

Ali felt sick. *How the hell did I not remember that?*

'Ernie was scared of heights,' Ali told the cat. 'Terrified. Absolutely terrified.'

Wildness passed over her eyes, blooming and then fading

like the dying embers of a fire ignited briefly on the wind. A single tear trickled out of her left eye and down her cheek. The middle finger of her left hand halted its journey and then drew up her face, wiping its tracks away. Then it was as if it had never been there in the first place.

It took her less than three minutes to fill a tatty old rucksack with spare clothes and a few toiletries, and usher the cat out of the flat. Later she would stop and think about the sadness of that, but not right then.

Chapter 2

Fifteen months earlier

The night can move around you. You can make it alive if you have a mind to.

That was what Ernie Lipkiss had said to Ali on their first evening call out together, so many years ago, his soft Scottish burr diluting the implied warning in the words. Back then, at the start of their friendship, Ernie had been withdrawn and wounded; divorced from his wife, estranged from his daughter, and relocated to the wilds of Wiltshire, about as far away from his home as he could get.

Day-by-day, week-by-week, Ali would watch Ernie growing into his new life, the weight on his shoulders easing, and Ali had hoped she had a hand in that transformation. Theirs was an instant friendship, a logical entwining of like minds that always seemed to have been there, somewhere. Despite only being ten years her senior, somewhere along the line Ernie had tried on the father figure role too, and liked the way it fitted. Ali didn't discourage it. They were placeholder family for each other, but neither ever articulated the fact.

That first call out together had taken them from New Salstone to Hanging Twitch, a few miles north. It had been nothing more than a few kids vandalising the old bridge out of town with sticks and makeshift clubs: one had thrown a rusted oil drum over the side; another had sworn at old Mrs Boden as she was returning home with her dog after its evening constitutional. Ali and Ernie had told the kids off, made a note of their names and given a few stern warnings that they would tell their parents, and that had seemed to do the trick.

Ali had told Ernie later that it was probably as exciting as Hanging Twitch was ever going to get. *It's a place in the fold of every map*, her father, the estimable DCI Davenport, always used to say. Nothing ever happened there. At least, that was what she had always assumed.

The night can move around you. You can make it alive if you have a mind to.

Ernie's words came back to Ali on the night of the madness at Lord Deveraux's estate. When she got the call she had been parked up by the side of the main road through Hanging Twitch, watching the driver she'd pulled over crawl slowly away in his car, his smashed tail light glaring at her like something demonic; a clinical brightness encased in jagged red teeth. Across from the squad car, Tanner was closing up the off-licence (general store, people in Hanging Twitch preferred to call it) and he proffered a friendly wave to Ali, which she returned on instinct.

'Hey, Ali-cat, you there?' Ernie's voice crackled through her radio.

She had been Ali-cat to him ever since she broke up a fight in their local pub in New Salstone. The Haven had decided to partake in a real ale festival one year and things had got a bit tasty between two old friends whose argument had spilt over to the alleyway outside. One had made the mistake of throwing a beer bottle at Ali as she tried to separate them. The other had been even more foolish and laid a punch on her. The two old friends left town the next day with two broken fingers, a scratched face and a black eye between them. Ernie hadn't bothered to contradict the assumption, as the men sobered up in the cells the next morning, that each had inflicted the other's injuries.

'Clocked off, I'm going home.'

'You still in The Twitch? We need you up at Lord Deveraux's place. I'm heading there now with Taylor.'

'What's happening, Ern?'

'Just had a phone call from Mrs Somers out in The Oaks. Says she was coming in to pick up her fella and she's convinced herself she's heard people screaming out near the woods around the Deveraux estate. Well and truly spooked herself, she has.'

'Somers?'

'Aye, that's Councillor Somers to you and me, kid. Told the chief we'd do a drive through, see what we see.'

'On my way.' Ali moved out into the evening, the darkness folding over her car.

The housing became sparser and then soon fell away altogether, and with it any sort of definition to the surroundings. Fields spread out on either side of the narrow, winding lanes, but a stranger wouldn't have known that. It was as if everything, except the part of the road picked out by the squad car's headlights, was smothered in black treacle. Ali crested the hill that led off towards the Bleeker guest house, swung the car right and then let it cruise down towards the large basin of land that would eventually feed out on to Lord Deveraux's property.

The night sky felt deep and impenetrable. She couldn't

see any stars, could barely even make out the hedges either side of the car. As the road levelled out again she slowly pushed down on the accelerator, but not much. Something was flattened in the road ahead of her, some poor creature that had been going about its business, and Ali gently manoeuvred the car around it. She took the speed down even further as she anticipated the split in the road she knew was near, left taking her towards the estate, right towards the towns of Little Lamp and Gracious Oaks.

Something suddenly caught in her vision; a shape bearing down on the car from the driver's side that seemed to have been pulled straight out of the night. Instinctively she jabbed the brake and jerked the wheel to the left. The night seemed to shift. The shape came again; this time it was right outside the window. Just beyond her door she saw that a deer was running alongside the car, the white of a scared eye finding Ali just before the creature jumped away and flung itself into the hedgerow.

Ali slammed the brake pedal to the floor, and the car came to a skidding, swerving halt, the seatbelt cutting into her shoulder as she lunged forward and then jerked back. Her hands slipped off the steering wheel and flopped pathetically into her lap. Unbuckling her belt, Ali leaned over the passenger seat and retrieved her torch, which had fallen on to the floor and slipped under the seat. As she righted herself she looked back to the windscreen. She blinked once and then took the heel of her left hand to both eyes and rubbed.

She must have been looking at it for several seconds before she registered that it was there in the road, less than thirty feet away, and even when she had registered it, it still took her even longer to believe what she was seeing. The headlights had picked up a man making his way towards her along the middle of the road, a shambling gait causing him to move from side to side. He was wearing a tatty old shirt, unbuttoned and hanging off him, a ripped pair of trousers and nothing else. His skin made her think of a whiteboard half rubbed out – brilliant white battling with smears of duller colours. It was only as he got nearer that Ali realised the darker patches were blood. His face was set rigid, staring down at the road with a determined look of concentration. He hadn't even noticed the car.

'What...' was all she managed to say, all she could think of that suited the moment, as the man walked into the front of the car and then started to clamber up on to the bonnet.

Ali's right hand gripped the door handle but she couldn't quite bring herself to open it. The man's face briefly rubbed along the windscreen and she saw he was actually a lot younger than she had assumed. He was not much more than a boy. A dirty pair of bare feet scrabbled across the glass, and then the roof of the car clunked as he began to crawl across it and then down the other side.

Chapter 3

Ali stood at the top of Mewlish Hill and stared down at New Salstone stretched out beneath her. Her hometown was a dark bowl of nothingness, broken only by flat smears of orange streetlights, and the occasional grey husk of a building. She tried to locate something down there that she recognised, some piece of her past that she could grab in the dark and use to find her bearings, but she found nothing. This November evening seemed intent on skipping dusk and rolling straight into night.

The night can move around you…

'Not this night, Ern, definitely not this one,' Ali whispered to the soft Scottish voice in her head.

Ali had already done a form of grieving for Ernie. Not yet for the finality of his passing, that pain was a promise still biding its time to strike, but certainly for what they had been when they were together; she knew they were a better pair of police officers than one night of madness had a right to undo. But it wasn't just that horrific night at the Deveraux estate that came to her in that moment – some things never left. It was also the phone calls they had shared over the intervening months – the laughter, the comfort, the support.

It was Ernie she had phoned whenever she felt she was slipping. The times when it all got too much and she felt smothered and unhappy, when she had wanted to scream at people – to get right into their faces and scream until she had no more voice left. Those were the times she needed him most and he never failed to talk her down, turn her away and make everything all right again. She hadn't seen him in a year, but those phone calls might just have saved her, she thought. But it hadn't just been Ernie talking Ali back down from the ledge; she had done the same for him. He'd never said – he had too much misplaced pride for that – but she had known. And now she felt utterly wretched.

A sweaty and out-of-breath Ali had caught up with Frank Gage outside Highgate tube station. She'd expected a smarmy grin, or perhaps a weak joke about her appearance, but her former colleague had merely given her the smallest of nods, and carried on towards the station, barely breaking his stride. Once Gage had reacquainted himself with the futility of small talk, and instead busied himself with a newspaper, the train journey from Waterloo to New Salstone had given Ali time to consider the questions that had started gnawing at her.

That Ernie Lipkiss would have jumped to his death had become less and less of a question the longer the possibility had played through her mind, and by the time the train had crossed into Wiltshire, the idea felt perverse. That the nightmares of that night, fifteen months ago, had left a stain on her dear old friend's life that had somehow contributed to his death, on that she was far less certain. She'd come close a couple of times to telling Gage about Ernie's acrophobia, but something had pulled her back each time. That Gage wouldn't remember himself was no great surprise. He and Ernie had never been more than casual acquaintances, as close a relationship as was usually had between New Salstone uniform and CID. That was if he'd ever known, or cared enough to listen, in the first place. Ali wasn't about to ask. Not until she could satisfy herself of the other question weighing heavily on her mind: she still hadn't decided if she trusted a word Frank Gage had said to her.

He stood about twenty yards away, the collars of his white linen jacket turned up against the sharpness of the cold, mobile phone to his ear, and his back to her. He talked in hushed tones, broken only by the occasional grunt of agreement or a hollow laugh. Not once had he tried to disagree with her assessment that what he was asking her to do was ridiculous. Gage had merely repeated his desire to see Maggie find some peace, to help his friend Dalton close the sale, and his wife to stop giving him a hard time. On the biggest question Ali had about the whole job, Gage was even less convincing.

'Why does Dalton need a security guard in a disused building, Frank?' Ali had asked him on the train. 'I put that to Ernie once. He never had much of an answer. Just that Dalton must have more money than sense.'

Gage had given a there's-your-answer-then shrug and returned to his paper.

'Make sense to you, Frank?'

'It's a bad area. You must remember that.'

'Sure. I remember that. But so what?'

'So, I don't interfere in my friend's business, that's what. You'll meet him soon enough; you can ask him yourself.'

Ali's skin prickled as she turned back to face the darkness of New Salstone.

What have you got me into, Ern?

'We're meeting Dalton at eight in the morning, if that's OK?' The light bounce was back in Frank Gage's voice as he pocketed his phone. 'We'll pick you up from the hotel. I've got you a room at The Lamplighter.'

'The high life.'

Gage laughed. 'Hey, you want to spring for an upgrade, be my guest. Come on, I'll walk with you.'

'No. Thanks. I'll see you in the morning.'

'You're sure?'

Ali gave a wan smile. 'I'm a big girl, Frank. And you've never been a gentleman.'

Gage returned the smile. 'Thanks, Ali-cat.'

Ali hitched up her rucksack. 'Don't call me that.'

The road was sparsely lit, the gloom hugging around the meagre spill of orange streetlight, threatening in its thickness. As Ali slowly ambled away from Gage, she started to see shapes in the darkness, people ready to jump out and attack her. She clenched her fists and, for just a fleeting moment, she welcomed them.

The Lamplighter hotel wasn't much to look at, inside or out, but all things being equal, it was still a palace compared to her squalid little kingdom. The reception still held the garish, seventies sitcom aesthetic she remembered so well, the buttercream walls and brown carpet leading her around to a creaking staircase at the back of the building.

An old community noticeboard hung on the wall next to the stairs, a sea of posters and flyers haphazardly pinned on, clogging every inch of the corkboard. Many were already weeks out of date; several were out of date by months. Adverts for yoga classes, art exhibitions and music lessons battled to be seen amongst charity event flyers and job adverts, and then in the top right corner the edge of one poster caught Ali's eye and made her freeze, one foot on the stairs. She pulled a handful of flyers aside and stared at the poster, another memory stirring an unpleasant feeling in her chest. The laminate sleeve covering the poster was loose in one corner now, the paper crinkled and torn in places and pierced with pin marks. At one time those posters had been everywhere, and the photo in the middle of it ingrained in people's minds, but Ali hadn't seen one for a long time. With one quick tug she tore the laminate sleeve free and scrunched the poster up into a ball.

Her room on the second floor consisted of not much more than a bed, seemingly held up by dirt and desire. A rickety shelf was opposite it, and on it a small TV. The toilet was only as big as it needed to be, and the bathroom sink was next to the bed, all rusting pipes and gurgling taps. She tossed her bag to the floor and slumped on to the bed, and something, somewhere, snapped and sighed.

She was exhausted, but sleep eluded her. She lay on her back staring up at the dead insects gathered in the pearl-coloured light fixture in the ceiling. Whenever she closed her eyes all she could see was the poster now lying scrunched up in her coat pocket. Yet not that version, not the faded memory; she saw the full colour version. The block capital letters above the photo in the middle said MISSING, and to her they always seemed out of proportion with the photo of the boy.

Tooley. He has a name. Jake Tooley.

She thought back to the time when those posters were

everywhere. When that photo was on the local news, then the national news, and Jake Tooley's mother was being interviewed all the time and was praised and applauded. People would always wring their hands in her presence and nod like she was royalty, and then no one would know what to say. Ali hadn't known what to say either. Once you've offered your sympathy to her, what else was there?

'You can only ask someone if they want a cup of tea so many times,' Ernie had told Ali during one of Mrs Tooley's daily pilgrimages to the spot, just outside Hanging Twitch, where Jake had last been seen, for ever trapped in hazy CCTV footage. 'Nasty business. You just can't square your mind to it, not when it's bairns. The things I've seen, Ali-cat, the bloodied and the battered. The stiffs. Not one of them sticks in my mind like that photo of Jake Tooley. Those eyes. That expression. One day someone's going to stumble over that wee lad. Find something. Find part of him. Hate to say it, but I sure as hell hope it isn't me.'

No, it wasn't you, was it Ernie? It was me.

'Woman's got steel in her veins,' Ali had said then. 'How do you keep going? How do you keep coming back to that spot day after day to light a candle? World's moved on and I doubt she's ever going to catch up with it again. How do you not crumble and give up?'

'You will see. One day you'll understand. Trust me, Ali-cat, when you have children, you'll know. You'd tear down buildings for your children. You would set the world on fire without so much as a blink of the eye. You'll see.'

Tears stung the corners of her eyes, and this time she didn't have the energy to fight them. Ali cried herself into a fractured sleep circled by old familiar nightmares.

Chapter 4

Fifteen months earlier

When Ernie's voice came through the radio Ali became convinced, just for a second, that he was actually outside the car talking to her through the window. Ernie was calling in an ambulance to the Deveraux estate; his voice was breathy and unusual, as if he had just run a race. He shouted for Ali, demanded back up, and then he disappeared.

Ali's hand went to her radio and then fell away and fumbled for the door handle instead. She craned around and looked through the back window – nothing but more unrelenting, impenetrable darkness. And somewhere back there, a young, half naked man stumbling along the road.

She whispered his name into the headrest. 'Jake.'

The penny had not so much dropped as clattered and then skittered across her mind. Her stunned realisation had come in stages, each connection made between that dishevelled young man crawling over her car windscreen, and that boy in his school uniform, smiling awkwardly from the missing poster, seemed to make her heart hiccup. That photo was a part of her now; she knew every inch of Jake Tooley's face, had seen the intelligence in his deep hazel eyes, and had understood the effort in the smile. The face she had just seen up close, less than a foot away, was an ugly distortion of that young boy. Ali turned on the blues as well as the hazard lights, opened the driver's door and stepped out.

'Jake? Jake Tooley?'

The summer air was sharp, the light breeze bearing a million miniature daggers that slid through her clothing and pierced her skin. Her breath left her mouth in wispy, white clouds, fragile formations that were soon consumed by the thick walls of the night. Instinct made her hands feel for the top of her baton, check for her CS spray and then adjust her hat. Ali thumbed the torch on and began walking.

'Jake?' She moved the torch beam to the hedgerows on either side, running the beam until the shapes stopped making sense. She did this twice more, alternating it quickly with a sweep of the ground. 'I'm a police officer, Jake. PC Davenport. Don't be afraid. I'm here to help.'

This time her torch beam found him straight away. He was crouched down and hunched over, his back to the road, rocking timidly on his bare feet and sobbing.

'Jake, my name is PC Davenport. It's OK, Jake. You're safe now.'

A strange sound suddenly started further up the road; a chaotic click-click above a feeble, soft mewling. Something was moving out of the curtain of the night, headed their way. Ali twisted one way, then the other. As the noises grew louder and bore down on them, she instinctively reached out for Jake by the side of the road to shield him, and as she did so he seemed to crumble under her weight and give himself to her completely, his arms flopping to his side like they were made of wet rags.

Ali started to drag him to his feet, and just as she had

him up, three fawns came towards them, careering clumsily down the road. Seeing the figures in the road, the three frightened creatures swung away from them, two darting into the bushes as the third carried on zigzagging down the road until it once more belonged to the night.

Ali turned Jake in the direction of the flashing blue lights. 'Let's get you somewhere safe, shall we?'

'Safe,' came a breathy little voice in her ear.

'Yes, sweetheart, come on.'

He tried to walk but every remaining ounce of strength seemed to have deserted him. Ali pulled his left arm up over her shoulders, and then wrapped her right arm around his waist, the torch now poking out at his side. She focused her attention on the blue lights up ahead, refusing to acknowledge the discomfort and the weight she was dragging until they were both at the boot of the squad car. In less than a minute Jake was bound up in her hi-visibility jacket on the back seat, and Ali was back behind the wheel.

Ali turned the keys in the ignition and switched off the hazard lights. Jake Tooley was staring at her in the rear-view mirror. It was an empty face, nothing to see, nothing to read. It terrified her.

'You OK, Jake?'

Jake wrenched his gaze away and slowly turned to stare from the side window. When he spoke, his voice was no more than a whisper, his words fragmented and distracted, his breath making condensation on the glass. 'Mustn't. Ever. You don't look him in the eye. No. No. Don't do that. Don't do that.'

'Who, Jake?' Ali turned in her seat, reached out and held his hand. His skin was cool to the touch, his palm clammy. Ali could see his reflection in the window; his eyes now open wide and unblinking.

'The ghost man.'

'Who is the ghost man, Jake?'

'It's what he wants. He wants you to see him.'

'Who does, Jake? Who is the ghost man?'

'Safe.'

'Yes, Jake. You're safe now. I promise.'

Jake took his free hand to the window and drew his index finger through the condensation, then his hand was curling loosely into a fist and his knuckles were knocking gently on the glass.

Knock-knock.

Knock-knock.

In the confines of the car, the sound was like a hollow, quickening, heartbeat.

Chapter 5

On the dot of eight o'clock, a cobalt-coloured Mercedes pulled up outside the Lamplighter hotel and a tall man with slicked back, greying hair got out. He smoothed the collars of his smart black suit and approached. Ali returned his smile with a nod.

'Ms Davenport?' he asked, extending a marble smooth hand. 'Nathaniel Dalton. Frank has been held up, asked that we get going. Is that agreeable?'

Ali shook the extended hand and felt embarrassed about the calluses on her palm. Then, almost instantly, she felt stupid for caring. 'Held up?'

'In the line of duty. Dog walkers found a body in Tanley woods apparently. Nasty business.' Dalton motioned to the car. 'Shall we?'

The inside of the car was as spotless and pristine as the man who owned it. Dalton was far more proficient at small talk than Frank Gage, but even this well-groomed and urbane individual gave up on Ali's economy of conversation after a few minutes, preferring to let the radio colour in the silence.

Ali rested her head against the passenger window and watched her hometown unfold and blur past. She had only been away a year, yet so much seemed different; shops and buildings appeared smaller, streets narrower, her many old haunts greyer and wearied. The New Salstone Arts Centre, home to so many cherished memories, remained closed down and boarded up, the wooden panels over the windows now replaced with metal ones, suggesting an air of permanence.

It was there, as a young girl, that she would spend so many Sundays with her father watching the weekly retrospectives. The old black-and-white crime movies had always been their favourites; the ones with tough coppers, hardboiled detectives and deadly women, though they'd also soaked up the big Technicolor westerns there too. Simpler times where the good guys wore white, and the bastards wore black. Ali had loved those films. So had her father. It was there in that building, so many years ago, that she had decided that she was going to join the police force. She was going to be one of the good guys. Just like her dad.

After another five minutes they were leaving the centre of New Salstone behind and moving towards the bones of a large industrial estate. It was like a ghost town. Dilapidated warehouses stood in large tarmac spaces slowly being reclaimed by nature. Burned-out cars were scattered around huge mounds of rubbish. One fenced-off space had become a white-goods graveyard. Another was home to a giant building now charred to its skeleton. To Ali, it looked like the carcass of some mythical felled beast with a long searching tongue squirming out of a flattened head, where a trail of rubbish now snaked out into the car park.

'You're familiar with this part of town, of course?' Dalton asked.

'Had a few call-outs this way. Back in the day.'

'Drugs?'

'Amongst other things.'

'Some things haven't changed then. This area has been falling apart for a long time. Going to be a huge regeneration project out here, sooner or later.' Dalton spoke in a tone as soft as his hands and Ali wondered if it was for her benefit.

'They've been promising that at every local election for as long as I can remember.'

'Oh, I think those wheels are beginning to turn. The council have drawn up some fairly grand plans. Have to get it right eventually, you would think.'

'So why sell up?'

'Time and tide, Ms Davenport. I'm not getting any younger. I promised my wife that when I hit sixty, I'd begin selling the portfolio. Make new plans. A quieter life. You know?'

'Sure.'

Soon the industrial estate fell away and empty land spread out on either side. Ahead, Ali could see the steeple of a church poking above a line of oak trees and she tried to remember its name. Further on from the church the land stretched upwards, a stark contrast to the desolation they'd just passed. Here houses poked out snugly from amongst small clusters of trees, and further on the trees gave way to a long patchwork of fields. Beyond, those fields would connect up eventually with Hanging Twitch and what remained of the Deveraux estate.

'Here we are,' Dalton said, swinging the car off the road and into an empty car park. The building appeared as if by magic from behind the line of sturdy old oaks. To the other side of the car park, a wall was holding back a chaotic jungle of bushes. Past the bushes a graveyard stretched up a gentle slope towards the church. The church itself looked as if it hadn't held a service for a long time, yet as they stepped out of Dalton's car, Ali felt sure she could see a little orange light glowing past the high arched windows. To one side of the entrance, a sign reminded Ali of its name: ST AUGUSTINE'S.

'So, Frank has told you what happened? You and Ernie were friends, I understand? Unfortunate business. I was very fond of Ernie.'

As they climbed out of the car, Dalton took position by the front entrance to the building and began jingling the keys in his pocket. Ali gazed up at the building. It spoke of cold and impersonal seventies architecture, yet she was sure it dated back further. A former office building, she seemed to remember, it now reminded her of her old college. It was wide, grey and dull.

A single stairwell ran up the right-hand side giving access to each of the floors, that much was evident through the continuous procession of windows that followed it up, most now either blackened by dirt, or boarded over. Floors two and three looked like they were open-plan offices judging by the wide windows there. The first floor had fewer windows, and those it did have were smaller. The ground floor windows were encased behind heavily graffitied, corrugated iron sheets that suggested this part of town still had a healthy share of night-time visitors.

The car park, too, looked an ideal place for young lovers to park up and make out – a forgotten building on one side, a neglected God on the other. Perfect for a youth that prized immediacy above romanticism.

Ali spun slowly on her heels and looked across the car

park to the church. 'So, Ernie's lady friend, Maggie, she's being a nuisance?'

'An extraordinary woman.' Ali turned back and frowned. 'I'm being polite. She's a monumental pain in my backside, and I need her…'

'Pacified?'

'Pacified. Yes. That's right. With any luck we can put this madness to bed before she scares away any more buyers.'

'And you really think me working Ernie's shifts will do that?' Ali fixed him with an unblinking stare. 'Some people might say that's a little crazy.'

'Fight crazy with crazy, I say.'

Ali tried to read his expression, to find something there that would either confirm he was being genuine or inflame her suspicions. As it was, Dalton chose that moment to stare at the ground, the toe of one expensive shoe scuffing at the gravel in the car park. He took a breath, held it and then let it out in a long sigh. 'Apparently you've seen a ghost.'

'Have I?'

'Have you?' Dalton met her eyes briefly with the question before brushing it away with a wave of his perfect hands. 'No. Don't answer. I don't want to look as if I'm indulging such lunacy. It really doesn't matter to me. Only thing that matters is she believes it. This woman. She needs to believe you. Frank seems confident she will.' Dalton pushed open the door of the building and held a hand out, showing Ali inside. A playful little smile danced on to his face. 'Well, you haven't run away yet, Ms Davenport. That's a start. What do you say?'

Ali walked towards him and, after casting another look up at the building looming over her, went inside. 'I don't believe in ghosts.'

The door opened on to a wide reception area. In front of them a huge semicircular desk ran around the main part of the room. Two discarded, smashed computers and a bank of phones were gathering dust on one side of the desk. On the other side of the room, two large halogen lamps on tripods were rigged up about ten feet apart.

'We have electricity, but no working light fixtures, I'm afraid. Ernie set these up, seemed to do him fine. You will need a torch. There are a couple behind the desk. There's a fairly powerful heater too. I think Ernie had a radio. Bring with you whatever you wish.'

'The other floors?' Ali asked, looking at a door-shaped space to her right, and the start of the stairwell.

'In worse repair than the ground floor; the third floor, particularly, can be a bit hazardous. Lot of detritus. Though I can't see why you would need to go up there. We've had a vandalism problem in the past, but blessedly the little urchins haven't yet mastered flight. There's only one way in. One would imagine that these two lights on ground level, and you making your presence known, would be sufficient dissuasion. There's not much left here worth snaffling anyway. Bastards have already stripped the copper out. Not much of a problem these days.'

'So why bother paying for a security guard if there's nothing worth guarding?'

'You don't get this far in business without making a few enemies, Ms Davenport. I've had threats against my life and my properties. You take most with a pinch of salt but there was a threat of arson against this place earlier in the year that I had every reason to take seriously. Still do. Nasty piece of work. Having someone here at night seemed a way to go. Can't put a price on piece of mind.'

'Why not go to the police?'

'I have my reasons. Does it really matter?'

Ali stored that information away and gave a small shrug of the shoulders. 'I guess not.'

'I wouldn't worry yourself about the threat. Really, I have a person here so I can sleep better at night. You'll have little bother, I'm sure. Nowadays, round here it's mostly junkies and deadbeats looking for a roof over their heads for the night.'

'Mostly?'

Dalton wandered behind the desk and took a seat in a large swivel chair. 'I can't really believe I'm asking you to do this, Ms Davenport. I'm actually a little embarrassed. But we are where we are. I try to look at it as pest control. That's how I quantify it. I'd not think twice about paying someone to rid me of vermin, so really, is this Maggie woman so very different?'

'I guess if you're used to paying past a problem, maybe not.'

'What does that mean? I think I'm being very generous in your payment.'

'You are. It's fine. A little too generous for pest control, but I won't complain.'

'Good.'

Ali crossed to the side of the desk, hands buried deep in her coat pockets. 'You've no doubt heard things about me, Mr Dalton?'

Dalton's eyes went straight to the scar around her eye. 'Well, Frank made it very clear to me not to mess with you.' The attempt at levity landed between them, dead on delivery. 'Frank mentioned how you got…' he gestured loosely in her direction. 'It's really not my business.'

'I think we are talking at cross-purposes. I'm talking about the job. *My* job.'

'Your former job?'

'Yes, Mr Dalton, my former job as a police officer.'

'The Tooley kid? That what you mean? Sure, I know about that business. I'm not judging you. We all make mistakes. Look, Ms Davenport...Ali...you're here because Frank tells me Ernie's lady friend is likely to believe what you tell her. She trusts you. Likes you. Something or other. I don't know, give it whatever name you want, but I'm in a situation here where I need this woman appeased.'

'Why? What does it really matter?'

'I dislike complications and irritations. I don't care for people turning up at my offices, haranguing my staff and potential buyers, making accusations. I'm hoping to close a deal in the next few days, but the interested party is slightly spooked by this woman's hysteria. Were it not for her friendship with Frank, I would have her arrested or get an injunction put on her.'

'Oh, yes, she is a friend of his wife?'

'They go back. I believe.'

'So really, I'm doing this for Frank, is that it? That makes more sense. He wants his wife's friend appeased, and you... what? You in Dutch with our DC Gage, Mr Dalton?'

'Let's not pretend you are here for anything other than the money, shall we? Why do you care what brought you here?'

'The death of my friend brought me here.'

Dalton's eyes narrowed, his lips pursing petulantly before easing into a smile. 'Look. I need this woman to leave me alone. You seem to be the person to do that. End of the week. Two grand. You won't make easier money.'

'I imagine Ernie didn't work here seven nights a week?'

'No. Morton did Sunday and Monday nights. He works the door at a nightclub in town the rest of the time.'

'Did?'

'He quit last week.'

'How many people have keys to this place besides yourself?'

'Why?'

'Because Frank said the building was all locked up when Ernie fell.'

'And what's that? An accusation?'

'Not yet.'

'The police are at least vaguely competent around here, Ms Davenport, even in your absence. Three sets of keys, Ernie's, Morton's and mine. Now I have them all. As much as I would put very little past Morton, he was working the door the night Ernie passed away, that much can be verified. As for me, I was out of town.'

'And that can be verified?'

'It has been,' Dalton said through gritted teeth.

Ali gave him a smile. 'OK.'

Dalton stood and leaned against the desk. 'So, what do you think then? Help me out here? Work Ernie's shifts until the end of the week?'

Ali crossed behind him and sat on the seat. As she scanned the meagre items littering the surface in front of her, she felt a dull ache twist in her heart. She saw Ernie's mug first. WORLD'S BEST DAD, it said in a big, childish font; an old gift that he had cherished so much. Tea stains still marked the handle. There were three dog-eared paperbacks neatly stacked next to it. Trashy thrillers, no doubt – they were Ernie's favourite. Tough heroes, badass villains and everything turning out all right in the end once the hero had killed the baddie. They were Ali's favourite books too. Somehow, it was the half-eaten pack of Garibaldi biscuits that struck Ali hardest. She reached for them, squeezed the packet and felt the top one bend and then snap in two.

Dalton stood at her shoulder, itching to move things on. 'There's a small room just behind you with a sink. Kettle, tea, coffee, and all of that.' He nodded in that direction. Ali ignored him. 'His lady friend didn't want the books. Or the mug.'

Ali turned quickly in the seat, making Dalton shuffle out of her way. 'Mostly? You said it's mostly junkies looking for a roof over their heads. Who else comes here?'

Dalton's lips seemed to disappear momentarily as his face became a rigid look of annoyance. He gesticulated towards the car park through the open front door, and the church beyond. 'St Augustine's has always had a few after dark visitors over the years. Kids with camcorders in the graveyard. Adults who should know better. All kinds of nerds and weirdos looking for things that go bump in the night.'

'Do you mean paranormal investigators?'

'You said that without laughing. Well done. Investigators? No. I could never use such a legitimising term. Sad cases who have seen too many films and have too much time on their hands more like. Ridiculous endeavour. Still, yes, they come looking for ghosts. Looking for answers to questions we have no right to ask. Reverend Barnard indulges them. Drunken old sod. Now, I fear, this woman's barmy bleating might just have breathed new life into these people. I don't want every local weirdo with their eyes to the sky and their head to the wall rolling up here looking for ghosts and ghoulies.'

Ali stood and gently rolled Ernie's chair back against the desk before wandering to the rear of the building where the reception area suddenly opened out into a wide rectangular space.

'You might not want to go back there, Ms Davenport.'

'And yet here I am. Going back there.'

Her boots stepped on to old and sticky linoleum flooring, a slight ripping sound coming with each footstep. Battered old seats and a couple of sofas lined the back wall underneath two giant windows, now partially boarded up. The far wall ran undisturbed all the way to the roof. It felt a bit like a small shopping mall; a great empty nothingness. There was even a large plastic fountain in the centre of the space. To the left, she could look up and see the edges of all four floors, open to the space but for a waist-high line of glass panels and metal supports that ran the width of each level.

Ali rested a boot on the edge of the fountain, plasterboard, rubble and shards of wood now clogging it up. A plastic nymph lay snapped off on one side staring up at the ceiling. Opposite her a small door stood partially open, a lopsided rectangular sign above it, hanging by one screw, read: TOILET. She followed the nymph's eyes upward and then, as she let her eyes drift away to the top floor, her stomach seemed to flip over.

Fourth floor, Gage had said. Ernie took a dive from the fourth floor. She scrutinised the glass panels and railings there. *Whereabouts did he do it? Am I standing where he fell?*

Ali looked down at the ground and fought the urge to gag as she stumbled away from the fountain. Dalton was suddenly behind her and Ali had to jerk to the side to stop herself from falling into him.

‘So,’ Dalton said, ‘what do you say?’ He reached one hand into the breast pocket of his suit and pulled out a thick stack of tens, twenties and fifties, held tight in a silver money clip. ‘A grand now; the other when you’re done and that woman is out of my hair.’

‘I will need to speak to her,’ Ali pushed past Dalton and headed back to the desk. Her breath seemed to be caught somewhere in her throat, as her head floated around her shoulders as if tethered there by string. She grabbed the back of Ernie’s chair and steadied herself.

‘I am sure you will. Do what you need to do. Be back here at nine.’

Ali fumbled in a pocket of her jeans and pulled out an old Biro, rubbing the nib against the back of her left hand until a blue lightning bolt shape appeared. ‘I will also need details for this guy Morton.’

Chapter 6

Ernie had been justifiably proud of where he lived, Ali considered, as she took in the cutesy houses, showcase gardens and military aligned blades of grass. He had always spoken fondly of his new house during their phone calls, and now she knew why. If this was what people referred to as chocolate box, then this particular box came with a big red bow on top.

Ali felt a queer mixture of jealousy and pride. She couldn't help but think of her ghastly, suspiciously stained bedsit in London and feel a little short changed, yet she also felt happy that Ernie had found this place, because she knew he would have been in his element here. He had always fancied himself a gardener; he pottered, fixed and built. She was sure there would be a shed in his back garden. Probably a pond too, because he had always wanted to keep fish, which Ali always felt was a slightly perverse thing for an avid fisherman to want to do.

It wasn't so much the beautiful garden that announced to her when she had arrived at Ernie's house as much as the woman's face in the window. As their eyes met, the face seemed to explode into a thousand emotions at once; fear, delight, amusement, hysteria, they all seemed to be there, so much being said all at once. Ali thought she heard her name being shouted through the double-glazing, and then the face vanished, reappearing a few seconds later through an open front door.

'Ali! Ali Davenport!' Maggie ran down the front steps and gathered Ali up into a huge hug, the woman's fingers digging into Ali's back as her hands clenched and grabbed fistfuls of her coat. Ali couldn't stop a quick flash of her mother from appearing in her mind. This was always how she used to greet Ali too, as if they hadn't seen each other in years, even if it had only been a few days. Then the memory stretched, blended and contorted into the image of an old woman sitting in a nursing home, staring at Ali with milky, confused eyes. She was asking her who she was, asking her what she wanted and why on earth was she crying? Ali swallowed hard and shook the memory away.

'Thank you.' Maggie's words were a whisper delivered straight into Ali's ear. Ali pulled back, the two women now face to face, both smiling with more convention than conviction. The shiny strawberry blonde hair and liberal application of make-up couldn't hide the fact that Maggie looked like she hadn't slept in a month. She wore one of Ernie's oversized jumpers and looked lost inside it. 'I've heard so much about you,' Maggie said, taking Ali by the hand and leading her inside the house.

Ernie's old cream-coloured Volvo was still in the drive, and still in need of a clean, both inside and outside. He'd had the car for as long as Ali had known him, and in almost as long the car had needed some serious valet service. Some hilarious wag had finger-drawn the words *Also In White,* along the top of the boot.

Immediately on crossing the threshold, as Maggie indicated down to Ali's boots – a silent request to remove them – Ali felt the unbearable, clinical cleanness of the house. It was a stark contrast to the heap of junk in the driveway, and that told Ali quite a bit. As cordial and pleasant as Maggie was trying to be, the house was so immaculate that Ali found herself instinctively on guard, worried about where she stood or what she touched.

Another old memory came calling from a deep part of her mind, brought forward in her father's comforting voice. Ali's small hand was in her father's big and protective one, her mother was to the other side of her, and up ahead of them Aunt Mary's grand house was falling into view, bringing with it snatches of childhood Christmases and a rich, warm bombardment of smells. But also the aroma of bleach, polish and the crackling sound of plastic whenever you sat on the sofa, and Aunt Mary's troubled expression as they all ate, her eyes looking for dropped crumbs or spilt drink, a napkin always in one hand. As they arrived at the garden gate, her father's giant hug of a voice had said: 'The house is so damn perfect it makes you feel as if a mouse fart would rip a hole through the fabric of time.' Her mother's laugh followed, a girlish snigger that she was trying to suppress, then Ali's own laugh erupted loudest of all, despite her not really understanding what her father meant, but finding the idea of a mouse fart hilarious.

'I knew you'd come,' Maggie was saying over her shoulder, as she busied herself in the kitchen with intricate tea preparations – doilies, teapot, tea strainer, best china, two-tier display of multicoloured biscuits and a small round pot of sugar cubes. 'I knew you'd believe me.'

'Why would you say that?' Ali caught sight of a photo of

Maggie and Ernie pinned to the fridge, and quickly looked away. 'I have to say I'm still not sure just what you think you need me for.'

'Yet you came, didn't you?'

'I came for Ernie. He was my friend.'

'He cared for you very much. He always said you were the only one who ever understood.'

'Understood what?'

'What happened. That night.' Maggie held the tea tray out for Ali to take. 'Oh, he told me, Ali. He told me everything.' Maggie held her ground, her face unmoving, just staring. She looked robotic, empty behind the eyes; a picture cut out of an advert for a kitchen in some glossy magazine. Then she suddenly came alive again as if someone had flicked a switch in the back of her head. 'Shall we go into Ernie's den?'

Ali couldn't equate the term with the man she knew. *The den.* What a ridiculous word, especially for that most unlion-like of men. She could see him pottering in a shed, maybe even working on an allotment, but not lounging around a den. Maybe it made him feel important, she wondered. Perhaps there, in that room, he became someone different and did great manly things like eating spare ribs with his fingers, his belt undone, belching beer-stained breath along to heavy rock or shouting great tribal invective at sports teams on the TV. Maybe. But probably not. Not Ernie. Ali came to the conclusion that, looking at the rest of the house, Ernie probably just needed somewhere to safely scratch his balls and have a good cry.

The room fed off the kitchen. It was small, cosy and lived-in. A desk was in one corner, a battered old leather sofa against the far wall and a giant TV opposite it. Photos of Maggie lined a narrow shelf above the desk, along with others of Ernie's daughter, Amelia. A child's drawing pinned to the wall above showed, in primary-coloured lines and splodges, a house at the end of a path and a big tree, in front of which stood a stick man, a woman and a small stick girl.

Are there always trees in children's drawings of their houses? There always seems to be. Why is that? Ali leaned in close to the picture, the paper browned now, crinkled and torn in places, and saw a scrawled *Amelia* in one corner.

'Have you been in touch with his wife?' Ali asked. 'Or Amelia? Do they know?'

'His ex-wife, you mean?' Maggie was at her shoulder, her voice soft with sharp edges. 'His ex-wife who poisoned his own daughter against him and made his life such a misery that he felt compelled to transfer to the furthest place he could find? No dear, of course I haven't. I'm sure someone will tell them. It shan't be me.'

Ali waited for Maggie to continue, to take the conversation elsewhere, but Maggie merely stared at her, as if waiting for some sort of response to a question she hadn't directly asked. Her eyes found Ali's scar, then dropped down to Ali's chest, then her legs and then back up to the scar. Finally, Maggie took a step back and settled herself on the desk chair, gesturing Ali to the sofa.

Neither woman spoke as they filled their teacups, Maggie moving the biscuit selection across the tray until Ali took one, both stirring their tea longer than they needed to. Then as they settled back, looking across the room at each other as if it were an interview, Maggie's smile levered away the awkward silence.

'You should have his car. He'd want that.'

'Don't be daft, I can't do that. That's very kind though.'

Maggie pulled open a small drawer in the desk; a second

later a set of car keys landed in Ali's lap with a light clunk. 'I will hear no more about it. He would be pleased to know it was in *safe hands.*' The strain Maggie put on those last two words wasn't lost on Ali. 'Despite appearances he was very fond of it. As he was of you. I imagine there is some symmetry in play there. Yes. Take the car. It can't do to have you taking a cab everywhere you go.'

'Maggie, I really can't—'

'Nonsense. You must. Either that or it's going for scrap. I can't drive. I have no intention of starting, either.'

'OK. Thank you.' Ali sipped at her tea, trying to remember how her aunt Mary told her ladies did it, before remembering that none of that mattered any more. Ali shoved a pink wafer into her mouth and chewed. Crumbs be damned.

'They all think I'm mad. I know that,' Maggie said. 'That in itself, in this day and age, with the things going on in the world, should be more of an insult than it actually feels. Maybe you think I'm mad too?'

Ali shook her head.

'No. No, I suppose you don't. Thank you.' There was a barely concealed bitterness inside Maggie, a raw look in her eyes. Ali knew these words had stewed for days, waiting to be served up for her, and she let them come. 'Madness, Ali, it's all we are allowed to feed on at the moment. Madness and hatred. Yet what indulgences can be offered to this silly woman? I know how I sound, but what else should I do but tell the truth, as I know it to be? Don't I owe Ernie that much? Of course I do. You knew him well enough. You were close. Suicide? You surely don't believe him capable?' Maggie's expression suggested no room for debate on this matter, so Ali merely nodded and let Maggie unload the words she was obviously so desperate to share. 'Quite. Frank patronises me, he always has. I really don't know why Kate married him. He tells me I need to accept it, move past it, and let it go. Let it go? I ask you, who would? Who could? Ernie was attacked in that place. I knew it from the moment I took the call. The only thing I was wrong about was what attacked him. Now it makes so much more sense.'

Ali thought it made very little sense but said nothing, just sipped her tea and nibbled at her biscuit, already feeling suffocated and uncomfortable in this woman's house. And it most certainly was *her* house. Maggie was right; Ali did know Ernie well enough, well enough to know he was never this house-proud anyway.

Maggie seemed to have stopped again. *Broken down*, Ali thought. She was staring over the rim of her teacup as if waiting for Ali to pick up the thread of the conversation and run with it.

'Ghost?' Ali asked, feeling rather stupid for saying it.

Maggie put her teacup back on the tray and shuffled forward on the seat. 'I don't want this, Ali. It's important to me that you know that. I don't want to be this person. I don't want to hassle Nathaniel Dalton. I don't want to have to talk to my colleagues at the press about this and be pitied and laughed at or tolerated with a dismissive pat on the head. I'd like nothing more than that wretched building to be sold and torn down, flattened, but not until the truth is known. Not until my Ernie has some justice. I need people to take me seriously. Something else you should know is that I never held any credence with the supernatural. I never read ghost stories. I never watched horror films. I never even believed in fairies at the bottom of the garden, even when I was young enough to be open to fantasy. Even...' Maggie laughed nervously. 'You know what, I even remember finding the notion of Father Christmas rather creepy when I was a girl. You see it wasn't that I ever even looked at these things with childish wonderment, even before I discovered adult pragmatism. It was just never part of who I was.'

'Yet you now couldn't be more sure of it?'

Maggie seemed to be carefully considering the words she was about to speak; once more she was distracted, not quite there. 'I'm sure of Ernie. I'm sure of the man I loved. It would be a stretch to say he was deliriously happy. I could accept that. But he was content. The pills…those pills he took. They helped. They righted him. Put him straight. We worked, Ernie and I, we fitted together. He simply wouldn't have taken his own life. When I last saw him. That night. Before he left for work. He was happy, Ali. Things were normal.'

'That's often how it will seem to the loved ones of people that take their own lives, Maggie. Normal. It's a word I've heard a lot over the years. Far be it for me to defend Frank Gage, but suicide is a fairly obvious conclusion to come to, wouldn't you say?'

Maggie took a deep breath, letting it out slowly. 'You're playing devil's advocate, yes, OK, I understand. It is an obvious conclusion to draw, of course it is, and had I not known Ernie, maybe I would have said the same. You know he was scared of heights, don't you?'

'I do. Yes.'

'His fear was intense, though he tried to hide it well. Would it seem likely that he would choose to jump to his death from the top floor of a building?'

Ali stopped short from voicing her agreement, not yet ready to fully fight from Maggie's corner. Instead, she gave a non-committal shrug and let Maggie continue leading her into whatever mystery Ernie had left behind. She found Maggie's tone unnerving; sweetness laced with steel. Ali could see how formidable she could be, could hear her shouting at Dalton and threatening anyone who doubted the tale she was telling. Yet she found it hard to doubt her sincerity, even if Maggie was latching on to lunacy in the absence of answers. At least Ali dearly hoped she was.

'There was something in that building, Ali. If it came for Ernie, then maybe you will see it too. That night tied you to it, I think. I need you to confirm what I know. It has to be you.'

Ali drained her teacup and placed it back on the tray. She knew where the conversation was going, where it probably had to go at some point. It was the thing that seemed to define her. Her and Ernie Lipkiss.

'That business at the Deveraux estate?' Ali asked, knowing the answer.

'Well, of course that. You saw a ghost.'

'Maggie, I don't know what I saw.'

'But the boy did. That Tooley boy saw something. Ernie said so. He saw a man with a head as white as the moon. The Knock-Knock Man, he called him.'

'Please don't say that name to me.'

'And you both defended the boy, you and my Ernie, and it cost you your jobs.'

'No. No it didn't.'

'Ernie would never have taken early retirement without all that happened. And you wouldn't have...well...you know, would you?'

'Wouldn't have what, Maggie?'

'Gone mad?'

Ali felt a small click in her throat as she spoke. 'That's

not fair. I was under stress. The doctor said it was stress. That's why I resigned.'

She heard a defensive tone in her words that she'd not heard for a long time. She didn't know why it still bothered her so much. Maybe because there was so much about that time that made no sense, that the one thing that she could say for sure – that she and Ernie walked and weren't pushed – should be defended to the hilt. If she let that certainty go then what the hell else would make sense any more?

'I always believed the story Ernie told me. I believed you both, even if no one else ever did. You were treated appallingly.'

'You know, Maggie…that night…'

'If this is where you tell me you don't think it was a ghost you saw, then please don't. I imagine you have spent all these intervening months telling anyone who asks that you saw nothing, that you don't believe in ghosts, that you're of rational mind and thought, and it must only have been a trick of the light, maybe, or just a man passing through the woods, an innocent stranger, or nothing much at all. Maybe after all this time you have even convinced yourself of it. But Ernie told me what you both saw. He never doubted it. I know you didn't either. Consider me a friend, Ali, you are free to tell the truth here.'

'The truth, Maggie, is that I've spent fifteen months trying to forget that night.'

'And how is that going for you?'

Up until that point Ali had been a little underwhelmed by Maggie, perhaps having built her up from Gage and Dalton's stories to be a merry lunatic, instead of this distracted, house-proud, empty-looking woman. But now she had started to change, booting up instead of breaking down. Maggie had crossed the point beyond which Ali's conversation was of any use, now it felt like her presence was an act of appeasement. But Ali wasn't quite ready to give that to her yet.

'The man we saw that night…'

'The ghost.'

'How can you possibly be so sure, Maggie? I wasn't.'

'Ernie was. Good enough for me.'

'You do understand how this sounds, don't you? Do you really expect Frank and Nathaniel Dalton to take it seriously? Do you expect anyone to?'

'That's why I wanted you here. They will listen to you. Who is going to listen to this mad, grieving fool? Countries go to war for their belief in ghosts. For their unwavering following of the echoes left of a person's life. For their need to be coloured by one who is no longer alive. And yet here I am, alone. Ridiculed.' Maggie leaned forward in her chair and pointed her teaspoon towards Ali. 'Something evil visited Ernie in that building. And I will have people know it.'

'And why are you so sure that it's the same man Ernie and I saw?'

Maggie settled back in the chair and casually rested the teaspoon on the saucer. 'Because I've seen him.'

A gentle coldness passed over Ali, stroking at her arms and making the hairs there prickle momentarily. She felt a small crumb of pink wafer on the back of her tongue and tried to swallow it, but her mouth seemed devoid of any saliva. She leaned forward and fixed Maggie with an expression somewhere between amusement and horror.

'Pardon?'

Maggie held a hand up and offered Ali a crooked smile. 'I should have said that earlier, I apologise. I tell you this as Ernie's friend, and someone I hope I can trust. Frank doesn't know about this, and Nathaniel Dalton certainly doesn't. So, I am asking you to keep this to yourself for the moment. You will meet a lovely young man called Will Kamen. He came to me last week. He was at St Augustine's the night Ernie was attacked.'

'Looking for ghosts?'

'Quite. He and his friends, they call themselves paranormal investigators.' Maggie gave a hollow laugh. 'He's a delightful boy. I'm not going to pass judgement.' Once more Maggie seemed to stall, her eyes glazing over and her expression blank. Then, suddenly, she came alive again and gave a wide, bright and deeply unnerving grin. 'Yes. Quite by chance they caught some of Ernie's building on film. There was a figure in a top floor window. You will see. He will show you and then you will know too. The Knock-Knock Man came back and he attacked my Ernie. You see, Ali. You see if I'm not right.'

Maggie stood and within two quick paces was standing over Ali, arms crossed over her chest, hands gripping at the sleeves of Ernie's oversized jumper. It felt like a cue to leave.

'Why not show it to Frank?'

Maggie gave a snort of disdain. 'I'll not have him patronise me further. No. This footage will go to my friends at the *Salstone Gazette* should it prove necessary. Though I dearly hope it will not.'

'And Will Kamen?'

'He will find you.'

Ali felt dizzy, her head thick with a disorienting fog of information, suspicion and grief. 'If I don't see anything there? If nothing...shows itself, what then? Will that be enough for you?'

Maggie gently inclined her head. 'So, you will do it then?

You will go to that building and work Ernie's shifts? You will help me get to the truth?'

Ali stood and offered Maggie her hand. The two women faced each other again. With her free hand, Ali surreptitiously swept pink wafer crumbs from her jeans. 'Of course I will, Maggie.'

Chapter 7

Fifteen months earlier

'He gave it a name?' Parker pinched the bridge of his nose and closed his eyes. 'I can't believe I'm even having this conversation with you.'

Ali felt the tears coming on again and made a valiant effort to keep them back. She imagined her face was a sopping red mess already, and she wasn't far wrong.

'I know. I'm just telling you what Jake said to me. I didn't…I mean, neither Ernie or I really…I don't know what it was we saw.'

Ali had wondered whether Chief Inspector Parker sitting on the side of the table where she herself had often sat, and her being on the side usually reserved for whoever they were interviewing, was intentional or not. Parker had certainly gone to great lengths to make her aware that it was just an informal chat, nothing more, just two colleagues talking through the craziest of nights. Parker had even got her a tea from the vending machine, asked if she wanted sugar, or maybe something to eat.

He was trying to put her at ease. She had to give him that. The fact he wasn't talking to her and Ernie together must have meant something. As did the fact that Superintendent Moss had already arrived with a face like thunder. Parker didn't believe her. She knew it. She even understood it. But she had gone too far already. The moment she had said that Jake Tooley had seen a ghost was the point when she had gone too far. But she was only being honest, only telling the truth. Just as her father had always told her to do.

'You need to talk to me, Ali. This is getting passed up the food chain, and then I'm not going to be much help to you. The super is already talking about stepping in. Help me understand what happened now, and maybe I can fight your corner before people start calling neglect of duty.'

'What about the IOPC?'

'It's a mandatory referral, twenty-four hours, Ali. You know how it works. You want my support, then give me something to go on, something other than albino ghosts.'

'Jake never said he was an albino.'

Parker gave her a withering look.

'Just that his head...his face, it was so white it made him think of the moon.'

'Fuck's sake,' Parker seethed before knocking back the dregs of his tea, scrunching the plastic cup up and lobbing it into a bin. 'For decades this town is barely even half awake, and then this...how did no one know this was going on again?'

'Again?'

Parker swatted a dismissive hand at her. 'Tooley's mother is on her way down, of course, and no doubt that means the press will be there too. This is going to stain this community for ever, you know that?'

'Are they all dead? The people that were in the house?'

'They are still being pulled out. Three so far. Taylor is

bringing in Garrett Lyman. Hopefully he might give us a bit more detail about numbers.' Parker read the confused expression on Ali's face. 'Deveraux's driver. Way things seem to be panning out he might well be the only staff on the books still vertical. He's been out of town visiting his sister this past month. But if he's so much as dipped a big toe in this horror show we'll have his arse. Christ, what a repellent thought. I played golf with him once. And Deveraux…good God, that man opened my boy's school fete one year.' Parker's face blanched, his fingers playing nervously with his watchstrap. 'OK, right, we need to start getting our house in order. You need to start telling me what happened, and it might serve you best to start with why you took Jake Tooley back to the place where he had been held against his will. What the hell were you thinking, Ali? Or perhaps you weren't thinking at all, is that it?'

'I didn't know,' Ali said to the table, tears spiking the corner of her eyes again, reminding her they were close by, ready to jump in. 'I didn't know he had been held at the Deveraux estate.'

'Really? What kind of police officer are you? Half-naked lad wandering down a country lane, nothing else but cow shit for five miles. Nothing, of course, except for the country estate less than a mile further down the road?'

'I…I…I don't know.' That was both the truth, and the trouble. Ali's memories were like flotsam on a vibrant sea, constantly being taken away from her despite her being knee deep in the water, just an arm reach away. She closed her eyes, tried to steady the sea, but nothing stayed, everything went.

She felt her heart begin to race again, a nervous fluttering against her chest. It felt like she had a bird trapped behind her ribs and that somehow that fluttering would make her expand and she would float away. And then her mind found the word it always searched for in times of worry and fear, and placed it before her.

Sparkleville, she said quietly, in a far-off secret place inside her mind; over and over she said it, breaking the word up, stretching it, slowing it down, and letting it breathe. Then she pushed it further and made herself hear her father saying it to her, as he so often had; it was his word after all. What a calming voice. Her father almost crooned that word.

The word repeated. The word swirled around her, going to work, doing its job, and then Ali felt her heart slow, the sea in her mind calm, and she reached out and grabbed at her memories. Just like other people do.

'Ambulance!' Ali suddenly blurted out. 'I needed to get him seen by someone. There were ambulances called to the estate. I heard Ernie. So, I thought...well, why would I drive him ten miles back the other way?'

'Was this before or after the gunshot?' Parker stared back at her dead-eyed. 'Where were you when you heard the gunshot?'

'I didn't hear that until I was at the estate. I wouldn't have...if I'd known, I'd never have...not with Jake...'

'Well, that's something.'

'I can't believe you think I would—'

'When one of my officers walks into a building after hearing gunshots, without calling for backup, and also leaves a vulnerable child locked in her car, I'm open to thinking they are capable of a lot of things.'

Ali bowed her head in shame.

'What the hell were you thinking, PC Davenport?'

Ali looked to the table as if searching for some inspiration there. She could already feel the waves building again, separating her from what she knew to be true. She held her hands over the top of the table, palms facing up to the ceiling. 'I don't know.'

'Well you'd better start to know.' Parker checked his watch. 'And while you are at it, let me tell you what I *do* know. See if it focuses your mind any. I know that you found Jake Tooley who has been missing for nearly two months. I'm pretty sure he was held for some, if not all that time, at the Deveraux estate. I know that somehow, he got away from there and that you, in your infinite wisdom, took him back. I know that shots were fired. I know that three people and counting have been scraped up out of that place. What else do I know? Oh, well I suppose I know that the kid, the fifteen-year-old kid, was so terrified by whatever happened to him there, that he had convinced himself he had seen a phantom. Or a ghost, or some such shit. So, I also know that I now have to consider putting a search together for a man with a head like the moon, that may or may not float a few feet off the ground. Possibly see-through. Answers to The Knock-Knock Man. How about all that? Any of that define the lines a little for you?'

Ali brought her hands to her face and laid the palms over her cheeks, fingers curling into her closed eyes, pushing, probing, nails scratching the eyelids; a fragile barrier against the tears that were going to come back strong, and possibly never leave.

'I also know that Jake Tooley is dead.' Parker gave the long and impatient sigh of an exasperated teacher, stood up and then turned to the door.

The night can move around you. You can make it alive if you have a mind to.

'Safe...' Jake Tooley whispered again, his breath causing more condensation on the glass in the car window.

Ali told him he was.

'Knock-Knock,' he said to his own reflection, a knuckle tapping twice on the glass. 'I saw him standing at the gap in the wall.'

'Who, Jake? The ghost man?'

'But not the window...' Jake shook his head quickly and then wrenched his eyes from the car window. 'He knocks on the window. Twice. Knock. Knock. But you mustn't look. You must never look at his face if he knocks on your window.'

'Jake, listen to me. OK? Did this man hurt you?'

Now his eyes found Ali. 'Away. I got away.'

'You did. You got away, Jake, and now you are safe. I promise.'

'It was always so dark there. But his face...white face. Bright face. Shining face. I thought the moon had fallen down into the room. He smiled at me. The Knock-Knock Man smiled.' His gaze once more found the condensation at the window. 'A ghost. Not safe. Not safe.'

Ali gently squeezed his hand; it felt as cold and unyielding as a block of ice. When he spoke again it was not just to her, it was to himself. Or maybe the boy he used to be.

'He told the old man that he spoke to the devil.'

'Huh? What shit is this now, Ali?' Parker turned back in the open doorway, one hand on a hip like the worst sort of catalogue model. 'What did you say?'

'The Knock-Knock Man told Deveraux that he had spoken to the devil.'

Parker dropped his arm, shook his head and lumbered away.

'And that the devil spoke back,' Ali told the empty interview room.

Chapter 8

The note Frank Gage left for Ali at the Lamplighter was short and not particularly sweet – MEET. 4. GRAVY BOAT. CONFIRM. His mobile phone number was scribbled underneath. The hotel receptionist had pinned it to Ali's door.

The Gravy Boat café held a lot of memories for Ali. A small, greasy spoon café, it had been offering the same fare, to the same people, from the same sun-faded menus for as long as anyone could remember. It was The Gravy Boat that Ali and her father would often go to on a Sunday, fuelling up on a late breakfast, before going to the cinema to watch those glorious westerns and crime stories where good and bad showed their hands in the first reel.

They would both have a full English and a giant mug of sugared tea. They would chat and catch up with each other; her father asking about school, and Ali pestering him to tell her about cases he was working on or criminals he had caught, and she would always get intrigued and a little frustrated on the occasions her father would say that he couldn't tell her. Or she would laugh when he said he could tell her, but then he would have to kill her, and he would take a ketchup-smeared knife and waggle it at her like some sort of amateur Norman Bates. She still missed it with all of her heart.

The café trips had been his special treat for them. Alongside their trips to the cinema, it was their thing. No one else was ever allowed. Before that they used to go ten-pin bowling together. They had loved bowling but had stopped going because both of them had been absolutely terrible at it, and they used to spend the whole time roaring with laughter at each other's inability to hit the pins. That seemed strange to Ali now – why would you stop doing something that made you laugh?

'So?' Gage asked, his elbows propped on the table. 'You've seen her?'

Ali took a big gulp of sugary tea. 'I've seen her.'

'And?'

'And what? Do you want me to tell you that she's completely crazy? Would that make you feel better?'

'It's nothing to do with how I feel.'

'How's your body?'

Gage looked momentarily confused as his own mug of tea arrived and was laid on the table before him.

'The one in Tanley woods?' Ali continued.

'Oh, yes, I'm sorry about not being there this morning.' Gage shifted on the cheap plastic chair and then gathered his mug of tea in both hands and took several delicate sips. Ali saw something pass over his eyes. She'd seen the look before on her counsellor. It was an expression that was guarded; a mask that was tentatively holding back any real emotion, and he only ever looked like that when...

'How's the hotel?'

When he was keen to change the subject.

'It's still a dump, Frank.'

Gage gave a watcha-gonna-do? shrug of the shoulders. 'Won't be for long.' When he looked back at her, Ali realised it was a question, not a statement.

'No. Won't be long,' she told him.

'Is Maggie going to listen to you?'

'No idea. Depends what I find there, I suppose.'

Gage gave her the same withering look she had seen so many times on Parker. *Perhaps they taught you that look at some stage on the police career ladder?* Ali wondered. She had never got far enough up to find out. Then the rung she'd been clinging on to had snapped off in her hand.

'Don't encourage her, Ali. It's not healthy having the inconsolable looking for answers in the unbelievable. Does no one any good. Where do you go then?'

'Weird places, Frank.'

'Well, I don't do weird.' Gage held an open palm towards Ali, as if presenting her to an invisible friend. 'At least she's got you now.'

'What do I know about weird?' Ali wasn't going to let him have it easy. That night at the Deveraux estate might have defined her to many people, but she wasn't going to be reduced to a tag, or be painted as some curiosity pulled out of the wacky drawer.

'Well, after what you've seen, at least you could entertain the notion of weird. Right?'

'I haven't seen anything. Ernie and I were just in the wrong place.'

'That's not how the story goes, you should know that. Truth doesn't matter as much as what people want to believe. For the purposes of what we need here it makes no difference if you saw the Holy Mother herself that night or a whole lot of nothing much at all. Only thing that matters is Maggie believes you saw something, and believes you aren't going to sell her short. Heaven knows Kate and I have tried to appease her enough times, but we are where we are, Ali, we play with the cards dealt and try to get a winning hand. Simple fact is, if you're looking for the bogeyman, you're always going to find him. I can't fight this with logic, and I can't waste any more of my time on it either.'

'Oh yes, you were telling me about your corpse?' Ali finished her tea, and settled back in her plastic chair like a child awaiting story-time from their parent.

'Just another dead body. Not the first round here, probably won't be the last.' Gage's eyes betrayed him again, the mask slipping. 'I was sorry to hear about your mother.'

Gage's eagerness to change the subject was piquing Ali's interest.

'Thanks.'

Gage threw a quick, instinctive glance at Ali's scar. She had grown so used to the looks that sometimes it didn't even register. People couldn't help themselves. Ernie used to call them 'push the button people', as in, if you are faced with a giant red button and a sign saying *Do Not Push The Button* there are enough people in the world that would do, regardless, because they can't help themselves. You could argue that it was human nature to do as the warning suggested, but Ernie Lipkiss wouldn't have agreed with you. He always felt human nature was to do the opposite. Ali could sympathise; she'd pushed a few buttons in her time.

Gage was cradling his mug again, his elbows once more propped up on the red check vinyl oilcloth. 'And, for what it's worth, I was sorry what happened to you and Ernie too. I know we didn't speak much at the time. But I think they treated you rough. It needn't have happened the way it did. We lost two good coppers. That doesn't benefit anyone.'

Ali shrugged. 'Don't worry about it. It feels like another lifetime, Frank.'

'Does it?'

'It did.'

'Sorry.'

'No, you're not.'

'No. Sorry for not being sorry then.' The light bounce was back in Frank Gage's words. He gave his remark a wide smirk, but his mouth hadn't told his eyes. There was no humour there. 'You know, people always said you were hiding from life up there in London. I didn't buy it. I told people they were full of shit. That Ali-cat could never hide, not with those claws.'

'Don't call me that.'

'They were right, weren't they? You *are* still hiding from life, aren't you?'

'I'm not hiding from life,' Ali returned, bluntly. 'I choose not to be an active participant. There's a difference. Don't try to evaluate me. Are we done here? We could have done all this on the phone.'

'I'm sorry, I didn't mean to poke at a sore.'

'I'm fine. Everything's fine. I haven't got any sores. I'm fine.'

Gage finished his tea and dabbed his lips on a napkin before standing and placing a hand on Ali's shoulder. 'If you ever wanted to come back, in some capacity, I have some clout, you know?'

Ali turned to look at the world outside the window and saw her ghostly reflection staring back at her. 'You probably believe that too.' She felt his hand slip off her shoulder and slap against his hip. 'You know I'm going to find out the name of this corpse in Tanley woods, Frank. It won't be hard for me to find whatever it is that you're trying to keep from me. And why. Maybe you should just save us both the time and talk to me now?'

Gage sighed, over-dramatically she thought, but she let him have his moment. 'The name Garrett Lyman mean anything to you? He was Deveraux's...'

'Driver. I know.' An old, familiar chill pulsed inside of her. 'What happened?'

'Suicide. Dog walkers found him hanging from a tree.'

'Lot of it about,' Ali muttered, wrenching away from that ghost in the café window. 'This suicide...lot of it about at the moment.' She looked back over her shoulder at Gage who was half out of the door. 'Wouldn't you say?'

Gage sucked his lips, contemplating her words. The well-worn mask was back on his face. 'Long nights. That's all. Nights seem to go on for ever, this time of year.'

'Normal for you to get the call to a suicide, DC Gage?'

'I was in the area.'

'Wrong place, wrong time?'

'Yeah, you know how that goes. Be in touch, Ali.'

'And with Ernie?'

The door closed. Gage was gone.

Five minutes later and Ali was back in the driver's seat of Ernie's car, staring out at the gathering darkness, that oppressive stranger that always came to visit. She could feel the threads of different people's stories running through her mind; Ernie, Maggie, Frank, Nathaniel Dalton, Garrett Lyman, and somewhere back there she knew that there would be a huge knot in these threads that tied them all together.

Back there.

There were too many coincidences, too many echoes of her past, and too many memories of that night. This puzzle was skewed and she held the pieces of the jigsaw in her hands without a clear picture, and no solid surface to build on. She was apprehensive, frightened even, but despite that, she had to admit to herself that part of her liked it too. There was a small, deeply hidden part of her that craved it.

Ali gripped the steering wheel tight, her knuckles turning a creamy white colour, and gazed at the pen marks on the back of her left hand as if seeing them for the first time – Morton's address and phone number. She had completely forgotten it. She took her mobile from her coat and quickly dialled the numbers. *Morton? First or last name?* When the man's answerphone kicked in, Ali was still none the wiser.

'Morton,' a voice barked. 'Leave a message.'

'Hello!' Ali said cheerily. 'My name is Ali Davenport. I've just started working for Nathaniel Dalton, covering the night shifts at the same building I understand you used to work at. I'd really like to have a quick chat with you sometime if that would be OK? Perhaps you could give me a call when you have some free time. Thank you.'

She gave her mobile number, hung up, turned the key in the ignition and then gently moved the car out of the parking space into a slowly assembling night.

Chapter 9

Fifteen months earlier

Ali sat alone in Parker's office with her fifth cup of tea. Outside the sky was growing lighter, another day rolling on despite all that had gone on during the night, a night that Ali felt might never end. She could see the vultures gathering in the station car park; saw the notepads and the cameras, a whole chattering macabre carnival picking at the bones of this horrible mess.

She had been left alone, told to wait, that people needed to speak to her, and things needed to be understood. Superintendent Moss had taken control and made himself highly visible to her. She saw him on the phone outside the office. Saw him having covert conversations with a couple of well-heeled strangers as well, strangers who stared at her as he spoke and nodded their understanding. She was on display, a freak in a glass cage to be scrutinised and jeered at. She wanted to see Ernie. She wanted to see her mother. She wanted to see anybody who would make her smile. She felt like a little girl and needed a child's comfort of reassuring words and gentle hands.

She saw Taylor leading who she supposed must have been

Garrett Lyman along the corridor outside the office. Taylor, that sweet kid, still carrying that same shocked expression on his face, as if those old wives' tales had actually been correct and the wind had changed and frozen his face, leaving his eyes as saucers, and his mouth in that silly little O shape.

Garrett Lyman was dressed in his Sunday best, a neat tweed three-piece suit, with a gold pocket watch chain hanging from his waistcoat. Shiny shoes and slicked back hair rounded off the image of an old man dressed in his finery. Only Lyman's face betrayed the intended statement; sagging jowls, feathered with white whiskers on a deathly pale skin. His eyes seemed lost in the sockets, no more than two drops of ink on a sheet of paper. He held his shoulders high, kept his back straight, and his feet in a precise step, and his face seemed to be carrying all the weight and bearing every year of the old man's life.

Ali held his image in her mind after he passed the office doorway, and tried to equate what she had seen that night to the man who had just arrived. She had dealt with enough criminals in her time. Even the best liars, from the shoplifters to the assaulters, past the burglars and the fraudsters, would all, in retrospect, carry something of their crime in their appearance. There would be a look, a movement, something in their walk or their manner or their words that connected up with what they had done.

Your crimes mark you, even the very smallest. That was what Ali had come to believe. With what had just gone on at Lyman's employer's estate, if that old man in the tweed suit being led past her by PC Taylor had any involvement at all, it would surely be screaming out at her in deafening stereo, or be plastered over him in neon letters. To Ali, Garrett Lyman looked like another victim.

Another Jake Tooley.

Except this man was alive, and Jake Tooley was dead.

'Safe,' she had said to Jake, reassuring him, saying that same word over and over again. It wasn't a token word. She had meant it. Because why wouldn't he be OK? She was a copper; she was one of the good guys. Ali Davenport had found Jake Tooley. The goodies had him back from the baddies. They had the happy ending. The long night would soon relent, and dawn would break and everything would be OK in the light of day. Ghosts don't come out in the daylight.

Even when they came out at the estate and he started screaming in the back of the squad car, she had just told him again that he was safe. She had truly believed that was enough. Even as he had tugged at the jacket she'd wrapped around him, pulled it so tight around his neck that he looked as if he was trying to choke himself, and when his screams began to sound like pained howls as he turned his head up to the roof of the squad car, she had just said that same stupid word again and again. She wasn't sure at what point it lost all meaning. She wasn't sure of much. But she did know one thing – neither of them had ever been safe.

The main house was bathed in the glow of the floodlights positioned in the ground about fifty yards from each corner of the building. It was showy and arrogant. The winding gravel driveway, even longer than Ali's own street, was always well lit, so much so that to see the opulence of the huge Georgian manor house basking in its own light seemed like overkill. Considering there was no other house for miles, and nothing but thick tangles of wood all around the building, Ali had always wondered whom the display of wealth was for. It was a beautiful structure, that much could never be argued; a building designed for Sunday teatime TV, or a tourist's gawping eyes, and in the right light, a thing of immaculate design. Yet in another light, in the false glare of those floodlights cutting into the thick summer night, it looked like something altogether different. No more the staple playhouse for TV actors to play dressing up in, this was now a horror house where crazed butlers and mad scientists frolicked about with ungodly creations.

She could see Ernie's car at the end of the driveway, just before the main entrance, the blues still on and the driver's door open. She slowed her own car, and followed the curve of the drive. That was when the hands came over the back of her seat and tried to kill her. At least, looking back at it all from a safe distance, tea-fuelled in Parker's office and watching the reassuring creep of dawn pushing aside the night, she thought that was what Jake Tooley had been trying to do. Right now, she couldn't blame him.

She screamed his name as his fingers dug into the skin at her throat and brittle, blackened nails drew thin trails of blood. She slung herself left and then right, trying to shake him off, then her hands lost the steering wheel as they wrestled with his tightening arms snaking around the headrest, trying to strangle her.

The squad car bounced up over a small concrete border lining a flowerbed, slammed off one corner of the building and skidded around until the rear of the vehicle was facing the property. She tried to scream his name again but as she opened her mouth the fingers on his right hand slithered in and grabbed at the inside of her cheeks, pulling and tugging as if he was trying to force her into some horrific grin. She could taste the filth on his fingers, a mix of ash and excrement, and then she could taste blood and didn't know if it was his or her own.

She bit down and Jake howled. She flung her head into the headrest, and felt him fall back a fraction, and as he did, she yanked herself forward and his fingers dragged along her teeth, scratching at her gum line. Now they were back at her face, searching, probing and striking out. Ali unlocked her seatbelt and half-turned in the seat, trying to face him.

'Jake! Jake, what are you doing?' How stupid those words sounded to her now. 'I'm trying to help you! You need medical attention, Jake! I'm just trying to help you! Stop it!' Even as she was screaming these things and fighting off the wild, animalistic attack by the young man in the back seat, her mind had just enough coherence left in it to highlight the fact that there were no ambulances there. There were no other squad cars yet, either. No more help or support. She was alone with Ernie and Taylor and whatever the hell was going on inside that great, opulent building. Her hand went up to her radio and immediately those dirty fingers clamped over her again, one hand at her throat as the other ripped her hand away, the radio and her wired earpiece tearing free too and clattering down between the seats.

'Jake! Stop! Stop this!'

He lunged now and was half over her seat, arms pumping back and forth, side to side, as his hands hit, slapped and grabbed. A couple of quick blows hit her in the left side of the head, pitching her against the driver's window, and then Jake was curling around the seat, leering down at her; that terrified face contorted into nightmare expressions of rage and desperation.

Ali hunched down against the door, her right arm up to shield her face as her left reached out behind her and scrabbled for the door handle. Jake's screams were snarls now, vicious unrelenting warnings from flared nostrils and spittle-flecked cracked lips. The index finger on her left hand curled around the door handle and tugged, just as Jake wrapped both hands around her right arm and brought his head down, mouth open, ready to bite.

The door gave, and then her back pushed it open and she felt the night-time breeze behind her. Jake's firm hold stopped her from falling out. Now Ali's left hand crossed over her chest and fumbled for the key fob jutting from the ignition, and as it did, she brought her left knee up, using Jake's hold as balance and shoved her foot hard into his belly. The boy gave a hefty grunt, his hands releasing her arm as he flopped to his side, his left shoulder landing with a crack on the dashboard as he bounced off, his legs now halfway between the seats. Ali yanked the fob free, tumbled out of the car and landed in a clumsy heap on the grass. Her right boot slammed the driver's door shut before Jake could gather himself and come again. She activated the fob and locked the car.

Ali turned over on the ground, regained her footing and then fell down again instantly at the sound of a gunshot. It came from somewhere deep in the house. Back up on her feet she sprinted across the grass to the driveway, determined to get to the radio in Ernie's squad car. She heard Taylor calling out for help, and then saw the young man running from the front of the house and diving over the bonnet of the squad car. Ali was no sooner out in front of the house, had no sooner registered the body of a woman lying on the steps leading to the front door, than a second shotgun blast exploded through the calm of the night. It shattered the windscreen of Ernie's squad car as Taylor lay flat on the gravel driveway just past the open door, his hands over his head.

Ali ducked low and landed against the broken concrete wall of the flowerbed. Backing up, she shuffled her way to the corner of the house, out of view of the shooter and then turned back the way she had come. She heard Ernie then from somewhere in the bowels of the building, his voice an angry bark of threat. She saw her dear friend, in her mind, being tracked through the corridors and vast rooms of this building by a madman.

Something took her over, some deep-rooted instinct. Her baton was out before her, tightly gripped in a fist; no time to consider its effectiveness, no time to question what the hell she was doing. She was detached, watching her actions from a distance; sitting in a cinema with her father, watching a character from any number of old movies, the good guy chasing the bad guy and saving the day. She had no time to consider just how stupid that was, either.

Just past the rear of her squad car, a small door led into the kitchen. It was wooden at the base, and the top half was made of four neat squares of glass in a thin crossed wooden frame. Beyond it a cream-coloured blind was pulled down and fastened tight. Ignoring any rational instinct, and closing her mind to the squad car rocking back and forth as that wild dog of a human continued his craziness inside, Ali smashed the bottom left pane and slid her arm in, pushed past the fastened blind and turned an old brass key in the lock. From somewhere, she suddenly heard her mother's voice: *'Always take the key out of the back door, Ali. You might not stop a burglar, but let us not make it easy for them.'*

The door squeaked open and she stepped in, a cosy warmth welcoming her almost immediately like a gentle stroke of the cheek. The old kitchen was partially coloured from an evening orange glow that was coming from a connecting corridor, making the edges and angles of everything soft and unreal. Her boots crunched on the broken glass before finding the smooth surface of a thick stone floor as she moved at the very end of the light, next to the safety of shadows. She passed an old range, felt some heat still coming from it, and just above her head she could see a line of birds hanging from a wire by their feet, limp heads wobbling at the end of wrung necks.

The room smelled of spices and alcohol, and a memory wafted past her, a snatch of family Christmases at Aunt Mary's grand home, where everything always smelled wonderful, and every image was sketched with a rusty winter hue. For a second the memory stalled her movement. Her childhood memories could be endless things at times; things so deep that she could dive in and never reach the bottom. Sometimes Ali teetered on the edge of allowing herself to fall back. Sometimes she welcomed it.

A scream shook her back to the here and now.

She stumbled through the door and into the orangey light. There were voices further on, deeper into the house, and there were noises below her too – rats, maybe, or just the sounds of a giant old house settling itself down into night-time slumber. Her free hand brushed her jacket where her radio should have been and felt torn material flapping free. She raised the baton in her right hand, but now saw little more than a bony twig in her grasp. Sweat was breaking on her forehead, as the heat of the corridor became something predatory and alive.

She crept on. Stern and accusing faces painted into history stared down at her from giant gilded frames hung on the wall. The floor creaked angrily at the pressure of her boots, and she imagined those painted eyes above her all turning on their canvas to glare with each sound she made.

'What the hell are you doing?' she asked herself.

Later on, people would ask her that same question directly and often, and not in the quiet voice she had used. The question wouldn't be a question either, not really, it would be an accusation, and she would have very little with which to back up her actions. The further she walked into that house, the deeper the hole she was digging for herself. But none of that registered. Not then. It only registered that her friend needed her. She knew only that she was supposed to save the day. She saw only white hats and black hats.

And blood, Ali. You saw blood too.

There was a line of it across a narrow cream rug in the corridor. Just a light smear. You could have convinced yourself it was something else, if you'd wanted to. There was a splat of it on the corner of one wall too, and it carried on around to the other side as Ali turned the corridor and found herself standing in another, almost identical one. There was a wide crimson puddle at her feet, and from here a scattershot line of blood wound away from it, disappearing around another corner. A smoky, acrid smell passed under her nose. She heard a whimpering sound.

She kept moving.

Following the blood.

Going somewhere.

The house felt like a maze. Corridor after corridor, all looking the same as the one before, seemed to lead her in a circle as she walked alongside the blood trail. She was convinced that at any moment she would end up back at the kitchen under that orangey glow. Instead, she finally found herself facing a giant set of wooden doors standing partially open. There was blood on the gold handles, a few angry streaks. A more-diluted orange light was coming from within the room before her, and as she stepped closer, she could see a shape on the ground, hunched forward. At first, she thought it was a chair, maybe a table, and then it moved.

The shape on the floor rocked back and then slowly started to unfold into something vaguely man-shaped, and ever so tenuously human. The back of his shirt was smeared with blood streaks, and seemed to hang from him in strips, and there was more blood congealed in sticky patches in his hair. With a huge effort the man pushed himself up to a seated position with his left hand, and then his face half turned and glanced casually down to his right side. With a quick, involuntary jerk of his shoulder the man's right arm quivered and Ali could see it was hanging together at the elbow by little more than exposed muscles, the forearm turned around and facing the wrong way.

Ali took one delicate step back from the doors as if conscious she was intruding on someone's privacy. Then she saw the woman across the room, sitting in the high-backed chair, and the sight was enough to screw Ali to the spot.

She'd seen Lady Deveraux a few times in the past, swanning around with an air of indifference as she took afternoon tea with equally aloof ladies, or gracing some piffling council function with her faded star wattage. But seeing that figure in the chair, something that just about resembled the lady of this particular house, Ali struggled to believe who she was looking at. Lady Deveraux had dressed up for her demise; deep red lipstick marked her marble face in two short slashes and elaborate jewellery adorned her ears and neck. Her head was tilted to one side as if she was considering Ali's appearance, and in her lap, hands that seemed to have been submerged in blood rested together.

The old woman had opened both wrists with a small knife that lay off to one side.

Ali's mind spun around like a child's zoetrope, showing her these ghastly sights in quick, repetitive strobe flashes until darkness came like a bottomless ocean and beckoned her to dive on in.

A hand landed on Ali's right arm and gripped tight, and then she was shoved roughly to the side and the wall seemed to open up around her. She was tilting forward, falling down into blackness. Her head struck something, once, twice, and then something else cold and firm slammed against her cheek. Disorientated and delirious, she had just time enough to roll over and look back up a small set of wooden steps, up to an open doorway hidden in the wall, and see a shape standing across the opening, before she was suddenly yanked backwards across the stony floor, a hand landing firmly over her mouth, to stifle her shouts.

'It's me, Ali-cat. I got you.'

Ernie dragged her into the shadows of this dank, basement room. At the sound of another gunshot, closer this time, just over their heads, Ali pushed herself back into his body, and let his arms wrap around her. She felt his chest moving up and down rapidly as he fought to control his breathing.

'Are you hurt? You hit those steps hard.'

Ali's right hand went to her radio and patted absently at the place where it should have been. Ernie rested his own hand over the top and slowly closed his fingers on to hers.

'I've called it in. Are you hurt?'

'Probably. What the hell was...' she trailed off, her eyes trying to adjust to the darkness, searching out shapes and angles. They were in some sort of cellar, that much was obvious enough. She could hear water dripping from somewhere. Heard the fidgeting scrabble of rodents. The air was ripe with age, mould and the tang of urine.

'You seen Taylor?' Ernie whispered.

'Yeah. He's...I don't know. He was alive.'

'You see the body out on the front steps? Mad old bastard has flipped. If I hadn't found this place he would have—'

'His wife...' Ali's free hand flapped around her face, the gesture trying to fill in gaps where her words were falling short.

Across the room something caught Ali's eye, a familiar shape was blurring into focus. She slowly disentangled herself from her friend's reassuring hold and as she did pain zigzagged up through her head, the start of a meaty purple bruise now breaking on to her forehead. She swayed, felt sickness hit her and then wash away.

'Where the hell you going?' Ernie tried to grab at her but she brushed him away and then scrambled forward on all fours, back towards the base of the stairs.

She only needed to go a few yards before her eyes did the rest and coloured in enough of the scene to satisfy her. There was a single mattress just ahead, a thin duvet bunched up on top. The smell of urine was stronger here, and as Ali reached out and pressed down on the feeble bedsprings, her fingers came away moist. Her hands ran across the floor at the end of the mattress, and then rummaged around under the duvet, along the sides, underneath it, searching for something that would turn her away from the grotesque realisation that was dawning in the darkest recesses of her mind. Then her right hand landed on something cool and metal, and her fist closed around the thick links of a chain. She gave a gentle tug. The chain went taut as the other end clanked against a large metal ring, screwed into the wall.

Her own disgust came first, even before the fear.

Then came his name.

Jake. Jake. Jake... and that name never left her.

Ali staggered to her feet. She could feel Ernie behind her now, moving forward to stop her, and she spun away from his touch. She lunged for the stairs in one ambitious leap, felt something in her leg object, but pushed on, outrunning the pain. She bounded clumsily up the stairs in a gangly dance, all legs and arms, headed towards the weak orange glow creeping around the open doorway in the wall.

Her ears began to prickle as adrenaline bloomed and started to course through her body. Her earlobes felt as if they were on fire, then soon enough that heat pulsed through her neck and down her arms as a deep, implacable rage tightened her body like a coiled spring. For a brief moment, Ali welcomed it all: the fury, the enemy and the release.

The gunshot had been so loud it had seemed like an explosion. That was what she told Parker later. Her ears were still ringing as she had said the words. She had told him she felt as if the ceiling was falling down on top of her, and that she had dived through the double doors to escape it.

She remembered a blast of heat.

The smell of burnt hair.

Her feet twisted underneath her. She fell again.

A hand was pawing at her. She rolled on to her back and saw the hideous sight of a man's bloody face leering over her, grimacing, within kissing distance. It was the man who had collapsed in the doorway, and now his left hand was in Ali's hair, trying to hold on to her, to life. He mumbled something incomprehensible and blood bubbled up between his lips and fell down his chin in one long, gloopy trail. Slowly Ali began to push back along the floor, her boots digging in and trying to find purchase on the slick ground. The man's hand released her hair and slipped pathetically down her face. A moment later he toppled over on to his side and moved no more.

The room seemed to shift slightly as another bolt of pain jabbed up through Ali's head. She heard a shuffling sound, or so she thought, something moving past her left-hand side and then disappearing. Footsteps, perhaps, but they were so slight, so gentle.

It couldn't have been Ernie.

With all the strength she could muster she flipped herself over on to her front and started to crawl across the floor. Her hands ran through lines of blood. She saw a lit candle on the floor, almost burnt out, just across from where she was crawling, and something that might have been another body. Bit by bit Ali pulled herself up on to her knees. She imagined the world around her spinning at a hundred miles an hour, rolling along without her.

Jake Tooley.

Oh God, what have I done?

'Ali-cat?'

His shape was there in the doorway. Yet something didn't fit. He didn't look like Ernie Lipkiss at first. Not the Ernie Lipkiss she knew so well. As she said his name, he raised his right hand, a gesture to silence her, and she saw that flattened palm was shaking. The reason became all too clear as Lord Deveraux walked out from behind him and crossed into the vast room.

He was dressed in a sharp three-piece blue suit, cream bow tie and black shoes buffed to a military shine. His healthy head of white wavy hair, so rigid and unmovable that it looked as if it belonged on a child's toy figure, was immaculate. Only his crisp white shirt, now decorated in splatters of blood, gave any hint as to what had been happening in his home. In many respects he looked just as he always had done the few times Ali had seen him over the years. Had it not been for the blood and the smoking shotgun in his right hand, he could quite easily have been off for an evening of bridge at the club.

His eyes found his wife.

'My darling Lisbeth.' Deveraux's voice was cold, at odds with his words, and cut through the silence like a sharpened sword. 'I am so sorry.'

Ernie stepped forward into the room and stood at Ali's side. Deveraux made no move to stop him. Instead, he leaned down to his wife and planted a kiss on her forehead. Holding the shotgun loosely at his side he then crossed the room, his shoes click-clacking on the wooden floor, and stopped at the candle on the floor, all but burnt out into a fat waxy blob. Using the shotgun as support, the old man bent down and scooped it up. Turning casually to one of the giant windows in the room he held the lit flame to the curtains until they caught, before dropping the candle back on to the floor. Ali watched in mounting horror as he returned to the centre of the room and another candle. She could now count four on the floor before them, even more behind, all seemingly placed at specific intervals along a never-ending line of blood. Deveraux tipped over the second candle before rolling it with a foot on to an old rug to their left. Within a few seconds he was holding yet another candle to a pair of curtains on the other side of the room.

Ali felt Ernie's hand on her arm. 'I'll distract him, you make for the door.'

The flames crackled as they ate their path through the

curtains, greedily grabbed for the walls, and then reached up for the ceiling. In the distance Ali could hear a siren, the first of a wailing cacophony that would soon drown the night-time peace around Hanging Twitch, and the noise lifted her heart.

Back in the doorway, Deveraux cast a wistful look around the steadily burning room before slowly, robotically, taking the shotgun up before him and blasting a hole through the window to his left. Wood splintered and glass shattered, and past the shock Ali had just enough time to notice the giant wooden boards nailed across the bottom half of the window. The window on the other side of the room was next, the blast punching through decimated curtains hanging in blackened strips, and the charring wood of yet more neatly fixed boards. Then, for one brief moment – a moment that would stretch in time for Ali, as the days and weeks and months rolled on – Deveraux seemed to be admiring his handiwork, gazing out through the large, ragged hole he had created, past the flames, the violence, the madness, and out into the treacle black night beyond. He looked as though he wanted to say something. Instead, the old man sunk to his knees, jammed the shotgun barrel up under his chin and squeezed the trigger.

It isn't like that in the movies. That was the ridiculously inappropriate statement that kept coming back to Ali in the days that followed. *In the movies, when the bad guy took one in the face or the head, it would fair explode like you'd dynamited a ripe watermelon. You had to have it like that in the movies, she supposed, wouldn't do to be too much like real life. No, in real life it was actually rather...anticlimactic?*

Yes, she was ashamed to acknowledge to herself that that was the word she kept coming to. That much she never confessed to anyone, not even Ernie, but she had certainly expected that old man Deveraux's head would explode in a riot of red. But it didn't really. There was a reddish splat on one wall, a few little bits of brain, but he kept most of his head on his shoulders. In the moment, no such dark thoughts came anywhere near Ali. There was only one thing that mattered – getting out of that house and getting back to Jake Tooley. Deveraux firing that last shot was as good as a starting pistol.

Ali tore out of the room, her body's aches and pains all coming alive as one, calling out their objections to her in chorus. But she didn't stop. She felt drunk, slightly out of step with her body, as if her skin and bones were a pace setter that she had to try to keep up with. Her eyes stung, her head throbbed, and she could taste that old coppery tang in her mouth, but there would be time for all of that later. Time to lick her wounds and make sense of all this insanity. She rode the adrenaline, carried her rage, and tuned to the gathering sound of police sirens. That was just about enough. Down those seemingly endless corridors she ran, back towards that orangey glow in the kitchen and then out of that small back door standing open. To her squad car, and then...

You knew he wouldn't be there, didn't you?

The driver's window was smashed. Jake Tooley had gone. Goosebumps covered Ali's body, ushered in by an unearthly cold that tried to caress her. She screamed his name. The sirens were blaring now, blue lights breaking into the night as three squad cars...four, five...all tore up the long driveway to the house. Two ambulances followed. More lights were flashing on the horizon. Across from her, Taylor was by the front steps waving his arms above his head to the oncoming cars.

'Jake!' she screamed like a scolding mother. 'Jake! Where are you? Come here now!'

She moved away from the car and started running, but Ali had no idea where to go. She turned in a large circle and called his name again. Taylor was looking towards her now. Then there was Ernie, walking down the steps of the house, past the body, and now he was starting to make his way over to her.

Again, she ran on, up to one of the floodlights nestled in the ground, and turned from the house to the woods, then back to Ernie. He was getting nearer, running himself now. He called her name. She ran on. Ran away.

'Jake!'

'Ali-cat!'

For the first time since he had started calling her by that silly pet name, Ali found she wanted to cringe away from the sound of it. She could feel him gaining on her, running faster. She was determined to get away from him, to not have to confess to him what had happened, to somehow make it all right before he found out.

She gathered the little energy she had left, and ran on again.

She got no more than a few feet before stopping dead.

There, just at the edge of the wood, her hi-visibility jacket, the one she had wrapped the half-naked Jake Tooley in, was spread out across the top of a bush.

When she ran again, charging into the wood, her legs didn't feel like her own. Thorny bushes jabbed at her, low hanging branches poked her, gnarled roots tried to trip her, but she felt nothing, saw nothing, only charged blindly on, screaming his name. Or at least she tried to. His name sounded little more than gibberish now as it became mangled amongst the sobbing she was powerless to stop.

Ernie was gaining ground. He'd grab her soon enough, plead with her to tell him what was wrong, then try to calm her down, and she'd probably break in his arms, confess everything, and maybe he would understand. Maybe he would forgive her. If he didn't, then no one else would.

She had no idea where she was going. She darted between trees, then tumbled through bushes, squelched through mud, turning left, then right. Hopelessly lost. His name was now barely a squeak on her breath. Bit by bit she slowed. Broke. Stopped. Her eyes felt like shards of glass. Her head a slowly crumbling rock. Her legs finally gave from under her and set her on her backside in a pathetic heap, howling up at the sky and the branches that leered over her like ghoulish spectators.

'Ali?' His voice was diluted, as if he'd just been woken from a dream. Ali saw a pale imitation of Ernie Lipkiss standing in the doorway of Parker's office, a plastic cup of tea in his hand.

'Hey,' Ali returned. Instinctively her hands moved off her lap and she held them out for him to take. Ernie didn't move. Embarrassed, Ali let her hands flop back.

'I keep seeing his face,' Ernie told her. 'Do you think he fell?' Ernie gently prodded an index finger against his head. 'Aye, tripped on a root, maybe, and that was how he…'

'Hit his head?'

Ernie blanched and seemed to fall down into his uniform. 'I'm sorry.'

'I'm sorry too. What are you sorry for?'

Ernie's gaze found the thin, bluey-grey carpet in Parker's office, his eyes widening as his mind replayed the image of Jake Tooley over and over again.

Ali saw it too. She would always see it. Their discovery of that boy slumped at the bottom of a steep slope, his bloody head smashed against a large, jagged rock, would be a private movie for the pair of them, played forever on a loop, unable to be unseen. The colours would always be bright, the smell always pungent and suffocating, the creeping horror always alive. It was their unshakeable bind, and theirs alone. Except...

'Tell me you saw him too?' Ali asked her friend. 'Tell me you saw that...man, Ern...when you shone your torch into the woods, tell me you saw that man watching us from behind that tree. Tell me I didn't imagine it.' Ali brought a hand up to her face and held it there. 'That face. You saw that face staring at us, didn't you?' She moved the hand out again for him to take. 'Tell me you saw it too.'

Ernie took a step back in the doorway, turned on his heels and walked away.

Chapter 10

The first shift

The hour-long nap Ali managed at the hotel was fractured, and troubled with a horrific nightmare. Jake Tooley often visited her dreams; sometimes he was a mute witness on the periphery, other times, like now, a central character.

She was holding Jake Tooley's hand as he led her through the identical corridors of Lord Deveraux's house. At least she assumed it to be him. Ali couldn't turn to look at the figure; her eyes, head and entire body were immovable. She wasn't walking. She seemed to be gliding as he pulled her along, past the hidden gap in the wall and up to the large wooden doors, which still stood tantalisingly ajar.

There was no blood this time, but Lady Deveraux – alive in this dream – writhed in discomfort on a sofa, her chest heaving as her crimson nails scratched at her eyes as though trying to claw something free. Ali couldn't hear her screams, but knew they were there. Her husband seemed to hear them all too well, because now he stood over her, helpless hands out before him. This version of Lord Deveraux was unkempt, wild and desperate. Now he was on his knees and he seemed to be crying, but again she heard no sound. Jake was squeezing her hand hard, trying to move her from the doorway, but Ali stood her ground a moment longer.

Something else there. Other things to see.

The man from the wood, Jake's very own Knock-Knock Man, now stood over Lord and Lady Deveraux.

She questioned in the dream whether he had been standing there the whole time, or if he had only just appeared. Even in dream logic, it seemed strange. He was there. He wasn't there. Like a ghost. She could see the shape of him, but couldn't tell what clothes he wore – they were black, dark grey or possibly navy blue. He was bald, and he also had hair that was black and streaked with white. The only consistent thing was his deathly pale skin.

Deveraux was no longer on his knees in front of his wife. He was kneeling to The Knock-Knock Man. Pleading with him.

The Knock-Knock Man rested a hand on Deveraux's head.

The Knock-Knock Man was looking at Ali and smiling.

Ali woke with a start, turning over at an uncomfortable angle, her left arm stretched under her back. Her right hand fumbled for her phone, knocked it to the ground, and a second later she was joining it, slipping out of bed and curling herself into a ball, smothering the irritating, tinny, beep-beep of the phone alarm.

'Sparkle…' she whispered. 'Sparkleville. Sparkleville.' Her mind took over, chanting the word, again and again. Ali switched off the phone alarm and stretched out across the carpet. She stayed that way until she found something within herself that felt vaguely human.

The communal shower room along the corridor was locked. She heard whispered voices coming from inside, voices that fell silent as soon as she knocked on the door and asked how long they were going to be.

The sink in her room gurgled and burped at her as she cleaned her face and washed under her arms. She tried to wash her feet but the sink was too small, the act too cumbersome, so she changed her socks instead and hoped that would be enough.

Half an hour later she was staring out of the window, down into the car park, counting the cars and the people. The streetlights twinkled in the distance. The moon was a cuticle inside a coal black sky. She could see thin fingers of mist combing through the light spill of the streetlight immediately beyond the car park, and further on, past the indistinct shapes of the centre of town, three firework tails streaked the sky, each ending in a popping pink flash.

She hit the desolate trading estate a little before nine, slowing the car as she passed the giant charred building with the searching tongue of rubbish. In the gloom of the evening it looked even more like the carcass of some monster. You could imagine it was sat there in the shadows, waiting to pounce, if you had that sort of mind. Ali moved through the gears and drove on.

She saw Dalton's Mercedes parked up on the road, just before the building's car park. He was standing on the pavement, one gloved hand pulled free of a coat pocket, and waved her into the car park. He had reached her car by the time she parked.

'Ms Davenport.' Dalton's voice was slow and deliberate. 'Thank you for being punctual. I was just asking myself if there was anything else you might need. I've switched the halogens on for you. Put a new filter in the kettle. There's a radio, and—'

'Really, it's fine.'

'You have provisions?'

'Yes. I have provisions.'

'Very good. You have my phone number, though I can't see that you would need it. Just...' Dalton gave a sideways look at the building. 'Yes. Boredom, I should imagine, will be your biggest inconvenience.' When he spoke again, his voice was soft, almost apologetic. 'You will remember why you are here, won't you?'

'Not likely to forget.'

'If there's anything else you need, do please...' Dalton's eyes flicked to the church, distracted, his mouth suddenly turning down at the edges. 'I told you!' he suddenly roared across the car park.

'Excuse me?'

Dalton brushed past Ali, ignoring her. At the far end of the car park, sat on the wall separating the car park from St Augustine's church, and just caught in the light coming from the open door of the building, was a tubby young man in a dark hoodie, slowly swinging his legs back and forth, the heels of his chunky trainers kicking against the wall. He had his arms folded against his chest in a defiant stance.

'Get off my property!' Dalton shrieked. 'I've told you before. How many times do you need me to say it? Do I need to call the police? Is that it? Is that what is going to get through to you?'

'I'm not on your property,' the young man on the wall said. 'This wall belongs to the church.'

'Don't try to be clever with me,' Dalton sneered. 'I don't want you on my property. I don't want you filming my property. I don't want you anywhere near my property, or me. Do we understand each other?'

‘As I was saying…sir…I’m on church property by invitation of Reverend Barnard.’ He gestured over his shoulder and Ali noticed a figure silhouetted in the light from the church doorway, watching them.

Dalton leaned into the young man’s face. ‘Barnard is a drunken old fool. Boy like you should be more discerning of the company he keeps. Boy like you should be careful whom he chooses to befriend and whom he decides to antagonise. Do you understand me?’

Ali wandered over and stopped just short of them. The boy on the wall pulled down his hood and smiled at her. This close to him she could see that he was much younger than he had initially seemed. Barely a man at all. She was pretty sure she had just met Will Kamen.

‘I think we’re all good here,’ Ali said to Dalton. ‘I’m sure you’re keen to get on home. Perhaps if you’d just let me have the key, we can say goodnight? How would that be? Are we good here?’

Dalton grunted and then took Ali’s right hand and pressed his key against her palm. ‘Oh, we’re good, Ms Davenport. But that boy does *not* go on to my property, tonight or any other night. I would consider it a grave betrayal if I find out that he has. Do I make myself clear?’

Ali nodded her compliance and then underlined it with a smile.

‘And I need hardly remind you that the same goes for… that woman. There’s to be no one in that building, save for you, Ms Davenport. No one.’

Ali stepped back, allowing Dalton room to leave. Dalton pulled up the collars of his coat and gave the figure in the church doorway a single, curt nod before striding away across the car park. Ali and Will watched until he was out of sight.

'Charming chap,' Will said.

'Isn't he? You're Will, right?'

'Yeah. You're Maggie's friend?'

'Friend might be stretching it. I'm Ali. Hello.'

'Hi. So, I don't know whether Maggie said anything to you, but I caught something on video—'

'So I hear.' At the sound of the Mercedes engine, Ali nodded towards the open door to the building. 'Fancy a cup of tea?'

There was a faint mix of smells hanging in the air: damp and mould and rotten things. The reception area felt different under the clinical glare of the halogen lamps. The whole front area of the ground floor room was bathed in crisp, clear light, making the hanging shadows in the rear of the ground floor – that wide space that opened up all the way to the roof – all the more oppressive. Ali spared it no more than a cursory glance before dumping her bag on the large semi-circular desk and walking behind to the small door where Dalton had told her she could find a kettle. The room was barely bigger than a cupboard, but Dalton had laid out the basics for her – kettle, mugs and two clear glass jars of tea bags and coffee. A tiny fridge, tucked away in the corner, held a pint of semi-skimmed milk, and there was a multipack of biscuits on the shelf of one open cupboard too. Ernie's pack of Garibaldi biscuits sat alone in a small plastic bin, just by the door.

Will had followed at her heels like a dog, and now stood in the doorway gazing up into the gloom of the rear of the ground floor. He pushed back a floppy fringe that then fell back again instantly and gently pivoted his body, his trainers squeaking on the floor as he did, and gawped almost reverentially at the open doorway to the stairwell.

'Never thought I'd get in here, thank you.'

'You need to set your sights a bit higher if this dump is getting you excited.' Ali held out the pack of biscuits to him.

Will shook his head. 'Dave and Ronnie will be really jealous I got in here.'

'And who might they be?'

'That's my team. My mate, Dave Spangler and his dad, Ronnie.'

'Right. Do you take sugar in your tea, Will?'

'No. I'm not allowed.'

'Who says?'

Will dropped his eyes to his stomach then quickly looked away. 'Can I go upstairs?' He plucked a small torch from a clasp on his belt, and looked at Ali with the pleading expression of a child asking to stay up late.

'Drink your tea, Will.' Ali passed him his mug and ushered him to the chair before shuffling herself up on to the desk, just next to Ernie's tatty paperback books. 'There are things I need to ask you.'

'Me too! When did you first see him? Have you only seen him once?'

'Who?'

'The Knock-Knock Man! That's what he's called, isn't he? That's what Maggie told me anyway. Why is he called that? Maggie wasn't too sure on that. She said that you and—'

Ali held her hand up to silence him. 'No,' she said, firmly. Like a police officer. 'You first, Will.'

Getting Will Kamen to speak wasn't difficult. The young man was garrulous and animated, spinning around in Ernie's chair as he spoke. Ali warmed to him immediately. She found something in his enthusiasm, and his seemingly overt innocence, utterly irresistible.

'So, I've been doing it for a year or so. Investigating. That's me and Mr Spangler and Dave. It was Ronnie that really started it. I knew Dave from school. I saw my first ghost when I was ten. No one believes me, but I really did.'

Ali's face was blank; it showed neither interest nor disdain. She kept her true feelings well out of Will Kamen's reach. Though quite what those feelings were, Ali couldn't have said. Her emotions were a running battle played out in her mind; she was scared and curious, suspicious and amused, but unable to alight on anything. The thought of this young man having video footage that might unlock this mystery was both tantalising and terrifying, and it was something Ali both needed and wanted to run from. Will seemed to look to her for a second, seeking permission before continuing his story. Ali nodded him on.

'We were on a school trip down at Corfe Castle. And I saw a civil war soldier a little off in the distance, looked like he was standing on one of the ruins. Little guy, sandy hair and a long pointy beard, and he was all dressed up in his gear. Mrs Alderton, our teacher, she said it would have been an actor doing one of those re-enactment things. You know? Like they would get people to dress up for school parties and things. Pretend to kill each other over and over again. So, I thought nothing of it. Even though I didn't actually see anyone else dressed like that the whole day. Just made sense. What she said. She was cool. So, we all go round in pairs, and I'm with this girl called Sally and after ten minutes she starts to cry and says she's feeling all funny. She just couldn't be there. Wanted to go home. And this is just at the very same place I saw the soldier earlier. And the really crazy thing is, now we're there, I can see that particular section of the ruins you can't actually stand on, there was no floor to it, just a drop. So, whoever the guy was that I saw, he was standing on a place where you couldn't stand.'

Will puffed up his chest and straightened on the chair, waiting for a reaction. Getting none, he ploughed on.

'I've always liked horror films. But paranormal horror films mainly. Like, I suppose, it was probably since that time at the castle. That was what started it all. That was when I really started watching horror films. Even when I was watching them off the telly at night when Mum was out. And we'd get some dodgy copies of the new films at school. I always liked going to the cinema. Not just horror. Any film really.'

Ali's impassive expression broke with a smile. 'Yeah, I'm the same.'

'I set up a film club at school with Dave. Didn't get many people. But that's when we got to know each other a bit better. Then he tells me about his dad, and we nag him to let us go out with him one night. And, well,' Will shrugged. 'Here we are investigating ghosts.'

'And what do your parents think about that?'

Will's voice dropped, his enthusiastic tone gone. 'Mum works a lot. I dunno.' He raised his shoulders high in an elaborate shrug and scrunched his face up. 'See Dad a few times a month. We haven't talked about it. He'd laugh, I think. He wouldn't understand about it. He wouldn't be happy. He was never really happy about me doing film at college either. That's what I'm doing now. Did I say? Film studies A-level. Dad says I need a trade. Something practical. He says studying films is a waste of time. He couldn't see the point.'

'You like films. That's the point.'

'Exactly! That's just the words I used. I like films! He said I was a dreamer. He said I lived in a fantasy world and that was why I liked films. He always said that sort of way of life was never going to get me anywhere. Dad used to be a journalist and he said that he met lots of film critics over the years and that in his experience they were all good-for-nothing drunks, and he'd be so disappointed if I ended up like that. I told him that I didn't want to be a film critic anyway, but then he just asked again why I was studying films, and I told him again it was because I liked films, and the conversation just kept going around in circles. But I did it anyway. I stood my ground and went for it despite him. Mum supported it. But I think that was more a case of her choosing whichever argument went against Dad. She just said to me what she always said to me. She said, "Will, if there's any justice in this world, you will never let your father have the last laugh. He barely even has a sense of humour."'

Ali laughed into her mug of tea. 'Good for her. And good for you, Will.'

'You know, you can find answers to most situations or relationships by studying films?'

'Is that so?'

'Yeah. I will tell you one thing I have learned from watching films, one great universal truth that you can apply to most aspects of life; it's that there are two sorts of people in this world. There are those that watch *Jaws* and see a perfect film, and those that watch *Jaws* and see a mechanical shark. I'm the first sort of person. My dad is the second.'

'Ernie used to say that you can find the answers to everything in books.' Ali looked to Ernie's old dog-eared paperbacks. 'Apparently there's a book for every question. Maybe not here though.'

Will spun around slowly in the seat again, his trainers tapping a tune on the floor as they scuttled around the chair legs. As he returned to face the desk, Ali extended a leg and planted a boot on his knee, stopping him, before slipping off the desk and standing over him.

'Tell me what you saw that night.'

'Sure. I'm sorry about the old...I mean, Ernie. I'm sorry what happened to Ernie. He was your friend, wasn't he?'

'He was. He was a good man. The best.'

Will's eyes went to her scar, and lingered a little too long.

'Say it if you want, Will. I don't mind.'

'It looks nasty.'

'Yes.'

'Did you get that when you were with the police?'

'No.'

A brief moment of awkward silence smothered any further questions. Ali took several small sips of her tea. Will was bug eyed and blushing.

'Go on, Will.

'Oh, yeah, OK. That night.' Will stood and stretched. 'Well, I should just go get what I filmed, shouldn't I?'

'You haven't got it on you?' Ali felt a flutter in her chest as a ragged breath escaped her. She didn't know if she was disappointed or relieved.

'No, I gave my camera to Dave. He's going to stick it on his YouTube channel. He's got way more subscribers than me. I can go get it for you though?' Will checked his watch. 'Yeah. His folks won't mind. I'll go get it now.'

'Sit down, Will.'

Will plonked himself back down on the chair.

'Does Maggie know you're doing that?'

'She knows Dave wanted to. She just asked that he doesn't make the link public until he hears from her because she said she might be going to the papers with it. Dave's hoping she will, because he reckons the traffic to his page is going to go insane.'

'How did you two meet?'

'Maggie? She was here one morning last week. Early. Really early. We'd just finished another session at St Augustine's, and we saw her at the door here, trying to break in. She was shouting for Dalton. Screaming for him. Banging on the door, trying to prise the windows. She wasn't in a good way. Dave and his dad headed off, but I stayed with her. Waited until she felt better.'

'No one else knows about the footage?'

'No.'

'The police?'

Will flushed crimson. 'No. Should we have given it to them? I said we should, but Dave reckons they would have just taken it and he'd never get it back, and Maggie said it was a waste of time, that they'd just laugh at us. So, we sort of agreed that as it was going to be going public sooner or later that we just would keep it between us for a bit. Is that OK? Are we going to get done for that?'

'Police have made their minds up. I wouldn't lose any sleep over it.'

Will nodded to himself and pushed his fringe back from his forehead. It flopped back again almost instantly.

'What were you doing here tonight then, Will?'

'Oh, I had to see Reverend Barnard. He...well, yeah, I just needed to see him.'

'Why? You need absolution?'

'No. I mean, I just—'

'That was a joke, Will.'

'Yes. Sorry.'

'Don't apologise to me.'

'No. Right. It's just...Ronnie asked me to pay him. That's all. We still owed him from the other week. When we filmed here. I didn't realise it was my turn, so I hadn't done it, and then Rev B had phoned Ronnie up and had a go at him. So, I said I'd do it. No big deal.'

'You pay the priest for permission to film at his church? You mean, you make a donation?'

'No. Whenever we film here, we take it in turns to buy him a...he's a bit of a...' Will mimed glugging down a drink. 'You know?'

'Met a few.'

'He's all right though. He's a good drunk.'

'You've filmed there a lot?'

'Yeah, five times now. Got some good EVPs.'

Ali's confused expression asked the question for her.

'It means electronic voice phenomenon. When you pick up sounds or ghost voices on electronic devices. Ronnie has this digital recorder – pretty cool. We were out in the graveyard the night we got the footage from here. There had been a story going round college that a couple in the year above me had been out here one evening, parked up, and, you know, sort of messing around, doing stuff, and the guy freaks out because he thinks he sees this little girl out in the graveyard, putting flowers on a grave that isn't there. Said she was sort of glowing. Well, his girlfriend said he screamed and drove off so fast that he ended up driving for a mile the wrong way back along the ring road. So, yeah, that was why we were out in the graveyard.'

'And you saw Ernie?'

'He was at his desk. Right here.' Will pointed between both of the front windows, either side of the door. 'These corrugated sheets weren't over the windows then. Someone has stuck them up quite recently. He used to use the right one to look out of, keep a check on the car park and whatnot. I could see him clear through the window. He was reading.'

'And what was it you think you caught on video?'

'That was on the fourth floor. I started filming your friend for a bit. I don't know why, shouldn't have really, but we were getting nothing that night, looked like it was going to be a washout, so I guess I was just bored. I didn't film him for long though, just a few seconds or so. Then I move the camera up, and…well, that was when I saw it.'

'It being…'

Will pulled a face that seemed to suggest he thought Ali was dumber than a village idiot on a city break. 'The Knock-Knock Man.'

'Please don't use that name.'

'Why not?'

Because Jake Tooley gave it that name, that's why.

And giving it a name makes it seem real.

'Because I asked you not to, Will.'

'But you saw something, right? You and Ernie. Maggie says you did.'

'Saw something, yes, maybe. In all honesty I don't know any more. I believe someone saw something that night. At least, I believe that they believe they did. The man that I saw, that Ernie saw. I just don't know.'

Ali wondered if he could see through her if her pretence was so very obvious. She couldn't allow herself to succumb to this notion, certainly not in front of Will; that path led nowhere but down the rabbit hole. And yet this boy claimed to have evidence on film, evidence that might just turn what she went through that night on its head. Maybe that would mean her life would be back the right way up again? Or maybe it might just open up a hole she would never get back out of.

'But if you're right, Will, and I have seen a ghost – if we both did, Ernie and I – then how is it that that ghost is suddenly here too? Ghosts haunt buildings, don't they? Or places? They don't move around locations. Or have the movies been lying to me about that too?'

Will nodded his agreement and then pursed his lips, as he seemed to consider this point. When he finally spoke again, what he said sent a deathly chill through Ali's body.

'You're right. But spirits have also been known, from time to time, to attach themselves to a person too.'

He was saying something else now, but Ali wasn't really listening. Her mind had been hijacked by grotesque images. She turned from the desk and walked towards the front door, her legs moving without her feeling them, her heart beating loudly inside the freezing casing of her chest, a bunched fist against a wall of ice. At the window to the left of the door, she stopped and found her right hand was up before her, her index finger running over the dirty glass. The corrugated sheet beyond the glass seemed to shiver in response.

A gust of wind swirled outside, hit the front door once, hard enough for it to rattle, and then fell away. The silence that came with it was heavy. Ali felt as if she was under water staring up at a surface that continued to pull away from her. She saw her right hand on the door handle and couldn't remember reaching for it. It gripped tight and then turned the metal. She was moved forward on those alien legs, and then she was shoving the door open wide with a dramatic flourish.

She walked out into darkness.

Emptiness.

Silence.

Will's words came eventually. The sounds of the night – distant traffic, the bark of a fox, and the gentle audience whisper of trees – they all came too, like an afterthought.

'I said, did you want me to go get the video? You OK?'

'You need to go home, Will.' Ali looked up to the roof, across to the stairwell on the right-hand side, and then stared at each floor in turn. Though now, in the night darkness and with most windows boarded up, it was hard to see any definition. The sharp light from the reception area bled out through gaps under the corrugated iron boards, to the left and the right of the open front door that, to Ali, was beginning to look a bit like a mouth. She reached into her back pocket and pulled out a Biro, before holding her hand out. 'Hand, Will.'

Will offered his left hand to her. Ali turned it over and wrote out her email address across the palm. 'Send me the link to the footage.' Ali pocketed the pen and returned her attention to the building. 'Weird.'

'What is?'

'Almost looks like it's smiling.'

The first noise came a little before midnight. At least, this was the first noise Ali could say for sure was real. That being a noise so loud, so alive, that it made her leap off her seat like she'd just been goosed. There had been other noises – in fact, her subconscious had a veritable orchestra of squeaks and whines and crunches-like-the-footsteps-of-a-monster going on – but deep down she had known they weren't real. Or if they had been, they were nothing more than an old building settling down. Everything aged makes noises. That was what she kept saying to herself during the first two hours as she sat idly thumbing through one of Ernie's tatty crime paperbacks – seeing words, not letting them in, not caring about the copper, the criminal and the dodgy dame talking in their diluted Chandleresque language.

No, the first real noise was something heavy and metallic landing with a hefty clang on the floor just above her.

Something was at her shoulder, and also just at the corner of one eye. Something else hid on the other side of the reception desk. A human form was being created from within the shadows behind her, just as another could be heard walking slowly down the stairwell to her left, getting closer. Fear was something icy, skewering her to the ground, and a thousand tiny spiders scuttling quickly from the base of her spine to the nape of her neck.

'No,' she said into the air, and then spun around to the shadows behind her, wafting an arm out as if brushing away a spider's web. There was nothing there. *Of course there wasn't.* Just the shadows and the merest hint of that fountain in the middle of the floor.

She stood that way for a minute, listening for other sounds. She turned to the windows, then across to the empty door shape at the start of the stairwell. She let her breathing slow. Let her fingers curl up against her palms, wiping away the sweat. *Sparkleville. Sparkleville.* It was her mother saying the word, her gentle and loving voice making the word dance, as she so often did. For another minute Ali stood that way, listening, waiting. Nothing came. Nothing was heard.

'No,' Ali said again, a whisper this time. Then her father's voice swam into her mind, saying one of his old favourites, something he would say to his pals on the force when he encountered someone with a tenuous grip on reality, and there had been a few over the years: '*She was wearing her craziness like a raincoat ten sizes too big for her.*' Ali had always pictured a woman trailing a grubby brown mac behind her like a train on the most hideous of wedding dresses. Then another from her old man, the venerable DCI Davenport: '*That show of madness was but a tinpot funfair that wouldn't divert a child with a pocket full of change.*'

He always had the right words. It was said by a few of his colleagues that he could talk a suicidal man off the ledge in less than a couple of sentences. And that he could make him jump in just a couple of words. Words were a weapon, and he was armed to the teeth.

DCI Davenport always had the right words for the right moments. Right up until the day he walked out on Ali and her mother, that was. That day he had nothing to say. Even as Ali stood there on the front lawn, in the stupid girly dress her father had bought her and that she only ever wore to please him, tears washing her cheeks, her throat sore from screaming at him to stay with her, he still said nothing. He had finally run out of the right words.

Ali walked to the halogen lamps, grabbing the stand of the one on the right and turning the tripod base with the toe of a boot, until the light spill hit the open space behind. The light cut a rectangular slice across the floor, illuminating the cheap, plastic fountain, the fallen cherub, and ending at the door to the toilet.

For a brief moment Ali considered moving the light inside that space, maybe seeing if the cord would stretch far enough for her to place it next to the fountain, assuming some light in that part of the floor would make things a little easier, but then her mind showed her something large and metallic dropping over the side of the exposed part of the floor and landing with an almighty clang just before her. Then, when her mind was done with that, it showed her a human body doing the same. Though now it wasn't a clanging sound; it was a heavy, sickening crunch.

Ali turned away. Now she was staring at the empty door shape at the start of the stairwell again. Somehow that sight was even more ominous than the shadowy emptiness behind her. She could see the first two steps, and then the third was at an angle to these as it bent around the corner, out of sight in the gloom. The white painted walls were peeling like giant scabs, the flaky paint skin littering the ground. Two lines of pinkish paint streaks ran haphazardly across the front wall; misplaced graffiti, she assumed.

Ali stared at that empty door shape, at the steps disappearing around the corner, into the darkness. Her mind showed her a dark figure descending the stairwell with a monster's casual arrogance, reaching the third step then turning around into the doorway to reveal itself as it gradually walked into the light. It was a man, but its face was a nightmare; his features glued to a face so pale it might make a child think of the moon, and he was walking right at her.

Then there she was again, back in the woods around the Deveraux estate. Out of breath and on her knees, Ernie Lipkiss at her side, Jake Tooley dead below them. They were looking further on into the woods, Ernie's torch picking out a face peering at them from around a tree. Was the face smiling? Ali had always thought so, but Ernie wasn't sure. It was a man, they both agreed on that at least, and his skin was a sickly white colour like curdled milk. And later on, when her senses returned, and she was able to remember her conversation with Jake, that head would for ever be like the moon to her.

Had they seen a body with that face? Again, they disagreed. He said yes, she said no. But both conceded they couldn't swear to it in court. Oh, and how that line always got dredged up when they needed a good laugh. But the boy had said he'd seen a ghost. He called him The Knock-Knock Man, and Ali had reported that, and she'd told how convinced she had been that Jake had truly believed it. That she was sure there was someone else involved and that she and Ernie might have seen him. She'd come close to believing she had actually seen a ghost. That night she wanted to believe everything Jake Tooley had said to her.

He knocks on the window. Twice. Knock. Knock. But you mustn't look.

Over the months, belief had been sullied by reality and now it was just another grey thing in her life that made little sense. The boy had said he'd seen a ghost, sure, and now the boy was dead, and it was all Ali's fault.

Spar...

She was wrenched out of her thoughts by something in the empty doorway at the base of the stairwell. It was a black shape, moving fast, low down to the ground; it shot around the corner, on to the first step and then seemed to crouch there, waiting.

For a split second it was Jake's Knock-Knock Man, scuttling down the stairs on all fours, coming for her. Ali's right arm shot out and grabbed for the second halogen lamp, yanking it around until it was in front of her, and the light was shining at the doorway. If he were coming to get her, she would damn well make sure she saw him.

But it wasn't any man.

Briefly it was a giant black, extremely furry spider, but then it moved again, startled by the light, and she saw a ragged black-and-white cat spring off the step and land gracefully before the front door. Ali's heart dropped down into her gut, whirled around then sprang back into place.

'You shitbag,' Ali said to the cat, as she placed the lamp back and made her way to the front door. 'How'd you get in here? You been knocking things off tables up there?'

The cat backed away from her, stepped into the door then straightened its legs and arched its back. As Ali bent down to it, holding out a hand, it began hissing.

'Well, you're a charmer, aren't you? You want out of here?' Ali unlocked the door. 'You and me both.' She had the door open no more than a foot before the cat jerked to the side and shot out into the night.

Ali was pulling the door to when a car turned into the car park, cut the headlights and came to a stop next to the wall of St Augustine's church.

The car remained stationary in the car park. Ali remained inside the building, peeking past a bent corner of one of the corrugated sheets on the windows. She was stooped slightly to get a good view and was starting to feel a dull ache in her lower back and down her calves. She thought she could hear noises out there, the low drone of voices and the occasional shriek of laughter. She waited for someone to step out of the car, for the light inside to come on, or for the headlights to come back on and the car to pull away, but nothing happened.

It was another suspicious noise that finally broke Ali's silent watch and turned her away from the window, back to the reception area and the empty doorway to the upper floors. She was at the desk, her fists balled up in front of her ready to lash out, before the sound came again, even louder this time, and the realisation slowly dawned that it was merely the sound of her empty stomach rumbling.

She rummaged in her bag for one of the sandwiches she had brought with her. It was thin, moist and smelled as if it was a day or two past, but she wolfed it down in three big bites and chased it with a large gulp of cold tea. When she belched a few minutes later the taste was acidic and sharp. There was a heaviness inside her now, something pushing down, squeezing tight. But there was nothing strange about this; after three cups of tea, and no desire to walk across the shadow-drenched open space to the toilets, her resistance had finally given out. She needed to pee.

Turning the second halogen lamp towards the open space behind the desk, the two beams cut across each other, connecting at the fountain. She jiggled the stand around and then placed both lamps side by side until the shafts were coming together into a single pathway straight to the toilet directly opposite where she stood. The darkness either side of this clinically bright pathway seemed to be swirling, pulsing almost. She knew the notion was ludicrous, her imagination ridiculous, but the idea was enough to stall her, her feet shuffling forward before stopping abruptly, her boots tapping a nervous tune on to the sticky linoleum as she hopped from side to side and her bladder seemed to fill with concrete.

All she could think of was those upper floors open to the empty space and if she dared look up, she would surely see The Knock-Knock Man gazing down at her.

'No!' Ali whispered to herself. *Enough. Enough!* She

coughed and tasted that hideous sandwich again at the back of her throat and then walked out on to the lit pathway and didn't stop until she was at the door. Her eyes never left that lopsided sign on the wall. Not even when one of her boots kicked up a piece of wood from the floor and sent it clattering against the wall, and not even when she felt a sudden wash of vertigo fall through her out in that open space that ran all the way up to the roof, when it suddenly felt as if her boots might rise off the floor if she kept on walking and she might float all the way up to the ceiling. Not even then.

A sweaty hand pulled the toilet door closed and then fumbled along the wall for the light switch, just as the other started yanking at her trousers, tugging them down. It was only then that she remembered there were no lights, just those halogen lamps and the long-handled torch that Dalton had provided, and that Ali had left on the desk. She scolded her stupidity, but had more pressing matters to attend to. Her hands felt around for the toilet seat, combing through air as she stumbled forward, trousers pooled around her ankles. Her knee found it first, the shinbone glancing off the porcelain and making her yelp. She turned, staggered back, and then slumped down hard on a thin plastic seat.

As she relieved herself in the darkness, other invading thoughts, rational and fanciful, fell away. Mostly. She did allow herself, on seeing the thin slither of light across the gap at the base of the door, the image of that light being broken by a shape passing across it. She even managed to conjure up the idea of a big fat rat in the toilet bowl, baby pink feet scrabbling on the wet porcelain, trying to get out. But those ideas were fleeting and weak.

The walk back felt easier. Still she didn't look up, but the idea that she was being watched by anyone up there no longer presented itself. Back at the desk she turned the lamps back to their original positions, crossed to the small room behind the desk to wash her hands, and then returned to the window.

Peering under the corrugated sheet, she could see that a tall figure was now standing at the boot of the car, side on to Ali. Seconds passed slowly into minutes that seemed to drag on for ever, and neither Ali nor the figure moved. Then a second, smaller figure suddenly appeared and stood before the first. The second figure then reached out and ran their arm down the chest of the first. A moment later the second figure was moving gingerly into a squat and bringing their head forward towards the tall figure and slowly undoing their trousers.

Ali felt another belch coming but it was chased back by a laugh of relief.

The midnight hour came and went and there was still no email from Will. Even more surprising to Ali was the fact that she hadn't heard from Maggie. But that soon changed. A little after one o'clock Ali's phone began vibrating on the desk. She didn't even question where Maggie had found her number; that she would have it was just about the only thing Ali knew with any certainty at that moment.

'Hello, Maggie.'

'How did you know it would be me?' Maggie's voice came in a cracked and dry whisper, as if she had just been woken.

'Call it a lucky guess.'

'Well, what's happened?' Maggie continued, her voice rising slightly now, finding its sharp edges. 'What have you seen?'

The image of the two visitors in the car park came straight to Ali, but she held back from reporting it, although the idea amused her. 'Maggie...'

'But the place, that building, you feel it isn't...right? There's something not quite right there. Tell me you agree with that too. Because Will said to me—'

'Will is an eighteen-year-old boy, Maggie.'

'What has that got to do with anything?'

Because I think the two of you are feeding off each other. The wide-eyed boy who wants to believe in ghosts, and the grieving woman who needs to believe that the man she loved could never take his own life. The thought stopped on her lips.

'You too then? You do think I'm mad.'

'I'm here, aren't I? As you wanted, to help you find some peace.'

'Peace? What peace do you think I'm going to find? My Ernie was attacked. He was killed. I don't know what possible peace you think you are going to find for me. What I want is people to accept the truth and to stop treating me like some crazy person. I want you to be honest about what you and Ernie saw that night. Have you seen Will?'

'I have.'

'And? The footage?'

'Not yet, Maggie.'

'Take a good look at what he filmed. You watch that and you tell me then what you believe.'

'Yes. I'll do that. I promise.'

Two loud blasts of a car horn suddenly made her jump out of the chair and drop the phone. When she retrieved it from the floor, Maggie had gone. A car headlight was now creeping in past the bent corrugated sheet. Ali could hear the deep purr of the engine as she approached the window, then the engine stopped and a car door opened and then slammed shut. She had just enough time to see that the couple from before had gone, and that this new car was parked right up alongside the building, before there were five quick, tuneful knocks on the front door.

'Hola, Señor Ernest, you perro viejo! I'm back from the land of anchovies!' The man's voice was light and bouncy, matching the way he knocked on the door. The knocks came again as he beat out another tune. 'Come on, you old bastard, don't worry, I've not got the holiday snaps.'

Ali went to the door. To her left, the open doorway to the stairwell – that third step turning around out of sight, those streaks of pink graffiti, the peeled scabs of paint – seemed darker than ever. Behind her, past the two lamps, the empty space looked to be just that – there seemed to be nothing there at all. A deep, bottomless ocean. Ali turned back to the desk and gathered up the long-handled torch. Holding it against her side like a small billy club, she returned to the door in three long strides, yanked down on the handle and swung the door open, almost into the man's face.

He jumped back quickly, and the glare of the halogens through the open door caught him like a frightened deer. He was short with dirty black hair streaked with grey at the sides, and was bound up in a thick winter coat with off-white fleece collars. Big ogling cartoon eyes gawped at her as she stepped outside and drew up to him, and the man's mouth opened and closed like a feeding fish. He moved to speak and then stopped, confusion colouring his face.

'Can I help you?' Ali looked past the man to his car. There was a taxi sign on the roof. She could also see lettering on the driver's side door and a phone number. 'I don't need a cab.'

The man began to back away. 'Sorry, I...sorry.'

'Who are you? How do you know Ernie?'

The man scuttled around to the side of his car. 'My mistake, I'm sorry. I'll come back when...I'm sorry...' As the man opened the driver's side door, the name Salstone Mini Cabs was clearly visible.

'Ernie's dead.'

Those cartoon eyes enlarged again. Ali imagined them popping out of his skull and hanging down from his face on the end of the optic nerves, clanging together like some grisly office toy. Again, the man went to speak but seemed to think better of it. His only response was a timid shake of the head, and then he was clambering back into his cab and starting the engine. Ali had just enough time to see a look of sheer terror creep across the man's face before the cab roared away, gravel scattering under its screaming tyres. She watched as the night swallowed up the cab, and when she blinked, she saw the trace of the rear lights in her vision, dancing around like fireflies, then they too went away and she was alone once more.

Except...

This time the feeling of being watched was something more than the feverish visions of a frightened mind, Ali was sure of it. And it didn't take long to be proved right. It was the soft orange light emanating from the open church doorway that she saw first. She didn't see the figure standing by the wall until she had locked the building up and was halfway across the car park, the beam of her torch sweeping left and right before her. He announced himself with a weak little cough, and Ali responded with a loud blast of swearing, and then the torch beam was in his face and he was shielding his eyes from the glare.

'If you could see your way clear to not trying to blind me, I'm sure we'll get along a whole lot better.'

'Maybe we'll start at you spying on me first, work back from there?' Ali moved the torch beam down until it was just under his chin, lighting up his clerical collar. 'Reverend.'

'Certainly, didn't mean to scare you.' As the reverend spoke, Ali could smell the stale reek of alcohol pass under her nose.

'Bit late for you, isn't it?'

'The church never sleeps.'

'Sure. Stay here overnight a lot, do you?'

'Sometimes. Am I under questioning?'

'Should I be questioning you?'

'I did speak to the police after it happened…that is why you are here, isn't it? The chap that decided to take his life in there? A shame. But I will tell you what I told them. My visitors here that night gave me a lift home. It has been verified.'

'Did you know him? Ernie?'

'No. Our paths crossed a couple of times here in the car park, but we exchanged little more than a nod. He never seemed a particularly chatty one. Although…'

'Although what?'

'Perhaps it was just with me. He wouldn't be the first to be unnerved by the clerical collar. He often had visitors there, in that building, so I suppose I do him a disservice.'

'Visitors?'

'Lost souls, I should imagine, wouldn't you? Are there any other kind at night? The night is security for the disparate and the strange. Eventually they find a home in each other.'

‘These visitors…the guy in the taxi just now?’

‘Yeah, I’ve seen him before, not for some time though.’

Ali took the torchlight from his face and shone it into the graveyard, the beam dancing between the gravestones. The feeling of being watched was alive again within her.

‘Looking for ghosts too, are you?’ Reverend Barnard asked with a light chuckle. ‘A young girl tending to a grave, perhaps? I hear that is a new one.’

‘You should look after this graveyard better.’

‘Someone should, certainly, but who will pay for that, I wonder? These parishioners of mine that have fallen away with such a tedious regularity? Or maybe you would have me rob a bank?’

‘I really wasn’t asking a question.’ Ali brought the torch beam back to him. This time she could see his face better; it was narrow and worn, yet his eyes were bright and cheery, almost twinkling in the torchlight. ‘Who else? What other visitors did he have?’

‘Well, let me see.’ Reverend Barnard stepped forward, rolled his shoulders until they cracked and then leaned on the wall, staring off at the building. ‘There was the dapper old chap, that was how I always thought of him. Immaculately dressed man. I saw him a few times.’

Ali thought instantly of Garrett Lyman, and how smartly he was dressed when Taylor had brought him in for questioning that night, so many months ago. She pushed Reverend Barnard to describe him further, and there was nothing in the description that made her think any differently. Could Ernie really have been having visits from the now-deceased former chauffeur of Lord Deveraux?

‘Did they ever come here together? The dapper old chap and the taxi driver?’

Ali turned the torchlight off and leaned her back against the wall.

'Believe they might have done. Couldn't say for sure.' Reverend Barnard crossed his arms on top of the wall. 'Creepy-looking place, isn't it? Whatever they are paying you, I should feel inclined to ask for more.'

'It's just a building.'

The real question she wanted to ask sat in her mind, waiting to leap. But before she asked it another question came charging forward and took her almost by surprise. 'You ever meet his partner? Have you ever met Maggie?'

'Can't say I have. We all know about her though. The poor woman. We've mutual acquaintances. I've offered her guidance, should she wish it. Her needs though seem to be something of a slightly different spiritual nature.' Reverend Barnard pulled himself up and straightened, his hands rubbing at his cheeks. 'You believe in ghosts, do you?'

'Do I?'

'That is why you are here, isn't it? I may be getting on a bit, but age has allowed me to meet more than enough people determined to make two and two add up to five. A grieving person wants answers. It is not to us to question where they choose to look for them.'

'You'd much prefer her to be turning to answers from your ghost, would you?'

'Touché.'

'Your God and I had a falling out some time ago. Don't take it personally.'

'Wouldn't dream of it. Want to talk about it?'

'The relationship became a little too one-sided for my liking. Nothing else to say. Tell me, these visitors Ernie had, you ever see...' she played the words back in her mind and found she wanted to laugh despite herself. In the most casual, nonchalant voice she could muster, she asked: 'Did you ever see him have a visitor – a guy, and sort of weird-looking. Very pale skin…deathly pale, I mean.'

The silence that fell between them unnerved Ali. Was he thinking? Or was his silence fear? Needing to see his face, she swung the beam back to where he stood, but Reverend Barnard was already turning away, one bony, long-fingered hand up over his shoulder in a parting wave. 'Don't believe I have. Sorry. Forgive me rushing off, but nature calls. See you around, I expect.'

'Hey!' Ali shouted after him. Reverend Barnard stopped and half turned back. 'No. Since you asked. No, I don't believe in ghosts.'

The reverend seemed to smile.

Ali turned the torch back towards the building and crossed the car park. A small, tinny pinging sound from her mobile phone greeted her return. A website link stared back at her from the screen. Ali took a seat at the desk, gripped the phone tightly and steeled herself.

After a cheap, scrolling title card announced that she was watching 'The Spangler Phantom Files', the face of Dave Spangler filled the screen on her phone. He was thin-faced and droopy-eyed with a large tuft of hair poking up on his head, half Tintin, half Stan Laurel. The short greeting to his YouTube video was spoken in a deep inconsistent warble, the teenage boy slipping through more than once and somewhat diluting his proud declaration that he was 'a purveyor of mysteries' and 'a ringleader for the strange'.

'And here we have something else unexplained,' he announced to his subscribers. 'An office building out on the edge of a business park in New Salstone, Wiltshire. An ominous and oppressive structure. Foreboding in daylight, deadly at night...one security guard protecting its four walls. But this guard is protecting the building from those outside. From the living.' Here the camera zoomed rather clumsily into Dave's nose and lips, the zit scarring all too evident, and the voice dropped even deeper. 'But what...' those lips asked the camera, 'if it isn't the living that he should be watching?'

The urge to laugh was overwhelming Ali, and had Dave Spangler continued his act any longer, she possibly would have. But that urge stopped abruptly, trapped somewhere in her chest like indigestion, as soon as the footage began. And then as the camera wobbled, zoomed and then gradually fell into focus on the small, hunched figure of Ernie Lipkiss sitting exactly where Ali was right at that very moment, her eyes began to fill. She mouthed his name into her palm and felt a tear trickle down on to her fingers. He was there for no more than a few seconds, and she considered that was just as well. She wasn't sure she could have taken any more of it.

The camera wobbled again as it pulled back from the building. She could hear voices in the background – Will, she was sure, and possibly Dave too. Up and up the camera went, all the way to the fourth floor, skirting along the edge of the roof. A jerk to the left and then the camera was swooping back down to the car park, alighting on Ernie's Volvo.

Someone walked in front of the camera then – it looked like Dave – and the camera moved back up, all the way to the sky. There it seemed to hold for a while, until slowly the building rose up into shot again as the camera lowered, past the edge of the roof, down to the fourth floor where it stopped at a long rectangular window with one end boarded up. Now the camera started zooming in at a sedate pace –

closer and closer, the image of the window sharpening, the shot steadying. Then, suddenly, there was a sharp intake of breath and the window was lost in a chaotic jumble of shapes – the sky, the building, the car park all seemed to change places in a quick blur, and then the camera was pointing down at Will's trainers. There were more voices, frantic, excited murmurings, then the camera was back at the fourth-floor window, searching left to right, before the image cut to black.

Ali's thumb moved to the screen, ready to run the video back for a second look, but it proved unnecessary. The footage of the window was repeated another three times, each time a little nearer and a little slower. The first time Ali saw very little, a shadow perhaps, hovering against a fleeting shape that moved ever so slightly past the window. The second time though, everything fell into view. The third time was merely another kick to the guts.

The shadow was human-shaped.

The shape belonged to a man.

The Knock-Knock Man.

She was sure of it.

Ali ran the video back and watched it again. She could make out a shoulder, an arm as well, and then that face, but only part of it, just a quick flash as it moved out from behind the boarded-up section, just for a few brief seconds, before moving back. It was fleeting, even slowed down as it was, so quick that you could easily be convinced it was something else. You probably had to be looking for him to know he was there. And if you'd seen him before, you were never likely to forget him.

She watched the video again. And again. She watched it

continuously until the battery on her phone was empty and she was staring at nothing but a black screen. Her eyes went instantly to the empty doorway to the stairwell.

Spirits have also been known, from time to time, to attach themselves to a person too, Will Kamen had very obligingly reminded her.

Ali suddenly burst out laughing. Her old friends, the army of tiny spiders, had lost all their direction now; instead of marching up her spine, they had set off on a thousand different drunken pathways across her body.

I have to go up there. Faces tumbled uninvited through her mind – Gage, Dalton, Deveraux and Maggie. Then there he was again, her constant nightmare, Jake Tooley, lying with his head against a rock. *Why do you have to go up there?* She was with Jake too. So was Ernie. And someone else was there too… *He called him The Knock-Knock Man.* Ali held her head in her hands, her eyes scrunched up tight as she tried to wrestle back the old rational logic that she had got used to holding on to so tightly. *This is ridiculous. Ridiculous!*

'This is fucking ridiculous!' she suddenly screamed, her fists balling up against her face. She gave herself one quick thump on the scar above her left eye. 'You hear me? I think this is ridiculous!'

The building gave no reply.

Fear and anger were a potent cocktail inside her, mixing together, diluting each other into something that at once made her stand up from the desk and pace across to the halogens, and then stall as soon as she began to move them. Two separate voices were haranguing each other inside her mind and neither sounded particularly like her.

Go up to the fourth floor. See what is there, one suggested.

Why the hell would I want to? the other countered, quite reasonably. *What do you think is going to be there?*

The argument went on as Ali began to drag the lamps past the desk and into the space behind. The cord stopped them just shy of the fountain. Ali moved the heads back and tilted them upwards. She didn't think the beam would get as far as the fourth floor, and a quick cursory look up confirmed it. But it was something.

So, you are going up there then?

Might be.

Otherwise you wouldn't be trying to light the floor, would you?

Gives me a choice then, doesn't it?

That beam isn't really touching the fourth floor, is it? Still going to be pretty dark up there.

I need to see it. The window. And where Ernie...

Why?

To that, the other voice had nothing. Ali gathered up the torch and crossed slowly towards the stairwell, all the while willing that second voice to come back and give her something, one small tenuous justification for what she was about to do. But the voices inside her head had fallen silent. She was alone again.

Rip the plaster off! That was another favourite saying of Daddy dearest. He would say that a lot, whenever Ali or her mother dithered or debated about something. Which had been often. Certainly, in her mother's case. Ali's mother had been a ditherer and a flapper. Ali often wondered what her father would have made of her over the last few years of her life, sitting in a nursing home, her mind hijacked by the ravages of dementia. Ali had no reason to think he would care. If he'd cared he would never have left them. As far as hereditary traits went, not caring was something Ali often wished he'd passed down to her.

She stood just before the stairwell, right hand gripping the torch, her left in a fist. But she couldn't walk through that open doorway. Her feet refused to climb those first two steps and lead her round into...well, who the hell knew what?

Just go for it. Just rip that plaster off.

The way out was easy enough. She was alone. She could make up any old guff and Maggie, Dalton and Frank Gage were just going to have to believe her. Did she even need to be here? Who would know? These shifts were for her to fill in as she saw fit. Because, if you boiled this stupidity down to its bare bones, all she was really doing was trying to offer succour to someone. She was playing a game, acting out a charade to help a grieving woman find some closure. She'd done it before; playing the caring copper with the comforting words, offering platitudes and singing the praises of strangers to make others feel better. This was just the same, really. Maggie just needed little more than a cup of tea and a kind word. But being that what she really needed to hear – or at least what people that cared about her needed her to hear – was something that would let her close this sad little chapter in her life and move on, then all Ali had to do was give it to her. It really was that simple. Why make it any more complicated than that?

Ali was in control of this situation if she wanted to be. She just had to sit it out and lie. Take her money and go home. She could do that.

But now Ali wasn't looking for a way out of this. She was looking for answers of her own, no matter how strange they might be. Seeing the video had merely underlined the fact. Seeing *him*. Now Ali knew, deep down inside, where she kept all her darkest secrets, that there would be no way out again until she found out who he was. What he was.

Anger bested fear in that moment. It was enough to yank that plaster clean off. Ali strode forward and almost hopped up on to the second step, swinging around into the stairwell. She held the torch up before her.

It was just a stairwell. A stairwell that led up to a small landing, and then around to another stairwell, and up and up three times more. There was a little rubble on the steps, some litter, and the peeling paint scabs here were far greater in number, but still – it really was just a stairwell.

The light from the halogens had caught the edge of the landing, and a few rather grotesque shadows were cast along the wall. She kept her eyes on these shadows as she picked her way gingerly between the detritus. Halfway up the stairs Ali's right boot landed on a broken bit of concrete, and she almost lost her footing and pitched backwards, but before she could she shoved herself into the wall, her free hand clutching the handrail. There she stood for a moment, the torch beam running up and across the landing, along the small section of ceiling that was visible, listening for any sounds, anything she couldn't place.

At the landing she held the handrail lightly as she turned slowly around to the next set of stairs, her palm running against the cold metal, brushing off loose chips of paint. She flashed the torch into the office space to her left as she passed. But she needn't have as the halogen lamps would have been enough for her to make out a long corridor running between shells of cubbyhole spaces, divided by occasionally still-standing chipboard walls.

There was more graffiti here, some of the walls now

with lurid pink, orange and green cartoon splodges covering them. At least they looked like splodges to Ali; maybe they were considered classic works of modern art round these parts. The ceiling was made up of squares of plasterboard, or it used to be. There were a lot of empty spaces there now, which made it look a little like a chessboard.

Ali began to climb again.

The stairs to the second floor were a little less littered with rubbish, and the paint scabs hadn't yet reached the ground. Instead, they hung in patches, bending forward to Ali as if in deference, ready to snap clear and fall. The graffiti here was on both the wall of the landing and the underside of the next set of stairs; words she didn't understand, and cartoon faces she didn't recognise, all created in fonts and colours that seemed to scream.

As she reached the landing, she started to smell something ripe and unpleasant, reminding her of the bins in the alleyway at the back of The Haven, and the tang of piss and puke and rotten food. But walking on, turning around to the next set of stairs, the smell seemed to break apart and vanish. Opposite her, the doorway to the second floor was partly blocked off by a filing cabinet that was tilted back, resting against the doorframe. She gave no more than a quick flash of the torch beam in the gaps above and below, before moving on up to the third floor.

There were no furnishings on the third floor, no cubbyhole shells or plyboard walls, nothing but rubble and litter strewn across a floor that was riddled with ragged holes. There was plasterboard missing in the ceiling again, and cords hung limply down through the holes. Ali slowed her pace but didn't stop.

Each step on the last set of stairs seemed to be uneven,

running at a slant, or it would feel like it was twice the height of the ones below. She knew it couldn't be the case, but the logic of it did nothing to stop her stumbling again. She felt drunk, untethered somehow. She sat halfway up the stairs and tried to gather her thoughts and calm the monotonous thrum of her heartbeat. The torch found the ceiling of the landing and sketched across it, down the wall and towards the corner of the door that would lead on to the fourth floor.

Get a grip.

You don't need to be here.

I do, though. Don't I?

Just lie. Tell them what they want to hear.

She gripped the edge of the handrail and staggered up the remaining steps. Her focus was at the open doorway further ahead on her left. The floor where Ernie fell. The floor where...

It's not real. Any of it.

I know.

She paused again to listen for any sounds, anything that didn't fit, but she heard nothing. The old building was silent and keeping its secrets to itself.

The halogen lamps were a mere suggestion on the edge of the floor, and what faced her as she moved into the doorway was a carnival of shadows and shapes, seemingly painted into a hanging gloom. She could make out the windows to her left, instantly finding the one that was partially boarded up, and to her right the light from the ground floor just about revealed the glass panels and railings. The rest of the floor was a mystery that her torch beam could only hint at. There was office furniture up here – drawers upended and scattered, filing cabinets that were doorless and dented, desk lamps tangled together in a heap in one corner, and smashed computer keyboards piled high in a moulding box. The floor was bad here too, not quite the hazard of the third floor, but enough broken flooring to turn an ankle or trip you over. Ali stepped over one such hole by the doorway and picked out a safe path to the windows.

It was the third one along in a row of six. The left-hand side was clumsily boarded over with an oversized plyboard square, loose at one corner, and the pane of glass on the right was smeared with dirt. There were two streaks in the dirt, just off centre, that she considered might have been made by fingers, and looking through these streaks she could make out the car park far below and the church further on. In the right-hand corner, a huge tangle of cobwebs was bunched up like greying candyfloss. Dead insects hung there like horrifying little decorations, and she could just make out one long, black, spindly leg poking out from the top of the web. It seemed to be twitching.

Ali ran the torch beam across every corner and line of the window, convinced that there would be something to see. Taking the torch beam back to the mysterious streaks on the glass, they now seemed wider than they had a minute ago, they were also less even, and she started to doubt that fingers would have made them at all. The torch beam found the railings again on the other side of the floor. And then her mind found dear old acrophobic Ernie Lipkiss.

'Was it an accident, Ern?' she asked the room.

Ali kicked a small cardboard box out of her path and picked her way slowly towards the railings.

'Because you wouldn't do it. Not you. You couldn't do it. What happened, Ern?'

The space beyond the railings opened out in front of her and she had to check her walk as a sudden wash of vertigo rose up through her feet and tried to tilt her off balance. Jerking down to a squat, Ali instinctively wrapped her arms around her knees, holding them tightly together in case they lost all control and tried to make her float away. Part of her wanted to scream. The other part wanted to jump.

'What happened, Ern?' Ali asked the silent building. 'What happened here?' She stared at the glass panels and the railings, and the emptiness beyond and gently began to rock back and forth on her heels. She gave a grim laugh before rolling on to her side, pulling her legs tight to her chest and scrunching her eyes shut. In her mind she was falling and somehow she knew she was never going to reach the bottom.

A phone was ringing far beneath her.

Ali-cat?

Call me back.

Chapter 11

Fourteen months earlier

'Ali-cat?' The voice on the answer machine didn't really sound like her old friend at all, although she knew it must be him. No one else used that bloody stupid pet name. 'You there?'

'Call me back,' Ali mumbled into her hall carpet as the lead balloon in her head pushed against her skull another few inches. Somehow, she pulled herself up to a seated position and rested her back against the hall table. The front door shimmered in her vision like a mirage. The vodka bottle lay to her side and she couldn't tell whether it was empty or not, although the taste in her mouth and the sharp smell of vomit on her jumper suggested the likely answer.

'Ali-cat?' Ernie was still on the line, still waiting for her to pick up. 'I need to speak to you, kid. I'm going to be... look, I think it's unlikely I'm going to go back. I don't think I can do it. I don't think I want it. This has... Makes more sense now. I want to speak to you, Ali-cat. So, crawl out of the bottle and give me a call. Yeah?'

Ali thought she heard Ernie curse under his breath, and then the answer machine beeped and a small red light started blinking. He was finally gone. She reached behind her and deleted the message.

She sat in her hall staring at the floor – at the bottle of vodka and the discarded post – for another twenty minutes, as her focus slowly returned. There was a cloying smell coming from somewhere and it was making her nostrils feel full. Rubbing at her nose, the back of her hand came away snotty. Ali wiped it on her trousers and then slowly got to her feet, leaning on the hall table for support. Then she saw the source of the smell – a bouquet of flowers was sitting in a small bucket at the bottom of the stairs. For a moment she glared at the bouquet as though it were something alien, then the recollection slapped her across the face and made the lead balloon in her head grind slowly around.

'Mum,' she whispered, before checking her watch.

Staggering up the stairs, she had already stripped her jumper and bra off before she had reached the top, dropping them on the landing and then stumbling into the bathroom and shoving two fingers down her throat, vomiting some acrid yellowy mush into the sink. Five minutes later she had washed her face, been overly generous with the deodorant and was standing naked in her bedroom gargling with mouthwash when there was a knock at the front door.

Ali made no move to answer it; instead she slipped on the first pair of jeans she could find and pulled on a baggy jumper that seemed to be clean. Picking up her boots, she crossed back to the bathroom, spat the mouthwash out and then padded wearily down to the front door.

Taylor's young, clean, and unbearably happy face was the last thing she wanted to see.

'Hey!' His smile stretched from ear to ear, and Ali didn't know what to do with it. She mumbled something that made as little sense to her as it obviously did to Taylor and then sat on the hall table and tried, with great effort, to pull her boots on. On the second attempt Taylor stepped in and crouched down to her.

'Here, let me,' he said, reaching for her.

'Don't touch my feet. We're not married,' Ali snapped, before tossing the boots across the hall in anger and picking up a battered pair of trainers from the shoe rack by the door. 'What do you want? Why are you smiling?'

'I'm sorry,' Taylor said.

'Why, what have you done?'

'Nothing. I haven't…I just wanted to see you.'

'Why?'

'See if you're OK?' Taylor was turning a crimson colour and averting his gaze.

'Oh,' Ali replied, and now it was her turn to smile. 'OK.' Ali looked past Taylor towards his car. 'I need to see my mother. Give me a lift?' Ali picked up the flowers and answered the question for him.

They drove for five minutes, Ali resting her head on the passenger side window, before either of them acknowledged the giant elephant on the back seat; the great thing unsaid. That night at the Deveraux estate.

Taylor's car carried a thick pong of aftershave and deodorant; the young lad hadn't so much gone to town with it, as tried to drown the whole postcode. She wondered if it had been for her benefit. Ernie had always told her that she intimidated Taylor, and she wondered if that was part of the attraction.

Was there an attraction, or had she imagined it?

'Who cares, right?' she whispered into the glass.

'Huh?'

'Nothing. Thanks for this. You didn't have to.'

'Sure. That's OK. How is your mum?'

Ali grunted and wound the window down a few inches, sniffing at the air like a dog. 'How old are you?'

'How old am I? Why?'

'You always seem to be eighteen. You've been eighteen ever since I first met you. How does that work?'

Taylor chuckled. 'I'm twenty-three.'

'Nice to be twenty-three.'

'It's not so bad.'

Ali opened the glove compartment and rifled around until she found a small packet of tissues. 'Mind?' she asked, before taking one and loudly blowing her nose. She glared at the flowers on the back seat and then rolled her neck until something clicked. She returned her face to the cool of the glass, watching the pretty hedge-lined roads of New Salstone blur past.

'Everyone misses you,' Taylor said.

'No, they don't.'

'You know that Ernie is thinking of pulling early retirement. Reckon Parker wants him to do it too.' Taylor laughed to himself. 'All the press attention is driving him nuts.'

'Good.'

'I probably shouldn't...can we...should I be talking to you about this?'

'Don't think it really matters any more. Any investigation into me stopped as soon as I quit. IOPC might as well file me away. What can they do to me now I've resigned? Does Parker still think that was the reason?'

'Probably. But you know I never thought that, right?'

'If you say so. Thanks. You know, you're the first

visitor I've had since it happened. Even Ernie hasn't...' Ali straightened up. The lead balloon did the same a few seconds later. 'I really thought Ernie would have come to see me. He's pissed at me, isn't he?'

'Not that I know of.'

'Yeah. He is.'

'Look, what you said you saw—'

'I didn't see anything. Just saw what you saw. Dead people. Whole load of dead people.'

'They pulled five out. The old girl, Deveraux and three staff. Fire took out half the house. Reckon it can be saved, but really, why'd you want to, right?'

'Did they hurt him? Jake? Did they make him—'

'No. No, nothing like that.'

'He had blood on his clothes.'

'Not his. Most was from Lady Deveraux, there was some animal blood in there too. As for how he died—'

'I don't want to know. I saw enough.'

'OK.'

'What about Garrett Lyman. What's he said?'

'If he's got a story to tell, I've not heard it yet. The super is all over the case, he's got the barriers up, and mere mortals like me aren't getting much on it. Word is Moss knew Deveraux. Moved in the same circles, and he's taking it personally.'

'That figures. Jake's mother?'

'You don't read the papers then?'

'I try not to.'

'Everything you'd expect.'

'She blames me?'

'Don't be daft.'

'I blame me. No reason she shouldn't.'

'His death was an accident. You didn't do anything wrong.'

'I did everything wrong.' Ali wound the window down a fraction more. Suddenly the inside of the car felt very small. 'Jake was held there, wasn't he? At the estate? They know that for sure now?'

'Yes. Ligature marks are consistent—'

'OK. I don't want to know.

'All right.'

'What else?'

'Couple of whispers about Lord and Lady Deveraux, that's about it.'

'Go on then, give me the whispers.'

'The old girl wasn't well, that much I do know. Back and forth to the hospital. Some mystery affliction just came on from out of nowhere. Apparently, she told her quack that she had someone living behind her eyes. He couldn't find what was wrong with her. Nutty old bird. As for Lord Deveraux, well, no one is saying much, or if they are, they aren't saying it to me. Did speak to Wallace Byram though. You remember him? The lawyer? He came to the front desk a few days after it all happened to volunteer some information. He'd been up at Deveraux's place the week before to help him rewrite his will and he said there was something amiss there, but he couldn't put his finger on it. Said Deveraux was very dark, morose.'

'His wife was ill.'

'Sure, it was probably that. But he also said Deveraux started saying some odd things. Things Wallace didn't understand, said he kept talking about the left-hand path. You know?'

'No.'

'No, me neither. I had to Google it. The left-hand path and the right-hand path are the two opposing sides to magic? Black and white?'

'Jesus.'

'I don't think Jesus had much to do with it. Wallace also told us he was sure that Deveraux had someone staying up at the house, and that from time to time he'd see someone out the corner of his eye and that Deveraux would get funny, creeped out, and move them to a different room.'

Ali perked up. 'And this person at the house, what did they look like?'

'That's just it. He was sure he saw someone, but has absolutely no idea what they looked like.

Ali sank back against the window. 'The Knock-Knock Man.'

'The what?'

'The man Jake spoke about,' Ali snapped. 'What's happening with that?'

'I don't know anything about that. No one has said anything.'

'Parker thinks it was bullshit. Moss will too. They're not going to do anything about it, are they?'

'The Knock-Knock Man?'

'It was in my report. He was the man who had scared Jake. Jake called him The Knock-Knock Man; he said that if he knocks twice on a window, you mustn't…' Whether it was because of the craziness of the words she was saying or the look of sympathy that suddenly tugged at Taylor's impossibly young face, Ali didn't know, but she quickly fell into a seething silence, her attention once more at the scenery rushing past the window.

'If it's in your report, then I'm sure Moss will deal with it.'

He knocks on the window. Twice. Knock. Knock. But you mustn't look. You must never look at his face if he knocks on your window.

Ali quickly lurched forward in her seat, the lead balloon grinding roughly into place a few seconds later. 'There were boards across the windows!'

'Huh?'

'There were boards nailed across the windows in that room. Deveraux's house. The room where he killed himself. Those windows were boarded up. Before he blew his brains out, he put a shot through each of those windows.'

'OK?' Taylor turned to her, waiting for more. 'I don't understand.'

The memory ebbed away so easily, the threadbare connection unravelling and falling away to yet more muddied confusion. 'No.' Ali slumped back in the seat and waited for the pain in her head to join her. 'Neither do I.'

Soon the main road to Gracious Oaks cut across them up ahead and Taylor slowed the car. The indicator clicked like a metronome in Ali's mind, the engine rumbled like an animal inside her gut, and as Taylor took the turning, bile rose in her throat.

'Stop the car,' Ali slurred.

'What?'

'Stop the car!' Ali wound the window down full and held her head over the edge, before vomiting down the side of Taylor's car. Taylor pulled the car off the road and into the start of a narrow lane. 'I'm done. I'm done.'

'Well, just give it a minute. See how you—'

'I'm done!' Ali shouted, tumbling out on to the lane and landing on her knees. 'I'm done with this. Go. Go home. Leave me alone.'

Taylor climbed out of the car. 'Hey, we're nearly there, let me—'

'Get away from me!' Ali staggered away from the car, her fists clenched, ready to strike. 'Please, just go away now. Please.' Taylor gave a whimper that could have broken another girl's heart, but made no move. He looked pathetic, Ali considered, much later. Pathetic and rather beautiful. 'Go away now. Go be twenty-three in someone else's nightmare.'

She only walked a mile, but by the time she turned into the gated car park of Gracious Oaks nursing home, she had to stop and lean on a fence to gather herself. Sweat was beading on the back of her neck and under her fringe, her legs were heavy and she stank. A transit van was parked alongside the small kitchen block at the side of the building and Ali checked her reflection in the wing mirror. The sight that greeted her was a perversion of a face that she used to know well. One she even used to like.

Sparkleville.

She closed her eyes and took a deep breath before opening them again. The same bloodshot eyes looked back at the same bloodshot eyes.

'Sorry, Toto. Seems we're still in Kansas.'

Ali could smell the familiar aroma of stewed vegetables, disinfectant and bodily functions even before she was buzzed in. As the doors parted with a delicate swishing sound the smell rolled at her as if in a giant cloud. Following in its wake came the bustling, always busy frame of the matron, Rose, her face for ever somehow stuck in the perfect balance between sympathy and happiness. With barely a pause Rose wrapped one short arm around Ali's back, brought her into a light hug and then turned her towards her mother's room and continued her bustle, Ali skulking along a few paces behind.

'Good day, today,' Rose chirped over her shoulder.

'Yeah?'

'We've had the photo albums out. Evelyn's been talking about your father.'

'OK.'

'Really rather lucid for a time, but tired now, bless her. She's been napping the last hour, so she might be a bit grouchy.'

There was much that Ali had had to get acclimatised to in the months that her mother had been living in the nursing home. A fact, in itself, that also needed some getting used to, and she had taken it all as it came, accepted it as another turn of the wheel and rolled with the punches – even though most turned out to be to the gut. Now, she found she fell into automatic, running on love, but the one thing that she still couldn't get used to was people talking about her mother as though she was an infant. The tone felt unnatural and misplaced. Yet everyone did it. There was no escape from that childishness. And there was no escape either from the stark reality that their roles had now irrevocably switched.

Deep down, on some level that Ali tried so hard not to acknowledge, that was the thing that really got to her. It was a terrifying truth for her to accept. She was the adult. She was in charge. She had responsibilities and commitments. When those old milky eyes recognised her, they looked to her for answers and help. And worst of all, this conversation, this convention, and this whole damn stewed vegetable stinking charade was not actually for her mother's benefit at all. It was for Ali.

All the colourful art on the walls, or the framed photos of happy days out, hanging against inoffensive neutral wallpaper, couldn't hide the vague prison-like feel of the place. A long, rectangular building for the most part, smaller corridors would feed off the central block like arteries, taking you to the gardens, the kitchens or the day room. Her mother's room was at the far end of the building, facing the overly maintained, ever-so-slightly clinical gardens.

The little old lady who pretended to be her mother was sitting, as she always seemed to be, in her armchair in the corner of the small room. The photo albums were stacked neatly on the table next to the window alongside her magazines and a photo of Ali that had haunted her for years; a young, painfully shy girl trussed up in that stupid girly dress bought for her by her father, that she only wore to make him happy, standing there on their front lawn, looking lost and confused.

Ali had given her mother other photos over the years, but none seemed to have taken its place in her affections, not even the one on Ali's first day on the force, so neatly decked out in her smart uniform, smiling proudly and so full of enthusiasm. She'd been sure her mother would have loved that, but it found its way inside an album and soon got forgotten. She wondered if it was because it reminded her mother of the man who had so casually walked out on her.

'Hey, Mum,' Ali said as she approached the lady in the armchair and gave her a peck on the cheek and a gentle squeeze of the hand.

'Come on, sleepyhead! Ali's come to see you. Are you going to wake up and say hi?' Rose bustled around the room, straightening things on the bedside table and fussing with the duvet. 'It's a lovely day; maybe you'd like to take her into the garden and see the frogs in the pond?'

'No, we'll be fine here, Rose. Thanks.'

'Would you like me to ask Ben to bring you a cup of tea?'

'No. Thanks. I'm fine. We're fine.'

'Well, as long as you're sure.' Rose finished her circuit of the room by running a finger along the edge of the small sink in the en-suite bathroom, nodding to herself and then hovering in the doorway, hands on hips. 'I'll leave you to it then?' She sounded almost offended.

'Thanks,' Ali said without turning around, and then heard the matron outside in the corridor offering her baby talk to someone else, her chirpy, happy voice gradually, blessedly fading.

Ali placed her fingers under her mother's left hand. Evelyn, her head drooping to the side, continued sleeping. Still holding her hand, Ali shuffled to a seated position by her mother's feet.

'Rose says it's been a good day? I'm glad you're looking at your photos. I'll bring you some more in next time. If you want.' Ali's eyes darted to the photo of her on the table, and for the briefest moment she could feel that horrid dress against her skin, prickling her, could feel the bunched-up hem and that wavy fabric that used to tickle her bare legs. 'I found a photo just the other week actually, it's you and me at Aunt Mary's one Christmas. Do you remember those Christmases we had there? Do you remember what she was like with her furniture? The way she would cover things in plastic sheets because she was paranoid about people making a mess? Well, this photo of you and me, we're sitting on her sofa with our drinks and plates of food, and we're laughing. Real big belly laughs, it looks like. And the sheeting on the sofa has fallen away from the back, so it's flapping free. And we're laughing and laughing and old Aunt Mary is there at the side of the photo and she has this look of abject horror on her face! She looks like she's just seen a ghost!'

The word threw her out of her reverie and swiped away the warm glow of Christmases at Aunt Mary's, returning her to the cold confusion of the here and now. There was Jake Tooley's face in her mind and he was asking her if he was safe, and then there was that other face too, that stranger in the woods. The Knock-Knock Man. Yet had she seen him at all? Or was she really just letting a child's overactive imagination infest her own?

He told the old man that he talked to the devil.

No, he didn't.

And that the devil talked back.

Ali rested her head in her mother's lap. Lifting up Evelyn's hand she gently rested it on her dirty tangle of hair, holding her own hand over it.

'I'm so scared, Mum. I'm so frightened. I'm not a bad person. You know I'm not. But they don't. Those people think they know me, but they haven't got a clue about me. They don't know that I'm one of the good guys. You know. Dad knew. But they don't.' She squeezed her mother's hand a little too hard and Evelyn shifted in her sleep and tried to pull it away, but Ali kept it where it was. Where she needed it to be.

'I can't find Sparkleville, Mum. I can't seem to get there any more. I think I might be lost.'

She saw that small girl in the photo crying and bawling in that stupid dress, sitting on her mother's lap, face nestled into her comforting chest. She remembered how unhappy and confused that girl had been back then. Those weeks after her father upped and left a hole in their lives, Ali had felt cut adrift from everything she understood, held down only by her mother and the comfort that she always gave. It was only in later years that Ali truly understood how broken Evelyn had become after he left, only when Ali herself had fumbled her own grasp on adulthood, and now she looked at her mother not just with love, but with awe.

That night the girl in the photo had dreamed, and it was lucid and seemed to stretch on for ever, outpacing all the hours of the night. The dream was a memory, yet somehow there was no corruption to it, no subconscious trickery or rearrangement. The memory was full, exact and perfect. Even in that period between sleep and waking when so often her dreams would tumble away in tiny fragments, never to be put back together, this one stayed with her, so strong was the recollection and so warm and happy the feeling. An adult would perhaps have analysed its meaning, picking apart what led to the subconscious choosing it, or someone of faith would maybe see it as some sort of message from the divine, but this little girl merely revelled in the good feeling it gave her. The safety she felt. She could corrupt it in years to come if she wanted to because, somehow, she knew that she would always remember it. No...not remember it, that's too weak a word. She would always own it. Even at her young age, the little girl knew that.

Sparkleville.

The old wooden sign actually said Hopeville, embossed in wiry black lettering. It swung on rusted chains from the top of an equally old and weather-beaten wooden post on the small stretch of path between the driveway and the beach. The little girl had run on ahead, her Cairn terrier Obi at her heels, and she had been the one to see the sign and the isolated beach house first and when she did, she jumped up and down on the sand in some sort of victory jig. She had no shoes on and she enjoyed the feel of the sand on her feet.

While the girl danced, Obi ran back across the beach to

the girl's parents who were trudging along a good hundred yards back laden down with their belongings, and battling the increasing sea wind. Her father's hat blew off – this had been the third time it had done so just on the short walk from the car – and the girl fell about in hysterics, just as she had done the two times before.

They had looked at the sign together, then her father had sucked his lips tight and gazed out at the darkening clouds and the foamy rolling waves, and he had laughed and told the girl he thought the sign might be ironic. She didn't really get it, but laughed anyway. Her mother was trudging up the driveway with Obi bouncing about at her side and she was calling to them, telling them to hurry up, and to not get cold, and that they better get inside before the rain came. They heard her, but they weren't really listening.

Her father dropped to his knees so that he was face to face with his daughter and he asked her if he could borrow the sparkly make-up sequins that she had been putting in her hair and on her face. Well, he called it glitter, until she had corrected him, and what did he know, anyway? She thought he was going to tell her off, because she had been a little liberal with this pot of sparkle that she had pestered her mother to buy for her, and she'd got them all over the car, her clothes and Obi too, but he didn't, he just grinned even wider as she handed the pot to him. He asked her if she had more of it and she told him she did, and asked him why.

Her father stood and drew her to his side. They both faced the wooden post and the old sign, creaking tiredly in the gathering wind, and then her father unscrewed the pot and gently tilted it over the sign until pink and red and gold and silver sparkly sequins tumbled out, caught the breeze and then danced and bent and flipped around before them.

She remembered them dancing. They *did* dance in front of them. Then those twinkling sequins caught the wind and blew on to their clothes and into their hair and their faces and neither of them cared.

'Sparkleville,' her father said. 'Let's call it Sparkleville from now on, what do you say, Alison?'

She didn't need to say anything because her smile said it all. Father and daughter high-fived and went on up to the house.

The rain came moments later, and then the storm that the weatherman had promised arrived within the hour. They unpacked – she chose the biggest room at the front of the house, facing the sea. They prepared food, they joked and mucked about, and they took it in turns to comfort poor old Obi who was cowering under the dining table as the storm raged. The house was old and a little rickety and it creaked and moaned and rattled, but the little girl was never once frightened, not like poor Obi. The waves crashed against the jetty further down the beach and the sky grew dark. The bony arms of lightning grabbed and swiped and the air thickened, and the girl was calm. She was happy.

Despite her mother's protestations, her father put the TV on. The reception was pretty good and the picture only went off a few times. Father and daughter flicked through the four channels on and off for most of the afternoon, uninspired by most of what they saw until they stumbled on a channel showing *White Heat* and they both voiced their approval, it was one of their favourites after all.

Her father did his Jimmy Cagney impression, and even her mother found that amusing. Not enough for her to stop fretting and waiting for the TV to blow up at any moment, but it was a start. The girl wasn't very good at impressions but couldn't resist climbing up on to the sofa and screaming, 'Made it, Ma! Top of the world!' at the film's end. Her parents laughed at that, and she didn't know if that was because they thought it was good or utterly terrible. But she didn't care.

They played games as the storm was overhead. Monopoly was her favourite, and she was always the boot. *Always.* As they were playing, her mother had told her that the thunder was actually God moving his furniture around and she'd really liked that idea. Her father gave her a small crucifix necklace after the game and told her that it used to be his and that he now wanted his daughter to have it instead. He looked funny that night; it was the first time she remembered him changing. Her mother said it was the job. A case. A none-of-your-business-young-lady. As her father put the crucifix around her neck, she asked him if the reason he didn't want the crucifix was the same reason why he'd stopped going to church. He had never answered her.

She went to bed and left her curtains open so she could watch the lightning, and the turbulent ocean, safe in the knowledge that she was untouchable in that moment. Obi wandered in and she let him come under the covers. She hugged him tight and he gently licked her face. He seemed to have finally scared himself into exhaustion.

Her father came to see her then with two mugs of hot chocolate. She sat up in bed and took hers gratefully. He perched on the end of the bed and then they both watched the dark, surely bottomless ocean moving under the bruised sky. The house had settled, yet still gave intermittent squeaks and moans as if to remind everyone it was still there. As if the little girl could ever have forgotten.

'Sparkleville is my favourite place in the world,' she told her father.

'Yeah?'

'Yes.'

'It would have been nicer in the summer, don't you think? Instead of autumn.' He sounded apologetic, almost slightly morose, and she didn't want him to sound like that. But he did from that day on. He changed. But there was still enough of him left that day, enough for her to hold. 'Sun and calm water and not howling winds and thunderstorms?'

'We can come back in the summer too,' she had said.

Her father hadn't replied. Maybe her father had known that they wouldn't. She gazed at his shape at the end of the bed, felt her warm dog snuggled up next to her, and then heard her mother cough lightly in the next bedroom. Her hand went to her throat and played absently with her necklace. 'But I don't care. I don't care about any of that. I certainly don't care about thunderstorms.'

'No? You always used to be scared of thunderstorms.'

'No. I'm fine. I'm not scared.' *Nothing can touch me here,* she thought. 'I feel perfectly safe. I *am* perfectly safe here. Why should I be scared?'

'You really feel that?'

'Yes. I do.'

'That's my girl. I'm glad. You should feel that way, Alison. Sparkleville is your place after all.'

And with that the girl closed her eyes on the dark figure at the end of the bed and fell asleep in the dream. And she slept with the comfort that came from the certainty that her father was right.

This is my place, and I am safe. This is a place where nothing can ever hurt me, because it is my place and I control the walls and the doors. I control the sky and the earth too. I will come here whenever I want. Nothing changes here because I don't let it.

Ali heard her name and slowly pulled her head up from her mother's lap. She could feel a line of snot across her upper lip and the lead balloon inside her skull reminded her of its presence too. There was a man standing in her mother's doorway. He said her name again, and then as her vision sharpened, she recognised the huge bouquet of flowers he was holding. Then she recognised the man.

'What the fuck do you want?' Ali said, straightening herself against her mother's legs.

'Your flowers. You left them in my car. I didn't notice until I got home.' Taylor was blushing again, not quite meeting her eye. 'Sorry, it's just they look expensive. I'm sure you must want—'

'Right,' Ali said to Taylor, 'let's go.'

'What? Go where?'

Ali got to her feet and felt the hangover awaken and seep around her body. Her mother was still sound asleep, her head still tilted to one side. 'I'm tired, hungover and have a headache as immovable as a builder's lunch break. I need air.' Ali bent delicately to her mother and kissed her again on her forehead. Taking the flowers from Taylor, she dumped them on her mother's bed and turned out of the room.

Outside Gracious Oaks nursing home, as the smell of stewed vegetables began to fade, Ali breathed deeply, sucking in the clean air. 'I feel like I've been submerged.'

'What's that?' Taylor asked, scuttling to catch her up.

'Nothing. Give us a lift?'

Taylor passed Ali on the way to his car. 'That much I guessed.'

They said nothing on the drive back until, three streets from her house, Ali told him to let her out. She walked off without looking back. At the sound of Taylor's car pulling away she quickened her pace.

As she stood on the discarded post on her hall floor, she noticed that the red light was flashing again on her phone. Ali pressed play and locked the front door, running the security chain across for good measure. The same small voice was back.

'You're right,' her old friend told her through the machine. 'Is that what you want to hear, kid? Aye, you're right. I saw him too. That night. I saw him too.'

'Yeah, Ernie. I know you did.'

'Call me back.'

Ali deleted the message and retreated into her house.

Chapter 12

Ali stepped out into a darkness feathered grey at the edges. The morning air felt as fragile as glass, something she could break, yet also something that could cut her deep. It danced its welcome all around her, whipping up her coat and ruffling the loose strands of hair on her head that hadn't yet been flattened to her scalp by grease. Somehow the empty car park surprised her; Ernie's car looked so lonely. St Augustine's too was no more than a gloomy suggestion this morning. She'd expected something, someone, but there was nothing.

Ali locked the front door and trudged to the car. She quickly glanced back at the building as if trying to catch it unawares. Her eyes went from the door, across to the stairwell and then up and up until any definition was lost in the dark. Then they went left, searching for that half boarded up window on the fourth floor, but the darkness still had it.

A dirty, maroon-coloured Volkswagen was parked on the road, just past the turning, the driver's door slightly open. There was no one inside. Further along the road, just before the start of the industrial estate, a taxi was parked up on her side. Not a Salstone Mini Cab this time, but a familiar old black cab that reminded her of London. She didn't see the figure on the pavement, their arm outstretched to her, until she was almost past it, and when she recognised the person hailing her, she had half a mind to just keep on driving.

'Right,' she muttered to herself, before pulling to the pavement, leaning over and unlocking the passenger door.

Maggie looked as if she hadn't slept in weeks. 'Well?' she asked Ali. 'Tell me.'

'Nothing to say, Maggie. Just as there wasn't anything to say at one o'clock this morning.'

Maggie climbed into the car. 'I find that very hard to believe.'

'Still the truth.'

'The *truth*, don't tell me you have as loose a grip on that as all the others. I expected better from you.'

'I don't know why you expect anything from me.'

'Because you know!' Maggie shouted. 'You've seen him!'

'Look, you wanted me here to investigate this. Seems to me there's not a lot of point in me carrying on doing that if you're not going to believe what I tell you.'

Maggie turned to the windscreen, her demeanour softening almost immediately. 'I'm being unfair on you, I'm sorry.'

'No need to be.'

'But the building…you felt something there, surely?'

'No. Not really.'

'So, I am crazy. OK. Then so be it.'

'Of course you're not.'

'I love him. Love can make you a little crazy, right?'

'I loved him too, Maggie.'

'Look at the video, Ali, you watch the video and then tell me if—'

'I have.'

'And?'

Ali had already given some thought as to her response to Maggie on this particular issue. Telling her the truth, and conceding that she thought she was right, would do nothing but change the course of her investigation, an investigation where she was still only fumbling at the edges. She could see Maggie taking centre stage, see Gage dragged into the way, obstacles piling up between her and the man she knew she had to find. Would Gage take it seriously? She doubted it. Could she even trust him? She still couldn't be sure on that either. But one thing she was pretty certain about was that Gage and Dalton would pull the plug on her inside track to the mystery. On the other hand, telling Maggie that she thought the video showed nothing at all, seemed too cruel to contemplate. So, Ali found the middle ground instead, and decided to come down on neither side, just buy herself a little more time to find the truth.

'I watched it on my phone. Screen's too small to see properly. I need to see it again. On a better screen. Clearer picture. You know?'

Maggie stared at her with narrowed eyes and Ali knew she was working her over to look for a tell, something to show if she were lying. 'You'll see, Ali. Then you'll know, and then you will tell them that I was right.' Ali held her poker face, giving Maggie nothing to work with in the hope that she would give up and get out of the car. But Maggie wasn't quite done yet. 'Don't ever lie to me, Ali. OK? Please don't ever do that.'

'I wouldn't dream of it,' Ali lied.

Maggie returned to the taxi without another word.

Chapter 13

Salstone Mini Cabs ran their operation from a small square building a few doors along from the train station. There was already a steady procession of cars coming and going, preparing for the morning rush, when Ali arrived and parked up across the road, tearing into a takeaway breakfast of a depressed-looking Pain Au Chocolat and an overly milky coffee.

A large crowd bundled out of the station and crossed in front of her, some scattering to the car park, others taking the two roads into town that ran either side of the station, and the rest crossing straight to the cab office, each person seeming to speed up as they neared the building, desperate to be the first there. A few moments later a couple of people filed back out and climbed into waiting cars. Cars left and cars arrived, people entered the building and came back out. In the half an hour Ali watched, the man who had so unexpectedly appeared at the building in the middle of the night, was nowhere to be seen.

As she was getting out of the car, Ali noticed a burly man standing in front of the train station, smoking. He caught her eye so easily she knew he must have been watching her already. Big of chest and wide of head, the man carried the sartorial aesthetic of the football hooligan abroad, and appeared to have all the cocksure confidence of one too. Flicking his cigarette away, he crossed his beefy arms over his chest and stood there, legs apart, glaring.

The cab office was little more than a narrow corridor from the door to the back wall. It passed in front of a small hatch where a woman with an obscenely cheery disposition for the time of day sat controlling the whole show, a headset seemingly welded to her head and a pen glued to her hand. Ali squeezed up next to the wall, standing at the back of the huddle that seemed to constitute the queue. From time to time the woman would call out someone's name in a joyful squeak and direct them to the door and then the huddle would shuffle forward a few inches.

At this close quarters Ali could smell the people around her, all clean and sweetly scented, ready for their day, and became acutely aware of her own rather rancid ripeness. At one point a woman in front of her whispered something to her friend, and then they both screwed their faces up and laughed. Ali wondered if she was the joke. Suddenly she was in front of the hatch, facing the cab dispatcher, and wondering just what the hell she had to be so happy about.

'Hey, honey, where you going?'

'Hi, I don't need a cab. I was hoping you could help me. I seem to have lost an earring and I think it must have been in the back of one of your cabs, last night.' Ali gave the woman one of her good smiles, trying to talk her own language. 'Has anything been handed in?'

'Oh, not to me. No. Sorry. Not expensive, I hope?' The woman looked genuinely distressed on Ali's behalf.

'No, not at all, but it was a gift from my husband, so sentimental value.'

'Oh, I hear that, honey.'

'Thing is, I was so distracted by my driver – he was nattering away, he'd just come back off his holiday, Spain I think he said – that I just didn't realise it was missing at the time.'

'Sounds like you had Mickey. Malaga, was it?'

'Yeah, that's right. Small guy, he was.'

'Uh-huh, that's our Mickey, but don't you worry. He's as honest as the day is long. If you've lost your earring in his cab, he'll hand it in.'

'Is he working now? Maybe I could—'

'He's on lates this week. You want to give us your name and a number and I can get someone to give you a tinkle when we've spoken to him? How'd that be?'

'Well, look, I'm actually getting a train home tonight; maybe I could call in beforehand, speak to him myself. I'd be happier about that. You phone home and you might get my husband, and I'd sure hate for him to know that I've lost something he gave me. How'd that be?'

'You can do that, sure thing. You come back here after six and I'll see what I can do.'

'Ah, you are a darling.'

The fake smile slid off her face as she walked back out to her car. Another surge of people alighted from the station and swept past her. As they dispersed, she looked for the man who had been giving her the eye, but the front of the station was now empty. Ali slid back behind the wheel and pulled out into the morning traffic.

From the train station car park, a dirty, maroon Volkswagen swung out of the exit and fell in behind her. The

Volkswagen tailgated her for two streets before falling back, allowing cars to pull in between them. By the time Ali turned into the road that led up to the Lamplighter hotel, the other car seemed to have vanished completely.

She felt filthy and wretched, and all she could think of as she climbed up the hotel stairs to the second floor was having a shower, staying locked in that little room under the warm spray until her skin was pink. Her heart sank at the sight of a man's work boots poking out from around the shower room door, an open tool box to one side, and a slow clanging sound coming from within.

'Problem with the—' she asked, from the top of the stairs.

'Pipes,' the man cut in, not bothering to look up.

'How long do you think—' Ali started, before the man cut her off with a grating blast of whistling. 'Right.'

Her room carried a whiff of fried food and something else, something damp and old. Ali crossed to the window, spared the car park a quick, cursory glance, and then pulled the curtains, shutting the world out. She plugged her phone into the charger, stripped down to her underwear and then flopped on to the bed.

There were five missed calls from Maggie and two from Gage. She ignored them both. Ali rolled on to her side and stared at a torn patch of wallpaper next to the window. Slowly she let the phone fall to the floor as a smothering tiredness began to crawl over her. She was powerless. She closed her eyes and gave in.

Someone held her hand and led her up the long, well-lit pathway towards Deveraux's home. She was stopped at a window, and through the glass she saw a room she recognised. Directly opposite her were two familiar doors, open a fraction. That autumnal, orangey hue caressed the walls. There were candles positioned on the floor, each connected together by a line of blood. More blood lines connected them up to a curious object in the middle of the room. She thought it was some sort of sculpture.

A voice in her ear corrected her. *An altar*, it whispered. Ali nodded at her reflection in the glass. It seemed obvious now. It also seemed odd that she hadn't noticed straight away that the lines of blood on the floor formed a shape that she recognised. *Pentagram*, the person at her side told her. She caught sight of the reflection standing next to her in the glass then. There was no shock in seeing The Knock-Knock Man there, staring directly at her. No fear, either, as he seemed to walk through her and disappear. It felt more like resignation.

Ali gave one timid little moan and then jerked awake, her eyes opening to the torn wallpaper. Rolling on to her back, she stared up at the dead insects in the light fitting until she was far enough away from the nightmare to move. She saw one small black fleck twitch inside the light; it flittered about, bounced off the glass and then fell back amongst its friends and moved no more.

So much of the previous night now seemed unreal and dreamlike. The only thing that felt real was the one thing that simply couldn't be – that face on the video. But there had been a blessed moment upon waking where she had convinced herself that that too was all part of some subconscious trick. Now as she drove through the rain-lashed streets of New Salstone, all she could see was that face moving into view in the window, and it felt like a taunt.

Will Kamen had answered her email immediately. Now, staring at Ali in the doorway to his house, his eyes were alight with questions. He gabbled a 'hello' as she walked past him into the hall.

'Would you like a cup of tea?' Will asked, shutting the front door and leading Ali through into the kitchen.

'Sure.'

As Will set about making their drinks, Ali poked around the kitchen and the adjoining living room. Both rooms felt sparse, the design purposefully minimal, a sedate riot of magnolia and showroom precision. She felt Maggie would probably approve.

Beyond the aching dullness, the strangest thing to Ali was the absence of paintings on the walls or photos on the mantelpiece in the living room – no photos of Will, of family pets or distant relatives, nothing much of anything. The single bookshelf in the living room carried a mere five books: nothing she had read and no one she had heard of. There were no plants either, or vases of flowers. It almost felt like a concession to the fact that nothing could live in a place so sterile.

'So, I didn't see a ghost. I assume that's what you're busting to ask me?' Ali said. Will turned to her, a mug of tea in each hand and an adorably stupid expression on his face. His mouth flapped open and then slammed shut. 'No bogeyman, no floating apparition and no one in a white sheet rattling chains and moaning. But I did see your video.'

His voice, when he found it again, came in a whisper. 'And?'

Ali shrugged. 'Do you have the original footage? Not what your mate stuck on the Internet, but the video you actually filmed that night?'

'Yeah. I got it back from Dave this morning.'

'I'd like to see it.'

In contrast to the kitchen and living room, the converted garage where Will had his bedroom oozed the chaotic teenage cliché in every inch, from the moment Will opened the door and a cloud of deodorant drifted lazily past them. Ali saw a teetering mound of dirty clothes shoved in one corner of the room, and a plate of half-eaten food under the bed. As Will passed by, she noticed him poking it further under the bed with the toe of his trainer. One of those hideous plug-in air fresheners that always gave her a headache was also pumping out its stifling scent. But despite the cloying mix of deodorant and air-freshener, the smell of teenage boy still hung in the room like low-level mist, unshakeable and impenetrable.

Ali leaned in the doorway with her cup of tea as Will started tinkering with his computer, rolling a chair across and then sitting hunched over, connecting up his camera to the back. The walls of Will's bedroom were smothered in posters and prints and stills from various films. She saw Lon Chaney in *The Phantom of the Opera,* Deborah Kerr in *The Innocents,* a large Italian one-sheet for *Suspiria* and a giant poster for the original *The Haunting,* in amongst a veritable rogues' gallery of monsters and creatures and nightmarish faces.

'How do you sleep at night with these things staring at you?' Ali asked, stepping into the room and taking a seat on his bed.

'It's all make-believe,' Will said. 'What's to be scared of?'

For a split second, Ali saw the smiling face and ghostly pale skin of The Knock-Knock Man staring back at her from an old black-and-white still hanging between The Wolf Man and Dracula, but then looking at it again she saw only the odd domed-shaped head of an alien from a cheesy old film that she didn't recognise.

'It's what your mind sees that you should be frightened of,' Will told Ali, as if reading her own. 'That's what I think, anyway.'

'Yet you hunt ghosts?'

'Ronnie says you have to be a bit of a masochist to be a ghost hunter.'

Will turned his computer monitor around so it was facing Ali. He had cued the footage up to start at the same point as the video Ali had already seen, the same out-of-focus shot of Ernie, the same wobbly rise to the roof of the building and the night sky.

'No, can you go back to the start? Take it from the first thing you filmed that night.'

'This is the only footage I have of the building. What are you looking for?'

'Something. Anything. Show me anything where you're filming towards a window, out towards the car park or the road.'

Will ran the footage back to the start. 'You know we were only there for an hour or so. When we left, your friend was—'

'Uh-huh.'

'Then what are you hoping to see?'

'Visitors.'

For a film fanatic, Will Kamen's camera composition left a lot to be desired. For a full minute he played back footage of the winding path through the graveyard at St Augustine's, as they ambled their way to the church, broken up only by the occasional swing to a gravestone or down to his trainers.

'Could you, perhaps, fast-forward parts of it, Will?' She saw the red creep back on to his cheeks. 'Sorry.'

For the next twenty minutes they sat there scrutinising

the footage in the few places the camera veered towards the windows. For the most part the large arched windows were too high to see anything, and Will would push the footage on, but a couple of times it panned across an open door at the side of the church that faced out towards the car park, and Will would slow the video down. But it was too dark, and there was nothing to see there, bar the wandering shape of Reverend Barnard passing through the shot. In these moments she would hear the self-important voice of Dave Spangler echoing around the church, calling out to spirits to show themselves, and Ali wondered just what he would do if one did. She imagined that his voice could break into quite a memorable scream. Soon the footage moved out into the graveyard and here Will slowed the video more often.

'I did the front of the church with Dave. Ronnie did the back. The ghost of the girl leaving flowers on the grave was supposedly seen out the front, so...' Will's words trailed off.

Ali leaned further forward now, almost shoulder-to-shoulder with Will. At one point the camera panned from the side of the church all the way across to the car park, and then back in a wobbly three-sixty, but a little too fast to see anything with any great definition other than Ernie's car. Slowed down, the footage was too blurry to give anything away.

'You know, there were no other people there that night, Ali. I'd have remembered. No cars. Nothing.'

'You can't know that for sure. You weren't outside the whole time.'

'We'd have heard.'

'Why would you remember? You weren't listening for anything. Besides, a slender thread from the noose that will finally catch your man is always better than any shot in the dark.'

‘What’s that, some sort of police motto?’

‘Something someone said to me once.’

‘Ernie?’

‘No.’

For another ten minutes they continued fast-forwarding the footage; the walls of the church, the oak trees and from time to time a gravestone, all jittering hyperactively in the sped-up, hand-held film, and the almost comical figure of Dave Spangler zipping in and out of shot. It made Ali think of very early film footage, where people in sepia hues all seemed to skitter about their life, and how that always used to scare her when she was a child, and how stupid that seemed now.

‘There!’ Will suddenly called out, stopping and then rewinding the tape. ‘I forgot!’ As he pressed play again, he pointed to the screen. ‘It’s not much but…’

It was more than Will could possibly know.

‘I’d nipped for a pee, put the camera on the wall, didn’t turn it off because Dave was doing EVPs, and I thought I might pick something up on my mic. Is that a car there? Something written on the side?’

‘Salstone Mini Cabs.’

The camera faced the oak trees and the turning into the car park. A shadow bled across the path and then retreated. Someone was on the pathway, just out of shot. The glimpse of the road was small, but there was enough there to betray the bonnet and driver’s door of a car parked next to the pavement. At least, it seemed to be parked at first, then slowly, bit by bit, it edged forward, crawling along next to the pavement, seemingly debating as to whether to turn into the car park.

Ali recognised the writing on the side of the car straight

away. She also thought she could take a pretty good guess at the face behind the wheel. It trundled forward until it was halfway across the turning and then suddenly gathered speed and disappeared out of shot.

'What does that mean?' Will asked.

'Quite. What does it mean? Threads, Will.'

'Huh?'

'All these threads are going to lead somewhere. I'm just going to pull on this, see if there's a noose on the end.'

'Shouldn't I call the police?'

'Police don't care about this. Police have never cared about this.'

'But...'

'No.'

She saw Parker in her mind, the exasperated looks that came so easily to him whenever he was in her company, and she remembered the ease at which both he and Superintendent Moss had shut her story down, all those months ago. She remembered their pitying and patronising demeanours. Most of all, she remembered the crushing realisation that she no longer belonged in the place she had always wanted to call home. Then there was Gage, and he might just be worse than them both. She didn't need any of them.

'I *am* the police,' she told Will firmly, ending the conversation.

Ali felt a knot in her stomach. For the briefest of moments, she had forgotten about where this video was going. Now she was looking back at her old friend again, sat alone at the reception desk, and she was watching the camera move up to the night sky before dropping back, and then there was that window with one side boarded up, and Will was slowing down the footage, moving frame by frame. She could see his leg twitching from the corner of her eye, could feel his stare, waiting for her reaction, waiting for her to tell him what he so desperately wanted to hear. She knew there was no hiding her expression from those eager eyes and, to her amazement, she found that she also had no desire to, either. More than that, she wanted Will Kamen to know the truth.

'Yes,' she said flatly, before that face had even appeared, 'it *is* him.' And then there he was on the computer screen, as if summoned by her words, moving out from behind the boarded-up window, one frame at a time. Will paused the footage. 'That *is* who I saw that night at the Deveraux estate. I'm sure of it.'

Ali leaned in close to the screen, staring back at that partial reveal of The Knock-Knock Man's face, looking into it as if it were some Magic Eye picture that might change and show her something else if she stared for long enough.

'How can it be him?' she whispered. Will started to open his mouth to speak, but then, perhaps realising he had no answers for her, closed it again. 'I don't want you to tell Maggie about this, Will. Not anyone. Not yet. Can I trust you to do that?' Will nodded. 'I'm relying on you.' Will's wide eyes got a little bigger at that. 'OK?'

'OK.'

'Right.'

'Right.'

'Will, please stop repeating everything I say.'

'Yes.'

'You should come tonight. If you want.'

Will certainly did. 'Thank you.'

'I don't believe in ghosts.'

Will nodded, unsure if the statement was for him or not.

Chapter 14

The rain had eased slightly by the time Ali parked up just beyond the train station. Weak drops danced on the breeze, swirling about under a dirty dishwater sky. Everything seemed drenched in greys and blacks. The first heavy bites of winter were snapping at people's skin as they bustled towards the station, coats tied tight, collars pushed up, umbrellas jostling for position.

She saw him straight away this time. Mickey was standing by the open driver's door of his car, just to the right of the turning circle, in heated conversation with another man. He was bound up in the same thick winter coat with the grubby fleece collars, but he seemed a lot shorter than he had been the last time she had seen him, almost as if he was lost inside the coat, struggling to escape. He looked greyer too, in his hair and his face, the Spanish tan already receding towards a soon forgotten memento.

The other man handed over a chunky wedge of money, which Mickey grabbed before squashing it into his wallet. Leaving his car, Mickey crossed back along the turning circle and quickened his pace, scuttling away as fast as his little legs could take him. Ali gave him a head start and then followed him into a long, tree-lined, residential street.

Mickey kept up his quick walk, only slowing every now and then to throw intermittent glances at his mobile phone, keeping his head down, moving against hedgerows and fences as if avoiding the orange glow of the streetlights. Ali stayed back, walking in the growing shadows thrown by the houses to her left. Halfway down, the road took a wide curve before two different roads intersected it. Aware that he was likely to disappear from her sightline, Ali decided to move across the road to follow him from the opposite pavement. Mickey quickened his pace before turning into the first road. Ali jogged across the road and took the turning.

She came to an immediate halt. Mickey was at the front door of the third house down, waggling his keys in the lock. A small porch light was on just above him and Mickey had his head turned down, away from the glare. He pushed the door with his shoulder and seemed to fall inside. A moment later the porch light clicked off.

Ali moved in slowly. Almost instantly the steady creep of headlights up her left leg pulled her attention from the house towards a maroon-coloured Volkswagen crawling alongside her. A familiar beefy slab of a man was behind the wheel, a cigarette dangling from his lips. She remembered him as the man staring at her outside the train station, recognising the thuggish cliché. Then, no sooner had their eyes met again, the car jerked away with a cocky screech of tyres, swung around and returned the way it had come, haring around into the next road.

'Right,' Ali said into the space where the car had just been.

Mickey's house remained in darkness. Ali pushed aside the spongy wood of the garden gate and wandered up to the front door. She waited for the porch light to click on, but it didn't. The door was slightly ajar, a slice of a deeper darkness coming from inside. She shoved the base with the toe of a boot and the door swung inwards, coming to rest against a large rucksack on the hall floor.

Ali could feel a redundant 'hello' on her lips, held back by old instincts and suspicions. Something wasn't right here. You didn't need a police officer to tell you that. She waited on the doorstep, her fingers flexing before curling into fists. Somehow, she knew he was inside that darkened house watching her, getting ready. She swallowed hard on a dry throat and stepped in, pulling the front door closed behind her.

The flash of metal came a second later and Ali was ready for it. She jerked to her right and ducked down, and as she did, she felt the air change over her head as the knife sliced through it and Mickey's elbow collided with the wall. Ali sprang up and slammed her left shoulder into a soft space just beneath his ribcage. The knife dropped, hit the front door and landed at her feet as Mickey's breath left him in a great, gasping wheeze and he staggered away from her. Ali snatched up the knife and went after him.

A second later something was knocked over with a hefty thud and Mickey gave a pathetic whimper. Ali stopped in the doorway of another room and let her eyes adjust. A small digital clock at waist level across the room told her where she was. She felt along the walls either side of the doorway before finding the light switch. The strip light in the kitchen popped and flickered before clicking on.

Mickey was cowering on the linoleum, the kitchen table

lying on its side next to him. 'Please!' he blubbered, 'please, don't!'

The room was cramped and cluttered and everything looked sticky to the touch. The digital clock on the cooker was telling the wrong time.

'Daylight saving was a couple of weeks ago. You need to put your clock back.' Ali stepped into the room and stood before him, the knife resting against her right thigh.

'You?' Mickey said, seeing her properly for the first time, his relief palpable.

'Oh, good. You *did* think I was someone else then? I'm glad. A girl could take offence. Hiding here in the dark, coming at me with a kitchen knife. Just who the hell were you expecting, Mickey?'

'Listen, please, you have to listen to me!'

'That's exactly what I'm here for. So that works out well, doesn't it?' Ali crouched down and he flinched away, scrabbling back until his head was next to the washing machine and he could go no further. Ali shuffled forward and then straddled his legs. She moved the tip of the knife down and wedged it into the linoleum, the blade resting just at the edge of Mickey's trouser zip.

Mickey's eyes found the scar above her eye. 'I know who you are.'

'Good. Saves a bit of time on the introductions then.'

'Ernie told me about you.'

Ali tensed the hand holding the knife. Mickey tensed his whole body in return. 'Then if I told you that I would jam this kitchen knife into your scrotum if you don't give me what I want, you'd know I meant it?'

Mickey seemed to quiver, his arms by his sides in submission. 'I heard you were mad.'

'So they say.'

'I didn't know it was you. I'm sorry for coming after you like that.'

'Who did you think I was? And what's with that wad of cash that guy gave you?' Ali reached into his coat and took out his wallet, now resembling some sort of leathery sandwich with a paper filling. 'That's a lot of money.'

'It was a debt. I was calling in a debt.'

'Holiday leave you skint, did it? I assume that's what the rucksack by the door is all about too. Haven't unpacked yet? Because the only other way of looking at it is that you were planning on doing a runner. Is that it? I noticed you left your cab at the office too. You'd think a cabbie might need that. Because if that is it, then I can't help but think back to last night when you came knocking for Ernie, so full of piss and merriment, and think that that is not the attitude of someone planning on disappearing. I then might be inclined to think back to how your expression just about slipped off your face when I told you Ernie was dead.' Ali gripped the hilt of the knife and started bringing her weight down on it, leaning forward and moving her face within kissing distance of Mickey's. 'I look at that guy and think, yeah, maybe that sort of guy might consider doing a runner. Because that sort of guy looks like he might know things, nice juicy things that other people might want to know. Or maybe things that other people might want to stop him from telling. Stop me if any of this is ringing any distant bells.'

'Of course I'm doing a runner.' He said it as though it were the most obvious thing in the world. Ali eased the pressure from the knife, her fingers still gripped around the hilt. 'I'm getting the hell out of this town. If you had any sense, you'd do the same. It wasn't suicide, was it? Despite what people are saying.'

'I don't know yet. You tell me, Mickey.'

'I turned that over all night. After I saw you, I called around to some of the late shift, and they told me what they'd read. Maybe, I thought. Maybe it was. Maybe he did take a dive. Who the hell knows what goes on in people's lives? I had all but convinced myself of it. I could live with that, poor bastard, but at least it had nothing to do with me.'

'What do you mean by that?'

His eyes passed over her face without really seeing her. 'But then I started to wonder just what you're doing here if it was all as cut and dry as the police say it is. You wouldn't be here if you didn't have doubts. And if you've got doubts then maybe I should have too. And if there's more to it, if there's a chance that he was murdered then that means he might have got a little too close to the truth.' Mickey's eyes rolled up to the kitchen window and then seemed to ping-pong around the sockets until they found her again. 'I thought he'd given all this up, let it go, you know?'

'No, I don't know.' Ali yanked the knife free and grabbed Mickey at the top of his coat, the grubby fleece collars closing around his neck like a trap. 'What the hell are you talking about?'

Mickey nodded over his shoulder to the mess on the worksurface. 'Local rag. On the side, by the cooker. When I saw that. When I saw that photo of him on the front, I knew that Ernie hadn't taken a dive. And I knew that if I didn't get the hell out of this place, I could be next.'

Ali raised herself up. The newspaper was there, neatly folded over like a life raft amongst the sea of clutter. She could only see half of the photo on the front page, no more than the forehead and slicked-back hair of the man it showed, but it was enough for her to know who it was.

'His name was Garrett Lyman. You heard of him?' Mickey said.

'How do you know him?'

'Because he worked for Deveraux. And so did I.'

Questions swirled around Ali's mind as it tried to piece together connections that couldn't be made.

'You had no idea, did you?' Mickey said. 'Did you really think Ernie Lipkiss contented himself with working night shifts in some shithole? That the guy you knew? I only knew him a few months and I'd never have bought that. Man had plod stamped through him like a stick of rock.'

'I don't understand,' Ali said.

'He's been working the case ever since it happened. Your case. That night at the Deveraux estate, the Tooley kid.'

Ali's heartbeat quickened.

'Ernie had been trying to clear your name because he reckoned there was more to it. He always said there was someone else there that night. And I knew he was right. There was. Because I saw them.'

Chapter 15

Twelve months earlier

It was a curious, macabre sight. For a moment she even thought it was real. It occurred to her later that maybe three months ago she would have seen it for what it was immediately, and maybe it would even have amused her. Somehow the fact that she even entertained the notion it was a real skeleton, even for a split second, made her angry. It was another symptom of that night. Rationality, another thing robbed from her. Another sign that her world, the things she understood and accepted as normal had been knocked off kilter.

As she approached the wooden bin by the side of the path, she noticed that the thing on the skeleton's head was a glittery party hat with a golden tassel hanging from the side, the thing jutting out of its mouth, a big fat rubbery cigar. The skeleton was wedged into the bin rear-first, its cheap plastic legs up in front of its crooked plastic head.

Ali hitched up her rucksack and walked on. Up ahead of her, the familiar old Volvo was parked on the edge of the grass. Her friend was a little further on, sat on a bench halfway down the hill. He didn't turn around as she approached; merely held a hand up to his side and jiggled it about in a stupid wave. Ali dumped the rucksack on the ground and took a seat next to him.

She knew why he had chosen this bench. She knew what he was looking at, but she refused to look too.

'Hey, Ali-cat.'

'Retirement treating you well?' Ernie turned to read her expression to make sure of the sarcasm. 'Old man, Ernie. Have you pottered yet? Isn't that what you do when you retire? I imagine golf can't be too far away either.'

Ernie shook his head in mock indignation. 'Kids of today.'

'All that daytime TV, it's not good for you, you know?'

'Aye, tell me about it. Milkshake for the mind, Maggie calls it. Whatever that means. It's not intellectually nourishing, I suppose.'

'Maggie?'

'A mate.'

'Nice to have a mate, partner.'

He smiled at that. 'Not heard that word in a while.'

'Almost sounds like you miss it.'

'I do. Of course I do.'

Ali felt the small talk dissipating on the November breeze. 'You could have stayed.'

'No, I couldn't.' Ernie rested a gloved hand on Ali's knee. 'But I'm still here for you. I'm always here for you.'

Ali moved his hand off her knee. 'I've got enough suffocating concern from Taylor. He's always there for me too.'

'He likes you.'

'That's not my fault.'

'He's a good kid. Heart of gold. Cut him some slack.'

Ali glared at him. 'You trying to matchmake? Don't do that.'

'You could do a lot worse, you know?'

'And he could do a lot better.'

'True.'

'You really think I need a man in my life? Haven't I got enough trouble as it is? Taylor needs a princess. Him and me, we come from different chapters of the fairy tale. I'd rather have a cat.'

There were two weak firework pops in the distance. Ali jerked her head up to the sky, searching the creamy winter clouds. Ernie lazily tilted his head back and did the same.

'Letting fireworks off in daylight. That's a particular breed of stupid,' Ali said. 'I hate this time of year. I always have. Even at school. That week between Halloween and bonfire night.'

'Did you see the skeleton in the—'

'Yeah. Maybe it's because of school? Do you think so? I still feel funny on a Sunday evening. Even now. Sometimes I get a twisted knot in my gut, deep down, a nagging fear, just as I always used to do on a Sunday when I knew I had to go back to school. Maybe Halloween and bonfire night are the same? The school term is new, Christmas still just that little bit out of reach. The weather turning to shit. Maybe it's all because it just reminds me of being at school?'

'Don't ask me, Ali-cat. Maybe you should see a shrink?'

'You have my permission to shoot me if I ever get to that stage, Ern.'

'I'd take a few nods back to my youth, these days.'

'So speaks the retired old man.'

'Maybe.'

'You really do miss it? Being a copper?'

Ernie dropped his head back and stared off into the distance. 'Some things never actually left. Some things I haven't yet had a chance to miss. Why won't you look at it? Since the moment you sat down you haven't looked over at it once. Why not?'

'Is that why you chose to meet here? Not very subtle.'

'Look at it, Ali-cat. It's not going to hurt you. It's just a building.'

She gave her old partner a contemptuous stare and then shifted on the bench, facing forward.

Threadbare fields were separated by an identity parade of angry-looking trees, the gentle rise and dip of the land lost in weak colours and dull tones. The fields fitted together like a jigsaw puzzle, crudely snapped into place. The basin of land dropped down to a huddle of yet more trees, these naked and fragile, stuck together in a tangle of reaching and probing limbs. The wood was shedding its secrets, opening up to more stories.

In the middle of the basin was the charred mound of the Deveraux estate, a broken beast in the woods. Scaffolding had been erected along one side and bright blue tarpaulin flapped and billowed like the sail of a ship, the only defined colour for miles. In the distance, just beyond the crude angles of the building, a deer galloped across the grounds and then disappeared into the bony and brittle embrace of the wood.

'Apparently kids go there sometimes,' Ernie said. 'They dare each other. Taylor told me that they shut down a Halloween party in the grounds last week. I don't get it. I really don't. It still feels too fresh to me for it to be a story for someone else.'

'Yeah.'

'Do you still have the dreams?'

'Yeah. When I'm sober. Sometimes. When I can sleep.'

'Aye. Me too, kid. Me too.' Ernie gently nudged her rucksack with his foot. 'Send me a postcard from Timbuktu when you get there. Tell me if doing a runner worked.'

'London, I was thinking. For now. Have an old school friend there. She's found me a dirt-cheap room. Sell my place here, and with what's left from Mum's house that gives me a bit of breathing space. Let's see how the cards fall.'

'I was so sorry to hear about Evelyn. I should have called.'

'I wouldn't have answered.'

'Aye.' Ernie looked up at the fresh scar around her left eye. 'Wanna talk about it, kid?'

Ali shook her head. 'I can't stay here, Ernie. I can't handle it. I can't breathe here. I can't sleep. The stares…I expect to be gossiped about, that's human nature in a place like this. I'm not daft. I know people are clucking about me over garden fences and whispering about me in post office queues. I'm OK with that, but it's the stares, Ern, it's the damn stares! And it's the little nods and raised eyebrows, the little acknowledgements they give to me too, like they haven't even got the guts to ignore me. I have to be gawped at because of some misplaced sense of politeness. I'd rather they spat at me.'

Ernie reached across and held her hand. They stayed that way for several minutes, both staring off towards the Deveraux estate and all the memories that swirled around it like chimney smoke.

'They found animal bones scattered across the north side of the grounds,' Ernie said, finally. 'Animal carcasses in the woods too. Butchered.'

'Meaning?'

'Meaning, this week they were devil worshippers.'

He told the old man he spoke to the devil.

Shut up.

'So local gossip has it,' Ernie continued. 'Lazy finds the fantastical to fill the holes. Cannae believe a word of it. Deveraux was a pious man.'

'He was also a murderer, so there's that.'

'I know. Religious hypocrisy, who would have thought it?'

'You can buy him shooting his staff and himself, but not that he may have started worshipping at a different altar?'

'If someone told me Lord Deveraux fancied himself a modern-day Matthew Hopkins, I could entertain the notion, but not this. No way. Not when you consider his family. The Deverauxs have been doing God's work round these parts for as long as anyone can remember.'

'Should have put more hours in.'

Ernie chuckled. 'Aye, well there's good and bad everywhere. Guess it's a little more pronounced in these quarters. You heard what happened to Deveraux's old man back in the seventies?'

'Haven't heard, never cared.'

'Well, I've been doing a little reading up on the Deverauxs these last few weeks. Not the most rollicking of yarns, truth be told, but Deveraux senior seems to have been a bit of a strange fish. He up and vanished from that stately pile. Not a trace of him. Fire still burning in the hearth, dinner untouched on the table, his wife asleep in an armchair. He was never seen again.'

'So?'

'So, somewhere along the line legend has caught the tail of that little event and there's people round here that will tell you now he fled the town with the devil at his heels.'

Ali turned to her friend, raised an eyebrow and offered a small hiccup of a laugh. 'You read too much.'

'Told you before, you can find the answer to anything in books. I've barely even dipped my toe into all this, but it's fascinating. Apparently, Daddy Deveraux was also a member of a secret club, a brotherhood of highfalutin big nobs. People reckon this whole area was run out of those clubs.'

'Brotherhood? What does that mean?'

'Well, I don't know yet. Drinking, gambling, that sort of thing, I guess. Just rich old men being rich old men.'

'Guess they should be allowed some downtime from that heavy burden.'

'I'm going to keep reading, see where it gets me. I've got nothing else to do anyway, as you so helpfully pointed out. There are other stories there, Ali-cat. In that house. Deveraux. His father. We are shaped by our parents, aren't we? For good or ill.'

A gentle breeze rolled past them, and just for a split-second Ali felt the material of a childish dress she once wore rub against her thighs, like sandpaper against her skin. The moment passed and returned to memory.

'You OK?' Ernie asked, gently. 'Someone walk over your grave?'

Ali tried to force a smile and then a nod and didn't really succeed in either. 'Let it go, Ernie. Deveraux shot three people then blew his brains out. Lady Deveraux slashed her wrists. That's it. They've got the *what*. Don't look for the *why*. That house is never giving up its secrets.'

Ernie took his hand back and folded his arms against the cold. 'I told them,' Ernie said. 'Parker, Moss. I told them what I saw.'

'What we both saw.'

'They *will* find him.'

'No, they won't. No one's looking.'

'Someone will find him. *I* will find him.'

'Not if he's a ghost.'

They sat in silence again, everything unspoken passing between them, a shorthand that neither needed to articulate.

'I don't believe in ghosts,' Ernie told her eventually.

'Neither do I,' Ali replied.

The muffled sound of crashing waves came to her in that moment, breaking into her mind. It felt as though she were holding a shell to her ear and the sound was blissfully separating a part of her, the part that really mattered, from her friend, and the reality he wore. Time fell away and ceased to mean anything. She was vaguely aware of him kissing her gently on the cheek and saying goodbye, and then she thought she heard her own voice telling him that she would call. She heard his footsteps retreating and she heard the car engine come to life.

Chapter 16

'I think he loved you.'

'Don't say that.'

They sat on the kitchen floor at opposite ends of the room, Mickey resting against the cooker, the incorrect clock just over his head, Ali by the door, blocking his way should he attempt to make a run for it.

'He always talked about you. Ali this, Ali that. He came alive when he talked about you. But then it was the case too, I guess. Dog with a bone, Ernie was. He wouldn't let it go. You try to tell him it was all done; you try to take it away from him and he'd show his teeth. I find it kinda sad now, looking back. It feels like the case was the only thing holding him together, that and you. He was obsessed. About the case, I mean. Not you. Not in that way. You, he loved.'

'Shut up.'

Mickey shrugged. 'Just the way I see it.'

'What were you doing there? And why haven't you been to the police?'

'I was there because Deveraux owed me wages. I did some driving for him. I was getting tired of waiting for him to cough up. So, I went to collect. Picked the wrong night, that's all. As for the police, fuck them. No offence.'

'How did you meet Ernie?'

'Drove him a couple of times, to his work. He was just a punter. Or so I thought at the start. He says to me, second time, that I should pop in and have a cuppa. Asks me if the night shift is as lonely for a cabbie as it was for him, and I say it can be, yeah. So, few days later I'm passing and, truth be told, I actually needed a piss, so I called in to him. We chatted. I liked him. A good guy. So, then I'd see him from time to time. Just two blokes on the night shift, shooting the shit, having some company. That's all. Didn't realise he'd orchestrated it. Not for a while. Then he starts to steer the conversation to Hanging Twitch, asking about the area, punters I take out there. Then he mentions Deveraux. Just drops him in the conversation, all subtle and nonchalant. But I saw his expression. That was when I realised I'd been interviewed.'

'And?'

'Didn't bother me. As I say, I liked Ernie. Not that there's much I can say. I never spoke to Deveraux all that much. The old girl I liked, spent a bit of time with her. She was sick, and I drove her to her hospital appointments. Totally hush-hush, had to keep all that quiet. Drove her maybe ten times, that was all. Never went into the house, and I swear I never saw the kid out there, the Tooley boy. Never.'

'Garrett Lyman was their driver. Why did they need you?'

'Garrett got me into it. I knew him a little from years back. He used to work for a private hire firm back when I was starting here, and I always fancied that. It was them that usually got the airport runs, and that's a good chunk of money. Well, when he goes off to work with Deveraux, he tries to set me up at the firm, put in a good word. I've got a record, you see? I did a little time. But I got stitched up for it. Police had it in for me. That was always going to be a thing for them. So, he tries to help. Tells them I'm a good guy, and all that. But it doesn't go anywhere. Then last year he phones me up out of the blue, not spoken to him in an age, and tells me that he's thinking of calling it a day and retiring, and maybe he could put in a word with Deveraux when the old man starts looking for a new driver. So, I'm all for that. Good money. Well, he says that the old guy needs someone to take his wife back and forth to her hospital appointments, but Garrett can't do it because his sister's not coping so great, and he needs to go see her. So, he says to me that I should do the chauffeuring instead, help out, do a good job and then maybe when the old man comes to replacing Garrett, he might give me a shot, right? So, that's what I did.'

'Ernie got to you through Garrett Lyman?'

'Yeah.'

Ali pulled her legs up to her chest, hugging her knees. 'Lyman visited Ernie as well?'

'Think Ernie had a bit of a revolving door down there. Weren't just Garrett and me.'

'People connected to that night?'

'I guess. Like I said, he never stopped working that case.'

'And did you meet any?'

'Sure, met one guy. He was leaving once as I was pulling up. Long hair, beard, scruffy-looking. Bob? Bobby? Guy was an oddball, something off about him, I tell you that much. Kinda weird-looking. Reckoned he was one of these homeless guys that always used to pitch up at that place. But then I also saw him few weeks later getting a mini cab from us, so maybe he wasn't. Maybe he was. I dunno. Ernie never said.'

'You didn't ask?'

'Didn't realise I would have to care.'

Three quick firework pops sounded in a neighbouring garden and Mickey flinched, his right hand dropping instinctively to the side, to a knife that was no longer there.

'Who are you so frightened of? Who were you expecting to walk through your door this evening?' Ali asked. 'Who killed Garrett Lyman? Because you clearly don't think he topped himself.'

'Neither do you. Either of them.'

'No. I don't think I do. What has Ernie stumbled on to?'

'I don't know.'

'I don't believe you.'

Another barrage of whizzes and bangs came overhead, followed by loud cheering from further down the street. Again, Mickey flinched and jerked away from the noise. He clambered up and rushed to the sink, filling a cup from the tap and downing the water in three big gulps. Ali stood too, leaning in the doorway, staring at his back and those filthy fleece collars as they rose and fell in time with his heavy breathing.

'Mickey?'

'What people said about them, about what went on up there, all that hocus pocus, do you think it was real? Black magic, and all that?'

'Satanism?'

'Not real, right? It'd be in the papers, wouldn't it? Police would have said something.'

'Would they?'

'You tell me, you're the ex-copper. What do they know?'

'They know that Deveraux killed three people, and that he then killed himself. What did you see that night, Mickey?'

'I never saw nothing, not a thing.' Mickey told his reflection in the kitchen window. 'But I hear the stories, hear what people are saying and you can't help but wonder, right? Makes you think about things in retrospect, the way people behaved, things they said. Garrett never bought it either. Said Deveraux was a Bible basher, said the closest they got to anything funky was when the old girl's sister supposedly came through to her during a séance. This that people are saying is a whole other level of crackers. But then no one knows what goes on behind closed doors.'

The knife twitched in Ali's hand, the tip of the blade jabbing her lightly in the thigh. 'Who are you so frightened of, Mickey?'

Mickey leaned over the sink and tugged at the cord to the kitchen blind, which responded to him in a series of clumsy jerks before falling into place across the window. 'They had someone up at the house. That much I do know. See, Deveraux was a bit of a hermit, according to Garrett, never liked to mingle. It was unusual for them to have guests, that's why it stuck with me.'

'How do you know they had someone up there?'

'The old girl liked to talk. We got on by the end. First few times I drove her, she was in too much pain...' Mickey waved a hand around in front of his face, 'Something with her eyes, it was. At the start. Then she told me she was dying. Said the man behind her eyes was killing her, whatever the fuck that means. I don't ask questions. Not in the job. But by the end, she seemed chilled. Couldn't see for shit, so I had to walk her in and all that, but she'd cooled the fuck out. Last time I took her out there she got real chatty. Kinda made me sad, because I thought it was because she'd accepted her fate, like, she was unfiltered then, unloading all these things to me, because it didn't matter no more. Do you know what I mean? So, last time I drive her, she mentions this guy, said he was a friend of her husband, and she talks like she's almost in awe of him. Said he was a great man that did great things. Said everything was going to be OK, and she'd not need me any more soon enough. I see her in the rear-view mirror and she's got this sort of wistful smile going on.'

'She mention a name?'

'No. No names.'

'"Great things?"'

Mickey held his palms out flat. 'Don't ask me. I assumed it was a quack that he'd found for her or something.'

'You never asked her any questions?'

'Wasn't in my remit to ask questions. You don't with people like that, do you? I was the hired help; you just do your job and keep your trap shut. Nod in the right places and laugh at their jokes. Not that they were exactly laugh-a-minute types.'

'The man you saw that night…it was this same man?'

'I don't know who I saw. Just a figure. Just a face. That's all. Honestly.'

Ali stared back, stony-faced and unblinking.

'See, when I get there that night, I see Ernie's copper car there already, so I park round the back, by the staff entrance.' His words trailed off as he looked back to his memories, and the darkness of that evening. 'The night sky was so…weird, that night. Do you remember?'

The night can move around you.

You can make it alive if you have a mind to.

'I do.'

'Felt…close. Alive, almost?'

'Yes.'

'North side of the grounds, out towards the wood, I see there's a figure standing there looking back at the house. Just the shape of someone caught at the edge of one of the spotlights, it was. I figured it was a scarecrow, didn't think anything of it for a moment. So, I'm sat there, looking at the house, looking for another way in, where I don't have to get up in front of the Old Bill, and then it suddenly occurs to me, why would there be a scarecrow out on those grounds? Just grass, innit? No crops or the like, just a whole lot of nothing.

'Then I hear the first gunshot. Funny thing is, I thought it was a firework at first and looked up into the sky to see it. Then it came again, and again and...I saw him through the window of one of the rooms downstairs. Deveraux. Well, no, it wasn't a window as such, because he had them all boarded up, but I'm looking at him through this big ragged hole in a piece of wood.'

The knife sliced into the skin on her thigh. Ali gazed down, momentarily confused by the sensation, before pulling the blade back and wiping the blood on her trousers.

Mickey continued, oblivious, trapped in his memory. 'All dressed up in his finery he was, looked like he was about to have a dinner party, and he's got the gun up before him and he's firing it off all around the room, firing at the windows until there's nothing but a great big empty space there in each one. I thought he was pissed.'

'And?'

'And I got the hell out of there, what do you think?'

'The figure?'

'I never looked back to where I saw him. But...you know what? I did have the strangest feeling, as I was reversing the car out of the car park, just as I hit the main path around the house and I was changing gear. I just had this weird sensation creep over me, because it felt like there was someone just on the other side of the driver's door, looking in the window at me. So, then I do glance round, and I see this face. This man is outside the car. Staring in.'

'What did he look like?'

Mickey turned his eyes to the recently drawn blind and then up to the ceiling. 'Just a guy. Didn't look like anything much, but there was something off about him, something that gave me a chill.' His eyes fell down and found Ali again. 'Guy had the palest skin I ever saw.'

Ali took a faltering step towards Mickey as a thin trickle of blood started to run down her right leg. 'I know I saw someone that night. You saw the same person. Do you know what I've been going through because of that?'

'I'm sorry.'

'Why did Garrett Lyman never mention you?'

'Garrett was my friend. He knew my history with your crowd, and what was I going to say that would have made a damn bit of difference? You said it yourself, Deveraux killed those people, that's that as far as the plod care. End of story.'

'They called me crazy.'

'Well, I'm sorry about that, but this is nothing to do with me, or Garrett.'

'If you're running from this same man, then it's got everything to do with you. Help me, Mickey. You need to go to the police. Tell them what you saw that night. Help me find that man.'

Mickey moved across the kitchen, and stood to the opposite side of the window, his back flat against the wall. 'No. Ernie has picked at the scab of that night and stirred something up that should have been left alone. I want nothing more to do with this. I just want to go. I've done nothing wrong. You can't stop me.'

'Speak to the police. And when you do, you can also mention to them the Salstone minicab that turned up at the building the night Ernie died.' Ali took a step towards him, the knife blade cutting tiny shapes in the air by her side. 'You?'

The last remaining colour in Mickey's face fell away. He quickly shook his head. 'No. Not me. I wasn't there. I wasn't even in the country that night. You can check that. Not me.'

Ali stepped closer, now barely a foot away from him. The truth was there in the look of horror on his face. 'Then find out who it was for me?'

'I'm out of here. I told you that. Ernie, Garrett, I'm not letting it be me next. You should go too. If you had any sense.'

Ali moved into his face. 'Find out who was driving that cab. You don't, and I will rat you out for all your worth. I will put you in Deveraux's life and I will put you there that night, and if that's not enough, I will put you standing next to Garrett Lyman's body with a smile on your face. Or maybe I will just stick myself with this knife and have you on attempted murder? How would that suit you?'

'You really are mad, aren't you?' Mickey whispered.

'I wasn't. But maybe I'm just catching up with the person people want me to be.' Ali took her pen from her back pocket and gently rolled up Mickey's right sleeve before writing her mobile number on his arm. 'Make sure you run far enough away.'

'And where would that be exactly? He's already found me once. Where do I go where he can't find me again?'

'What do you mean he's found you?'

'What do you think I mean? I saw him. Here. This morning, just after I finished my shift. Why do you think I'm not hanging around?'

'He was here? In your house?'

'Not quite. I heard a knocking on my kitchen window. I turn around and he's just staring in through the window at me, with a great big grin on his face. Then, before I can do anything, he's gone. Just like that. Like he was never even there.'

Chapter 17

The second shift

Ali watched the low-level mist gather at the base of the oak trees and glide across the car park. The building looked different, somehow smaller and less oppressive. The feeling of being watched, however, was overwhelming. She was sure there were figures out there, hiding behind the oak trees, maybe hunched down behind gravestones too.

Shadows moved. The night shifted. There was a strong mix of smells; dampness and smoke, thick earth, and then from close by, past even her own ripeness, the sharp smell of the antiseptic wipe balled up in her hand.

I heard a knocking on my kitchen window. I turn around and he's just staring in through the window at me.

Mickey's words played through her mind, each syllable stretching and distorting, and then it wasn't Mickey's voice at all. It was Jake Tooley's, and her mind snatched at the words and tried to make sense of what that poor boy had been telling her, warning her…

Knock. Knock. But you mustn't look. You must never look at his face if he knocks on your window.

She saw that face in the woods again, that pale face staring at her and Ernie from behind a tree as they stood looking down at Jake Tooley's lifeless body. That face that had not yet been corrupted by time's relentless march or the mind's diminishing recall. The face of The Knock-Knock Man.

'He was smiling at me,' Ali whispered.

Two timid knocks on the door just behind her made her jump.

'How does it feel?' Reverend Barnard motioned to her leg and the chunky plaster now peeping through the slit in her trousers where she had absently cut herself with Mickey's knife.

Ali was lost in the thickness of the past and gave no answer, merely staring at him.

Reverend Barnard reached down and picked up the first aid kit. 'I'll return this to the vestry and make us both a cup of tea.' He offered a smile.

Ali tried to return it but it looked more like a snarl. 'I'd prefer something stronger.'

'Very well.'

A fox trotted up the road alongside the oak trees and scampered into the graveyard through the open gate. In the distance Ali heard the bark of another. The graveyard fox checked its path before carrying on, disappearing into the mist that was stroking at the gravestones. Ali gently pushed the door closed with a boot and ran the bolt before returning to the nave.

When Reverend Barnard appeared with a half-full bottle of whisky and two glasses, Ali was standing by the pulpit gazing up at a marble Christ, about twenty feet up, hanging on a wooden cross suspended from the roof, his face turned away. Her left hand brushed at her throat, fingers tracing along her collarbone.

Reverend Barnard took a seat on the first set of pews. 'When did you take it off?'

'Huh?'

'Your fingers at your neck. I'm thinking perhaps you may have had a crucifix there once. I'm wondering when you removed it?'

'My father gave it to me. I have no idea where it is now.'

'Churchgoer was he, your father?'

'He was. For a time at least. Then he just didn't go any more. Said he'd stopped believing in God. I like to think he just preferred movies. That was our thing. For a while. Until he stopped believing in his family too. I don't know how much either of them ever really believed in God, but I know they feared him. That's enough, I guess? Subservience is easier through fear than through love, isn't it?'

'God is love,' Reverend Barnard said, filling each of the glasses with a healthy measure of whisky.

'Then what is the devil, Reverend? Because surely the devil must exist if God does. If there is good, then there must be evil. Without evil, you have no way of measuring goodness.'

'If you're thinking cloven hooves and horns, I have to disappoint. I'm sure I could find you a fire-and-brimstone preacher who might see it differently, but for me the devil is a metaphor. Nothing more.'

'So, all that forty days and forty nights business?'

'Parables. Take from them what you will. Evil exists, it always has. Some people choose to give it a form or a face.'

'Do you talk to God?'

'I do.'

'But you don't believe that someone could talk to the devil?'

'Why would you be asking me this?'

'What if your guy is a metaphor as well?' Ali took her glass and knocked back the whisky. She turned to the marble statue. 'Isn't it arrogant for anyone to think they have the answers to anything that can't be seen?'

'Open your eyes then.'

'That's such a cliché, Rev. Open my eyes! How about I open my heart too? Isn't that how it works?'

'There's no instruction manual. There's no one path to God.'

'What is it that keeps you coming back here, day after day to this empty church? What good is the word of God if there is no one listening?'

'You don't need to attend church to follow God. In fact, I'm inclined to think that I feel closer to God volunteering at our foodbank than I do standing at that pulpit. You ask how we can alleviate the suffering of others. What comes after that is your path.'

Ali took a seat beside him and picked up the bottle. 'Thanks for this.'

'When did you lose it? Your faith?'

'What makes you think I had it to begin with?'

'You told me before; you said that my God and you had had a falling out.' Reverend Barnard nodded to the statue above the pulpit. 'Also, I've seen people look at that with awe, and I've seen them look at it with contempt. You… you looked like you were trying to find something. Maybe something you used to have. Something a little more than the chain around your neck.'

Ali took a swig from the bottle of whisky. 'I just want answers. Just not the answers you're thinking of. I don't need to know about heaven and hell. I've no need to know whether we all troop up to the Pearly Gates and get given our own cloud to float on. Why does anyone need that?'

'Somewhat simplistic, but I take your point.'

'It *is* simplistic though, isn't it? We go to heaven, or we go to hell, or we rot in the ground and go nowhere at all. Not a lot we can do about it either way. It's as if the element of surprise doesn't mean anything any more.'

'What answers do you need?'

'I need to know what happened to my friend.'

'Sometimes all you get from answers are more questions.'

Ali laughed. 'You sound like my shrink. That's the sort of impenetrable doublespeak that he comes out with.' Ali took another swig from the bottle and then topped up Reverend Barnard's glass before jabbing her thumb towards the figure of Christ. 'Your man there, or the big guy upstairs, whoever is pulling the strings, they took my friend away. He really was a good person. But they let someone tip him off the top floor of that building. Your God sat by here and let that happen to Ernie. And to Jake Tooley as well. This world celebrates the cruel, the stupid and the vain. And my TV and my newspapers are full of all the things that somehow got forgotten by your God, the people that fell by the wayside while the self-righteous sat around telling stories. Old people dying, and children dying, and good people all over the world dying. And here you are rattling around in your empty church, with a message no one cares to hear. And why not? Because your God let all this happen. All you blessed folk with your beliefs let this happen.'

'Is it so bad, having beliefs?'

'Beliefs get you killed.'

'I think the person who believes in nothing is a person to fear.'

'No. The person who believes in nothing is the only person who gets out unscathed.'

Reverend Barnard leaned back on the pew, his eyes slowly rising up to the roof of the church.

A car horn broke the silence and Ali heard her name being called from outside in the car park. She stood and, feeling a twinge in her leg, patted at the plaster.

'I had a parishioner once,' Reverend Barnard said, 'a young lad, and he would come every Sunday with his parents, in his tie and his neatly pressed trousers, hair perfectly in place. He'd always sing loudly, joyously, and when he prayed his mother told me that he would always screw his eyes up really tight, comically so, like children do when they are pretending to sleep. Then after service one Sunday, I was talking to his parents and this boy is gazing up at the roof of the church, a confused expression on his face. I ask him what is wrong, and he says, "How do the prayers get out? How does God hear us with the ceiling in the way like that? Don't the prayers get trapped?"' Reverend Barnard rolled his head to the side and found Ali staring down at him. 'What do you reckon?'

'I've got to go. Thank you.'

'Don't you believe in anything at all?'

Ali walked down the middle of the nave, her footsteps counting her out. Reverend Barnard remained where he was, his face turned up to the roof and a thousand trapped words.

They stood in a line in front of the building, three silhouettes in the mist. She saw Will straight away. Her friend was standing a few feet away from the other two, his eyes on the graveyard. As she got to the wall separating the two properties, he waved. The others turned, eyeing her up as she crossed the car park and rummaged in her trouser pocket for the key. Will introduced them in turn. Ali recognised Dave, whose tufty hair was even more raised than it had been on the video, as if he had already received a fright. He gave her a single nod and then backed away, moving behind his dad. Ronnie was a tall man with a friendly face, and carried a smile that didn't even waver when his attempt at a handshake was ignored.

'Right,' Ali said.

She unlocked the front door, and then a moment later the reception area was bathed in the harsh light of the halogen lamps. One by one, they followed her in.

'Car!' Will's voice came down the staircase.

Ali was at the front door. She had already seen the creep of headlights through the slits between the corrugated sheets over the windows and now stood there waiting, the knife behind her back. She heard Will's footsteps in the stairwell a moment later and told him to stay where he was.

Outside there was the sound of an idling car engine.

She bowed her head and listened. The engine stopped and a car door opened and then closed. Footsteps approached. Three small, almost apologetic knocks tapped on the other side of the door.

Ali's stomach lifted as she slowly pushed down on the handle and eased the front door open. The smell of dampness and smoke and recently turned earth swam inside the room.

He stood there; a short figure shrouded in the mist. Holding a cat in his arms. 'Look, I've found a genuine Ali-cat!'

Frank Gage was trying hard not to laugh at his own wit. His white linen jacket was buttoned, the collars up against his neck. Leather-gloved hands tickled the cat's head and stroked it under its chin. It was the same black-and-white cat Ali had encountered during her first shift. It started to wriggle in Gage's arms as soon as it saw her, claws catching in his jacket, its tail flicking around wildly. It hissed once and then Gage released it. It landed soundlessly on the ground before bolting off into the car park.

'It's got your claws too.'

'What do you want, Frank?'

'You don't answer your calls.'

'You've come here to tell me that?'

'I've come here to see how this pantomime is playing out.' He pushed in past her. 'You catch any ghosts yet?'

Ali followed behind, running the knife into place against her belt, and pulling her top down to hide it. Gage saw the torch beams cresting the far wall and raised a finger in their direction.

'Friends,' Ali said.

'You have friends?'

'Fuck you.'

'Fuck you back with a hat on.' Once more, Gage struggled to hide his amusement. 'Who have you got in here?'

'They hunt for ghosts.'

Ali waited for Gage's smug smile to return or for him to start laughing. As it was, his reaction took her completely by surprise.

'Great idea! Nate said St Augustine's has a few nerdy paranormal nutjobs. You've got them on board? Yes, makes sense. I get what you're doing. Maggie may believe you when you say there's no spooky shit going on here, but she sure as heck is going to believe the Ghostbusters here, isn't she? Yeah, good call, get them in to debunk it as well. That will shut her up. Two-pronged attack. Good work. We can put this to bed tonight.'

Ali stared back at him, expressionless.

'I'm paying you a compliment, crack your face.' Gage checked his watch before sitting on Ernie's chair and idly spinning around. When he returned to face Ali, she was still staring at him.

'What?' Gage took out his mobile phone and checked the screen.

'What are you really doing here, Frank?'

Gage held his hands up in mock surrender. 'Oh, OK, OK, Sherlock. You win. I'm killing time, truth be told. Drug boys are busting a couple of clubs in town. Big things expected. No way I'm catching any shuteye until I know how things went. Kate doesn't like me pacing.'

'So why do I get you? I don't want you.'

'Never were much of a conversationalist, were you?'

'No.'

Still the suggestion of a laugh carried his words. 'Okeydokey.' Gage slapped his knees and stood, but instead of turning to the front door he wandered behind the desk to the large open space, taking position at the nymph and gazing up at the four floors. Ali followed a moment later.

'Creepy place,' Gage said. 'How was it last night?'

'Fine.'

'I would think this place could spook even you. Nothing?'

'Nothing.'

Gage slipped his hands into his pockets and rolled back on his heels, taking in the view like a tourist. Will crossed by the railings on the first floor, a video camera in hand. 'Hello, young man! I'm Detective Constable Gage.'

'Hello,' Will said.

'Hunting ghosts? Jolly good.'

'Just…' Will raised the camera slightly, his words trailing off. 'Yeah.'

'Found anything?'

Will shook his head and then looked to Ali.

'Oh, that *is* good. Good to put people's minds at ease, isn't it?'

'Leave him alone, Frank,' Ali said, tugging at his jacket sleeve.

Gage pulled his arm free and straightened his jacket before strolling back to the desk. 'Just a conversation, Ali-cat, put your claws away.'

'Don't call me that.'

'I imagine Maggie should like to hear of your uneventful evening, Ali. Maybe you will be calling in to see her first thing tomorrow? Yes. Go see Maggie. Get this off my back. I've real police work to deal with.'

'Garrett Lyman?'

Gage bristled at the mention of the name. 'Amongst other things.'

'Suicide though, wasn't it?'

Gage grunted.

Ali stood by the halogen lamps, arms folded, knife hilt resting against her spine, and watched him rearrange his jacket and pull his gloves tight to his fingers. He didn't look around. 'Put this to bed.' His words didn't sound like he was smiling this time either. Gage opened the front door and disappeared into the mist.

Ali locked the door and slipped the key into her pocket.

She sat in the doorway of the fourth floor and watched them; Will circling around the far end of the room with a video camera; Ronnie by the window, staring out at the mist choked night, lost in thought; and Dave standing by the railings with a digital recorder hoping to catch a communication from the great beyond.

Ali's initial amusement at the three of them had diluted. Now she felt something else, something she had eventually pinpointed as jealousy. It wasn't so much the camaraderie, the feeling of belonging, even if just to two other people, it was the total immersion in a passion. To see them diligently going about their business, showing a patience and a perfectionism so alien to her own life, Ali couldn't help but feel pangs of envy. Not for something she had lost, but for something she had never had in the first place.

'You OK? Stomach ache?'

Will motioned to her right hand, which was resting on her stomach.

'Yeah. You OK, Will?'

'I'm OK.'

Will shuffled down next to her, placing the camera in his lap, his legs jutting out before him, trainers tapping absently together. 'What that policeman said…'

'I wouldn't pay too much attention to him. I don't. It's easier that way.' Ali checked her mobile phone. Nothing yet from Mickey.

'What about Maggie?' Will asked.

'What about her?'

'Do you want me to go to see her, tell her that there's nothing here?'

'And is that the truth, do you think, in your expert opinion?'

Will sniggered. 'Well, I'm hardly…'

'Just because nothing presents itself tonight,' Ronnie

suddenly said from across the room, 'it doesn't mean there are no spirits here.' He was sitting underneath the partially boarded-up window, his arms folded across his chest. 'Two weeks at the inn in Heroes Ridge, wasn't it, Will?'

'Uh-huh.'

'Yes. Two long weeks of visits before we saw something there, but worth the wait. Only three people had seen the Old Lady of Heroes Ridge before we did. Three people! In the whole world! Many had been there; many had spent hours looking, waiting. But she came when we were there. Why? Well, I think you need to get a feel for a place. That is what I have always believed. Every building, every location, has a different tone, a different demand. Sometimes you work a place out quite quickly, and when you become attuned to your location it is far easier for any spirits wishing to communicate to become attuned to you. I don't claim to have the touch, or any sort of gift for these things, you understand? No. But I do believe I have a talent for becoming at one with a location. You need to feel it. Breathe it. Become part of it.' Ronnie took three big dramatic breaths and held his hands out wide before him as if about to burst into song.

'He does this sometimes. Sorry,' Will whispered. 'We didn't really see anything at the inn. It was Dave's shadow he saw; neither of us wants to tell him. You can't talk to him when he's convinced himself of something.'

Ali chuckled to herself. 'Will?'

'Yeah?' he mumbled.

'Why doesn't your mum have any photos of you up in the house?'

'She doesn't like clutter.'

'Oh.' Ali rolled her head to the side and stared at him. Will was gazing at his trainers, refusing to meet her eyes.

Dave Spangler's teenage warble echoed around the building, his grandiose words rolling up the staircase from the ground floor. It was all Ali could do not to laugh.

'Speak to us, spirit! Show yourself now. I command thee! Tell us your name!'

Ali was sitting on a battered office chair, just to the side of the door. Ronnie had returned to the half boarded-up window and Will was now by the railings fixing a camera to a tripod. From time to time he would look out over the edge, and Ali felt sure that, even in the gloom of the fourth floor, she saw him shiver.

'Why do you stay here, spirit?' Dave shouted, far below. 'Why don't you leave this place? Tell us your name!'

'The Knock-Knock Man,' Ronnie said with a chuckle. 'A curious moniker. Sounds like a children's entertainer.'

'Don't use that name,' Ali said. 'I don't like it.'

'My apologies.' Ronnie ambled a few steps towards her and leaned against the wall. 'I was forgetting where it came from. The Tooley boy gave it that name, didn't he? Being inside the story, it must be difficult to see the fascination it may hold for others. I would be very interested to know the story behind that name.'

'Why?'

'Stories are our trade, Mrs Davenport.'

'Ms.'

'Our characters, our stories, they are all held inside the buildings we investigate. A mere trace, a suggestion, no more than that. Characters in a story long gone who may still need to share their tales. I should think the Deveraux house has more than its share of tales that have yet to be told, wouldn't you agree?' Ronnie gave Ali an ingratiating smile. 'I should certainly like the opportunity to do an investigation there.'

'You need to get out more.'

Undeterred, Ronnie kept fishing. 'I can only imagine what you must have seen that night.'

'Yes.'

'And your...' Ronnie knocked twice on the wall, 'man. I wonder if there's a connection to be made with the legend of Chillman Grove, that was my first inkling. What do you think, Will?'

Ali heard the squeak of Will's trainers as he delicately tiptoed around the broken flooring. 'Gamble and The Brotherhood, you mean? Could be.'

'A reasonable assumption. I'm rather surprised you didn't get there yourself.'

'Brotherhood?' Ali sat up. 'Go on.'

'You don't believe in ghosts, do you, Mrs Davenport?'

'Ms. No. I don't. But don't let that stop you.'

'But, I suppose, being a former police officer, you may well believe in the darkness of man? That's probably sufficient. Anyway, The Brotherhood...'

'Under the Moon,' Will chipped in.

'Quite so. Yes, The Brotherhood Under the Moon, a club, a society...I'm not sure how you would term it. A gathering of men from a certain social standing, let us say. New Salstone, Hanging Twitch, The Oaks, Little Lamp and Chillman Grove, judges, police officials, politicians, lords and ladies, some say the clergy too. The best and the brightest, according to society's definition. Your Deveraux was said to be a member. His father before him, of course he certainly was, and his grandfather, and so on, all the way back. They've been around these parts for quite a lot of years.'

'1901,' Will offered.

'1904, actually. At the start it was assumed that they

were resurrecting the old Hellfire Clubs. I wonder, have you heard of Hellfire Clubs, Ms Davenport?'

'Why don't you assume I haven't?'

Ronnie gripped his lapels and stood erect against the wall, like a teacher about to give a lecture. 'The Hellfire Clubs go back to the eighteenth century. Exclusive gatherings for the upper echelons of society to indulge in various hedonistic acts. *Fais ce que tu voudras*, that was the motto they lived by. No rules. Do whatever you want. Perhaps you have heard of Sir Francis Dashwood?'

Ali opened her mouth to speak but Ronnie was on a roll and quickly trampled over the brief silence.

'Founder of the most notorious Hellfire Club. He had caves created for his club beneath the abbey where he lived. Drinking and whoring, debauchery, a libertine life. No one really knew for sure what went on at any of these places. There are stories. Legends.' Ronnie began to pace back and forth in front of the windows, and Ali could see where Dave had inherited his taste for the theatrical. 'There are stories that in some of these clubs, darker affairs eventually took over. Black masses, Satanism. No reason to doubt that such things did occur. Anything could happen, couldn't it? When anything goes. When you have no rules, you leave yourself bare to other…elements. Dark elements.' With a nonchalant air he returned to leaning against the wall. 'Evil could be sitting at your table, eating your food and drinking your wine before you even knew it had walked in through the door.'

'The Deveraux family were heavily religious though, so I hear.'

'Quite right, and once your Deveraux's father broke cover, the Hellfire Club rumour was rather dispelled. Then it was believed that The Brotherhood were actually under the auspices of the church.'

'Deveraux's father vanished, didn't he?'

'He did. Yes. After the Gamble murder. An easy conclusion to make was that Deveraux's father was the one who killed him, but there are some who think other Brotherhood members were equally culpable.'

'Gamble? Who is that?'

'William Gamble, from Chillman Grove.' Ronnie stared at her as though waiting for her to pick up an obvious answer that he'd laid before her. 'The Gamble family? Really?'

Ali shrugged.

'Necromancers, some say. Satanists, certainly. Chillman Grove was born from the Gambles' wealth and their dark deeds. It's a cursed place. William Gamble was the worst of them all. A maniac. A man who thrived on the misery and madness of others. He claimed to be an emissary of the devil, maybe even Mephistopheles himself. That family sold their souls to the devil for worldly riches and power.'

'Quite the tale.' Ali was unable to hide the sarcasm in her voice.

'Isn't it?'

'Don't see the connection though.'

'To Jake Tooley's Knock-Knock Man? I'm getting to that.' Ronnie cleared his throat and pointedly turned his face away. 'They found William Gamble, bits of him anyway, back in the autumn of seventy-seven.'

'Seventy-eight,' Will mumbled quietly from across the room.

'Twenty-five different bits of him, in three different graves, between Hanging Twitch and Chillman Grove. They never charged anyone. I don't think they ever really looked.

It will have been covered up, some sort of fiction created that satisfied anyone that bothered to ask. Which naturally points in only one direction. The Brotherhood Under the Moon.'

'And?'

Ronnie pursed his lips and sucked at the musty air. 'You know of the vampire lore that states a vampire must first be invited into a home before they can cross the threshold?'

'I've seen enough films. Yeah.'

'Well, it is said that William Gamble marked his victims by first knocking at their windows. If they looked at him, their fate was sealed. He would infest their lives. He would take their soul. There have been five such recorded accounts over the years. Five people in Chillman Grove all claimed to see William Gamble at their window smiling at them shortly before they passed away.' Ronnie flapped a hand around between himself and Ali as though shooing away a fly. 'Still, merely a story, isn't it? Shall we get on?'

A scream from far below them drowned Ali's answer.

Ali looked to Will, Will looked to Ronnie, and Ronnie looked to the doorway. Then the scream came again with a barrage of Dave Spangler swearing behind it and the three of them were charging out to the fourth-floor landing.

'David!'

'I've seen a man! I've seen him, oh my God, I've seen a man on the first floor! There's something here! What do I do?'

'David, where are you?' Ronnie called down.

'I'm in the stairwell between ground and first. I was just…' Something fell over with a hefty thud on the first floor and Dave screamed again. 'What do I do? Dad! What do I do?'

Will juggled the camera in his hold and collided with Ronnie as they both tried to turn to the top of the stairs at the same time. Ronnie lost his footing, tripped and sent them both down into a heap.

'Stay here,' Ali said calmly as she unsheathed the knife and stepped over the tangle of limbs on the top step.

She was aware of Will and Ronnie untangling themselves behind her, caught sight of Ronnie running back along the landing to the fourth floor, and then she could feel Will getting to his feet and following.

She held her hand behind her and extended the index finger. 'Don't follow me.'

Dave was whimpering like a wounded animal, the sound carrying up to her as she descended the stairwell to the third-floor landing.

Ronnie was back on the fourth floor, shouting over the railings. 'David? Stay where you are. It's OK!'

Dave replied with a screechy noise and another whimper.

'Dave?' Ali shouted. 'Tell me exactly what you think you saw.'

'I don't *think* anything!' came the voice echoing back up the stairs. 'I know I saw a man! I was coming across the first-floor landing, and he was just standing there in the middle of the room. It was a man. A shape. The shape of a man.'

'What else?' Ali asked as she turned down on to the stairs to the second floor.

'What do you mean what else? What does that mean?' Dave's warble was back, making him sound even more pathetic than he did already.

'What did he look like, Dave?'

'I don't know! It was too dark.'

Halfway down the stairs to the first-floor landing, Ali stopped and fell into a crouch, peering through the stairwell railings at the entrance to the floor. She heard nothing in that moment except for Dave's laboured breathing coming from the next staircase. Her sweaty hand gripped the knife hilt and, for a brief moment, she considered how much she liked the feel of it.

She stared at the doorway, imagining that ghostly face appearing from around the door jamb, the rest of her mystery man following it around on to the landing, heading towards her with some demonic grin on his face. She saw herself standing to meet him, her hand up before her, the glint of the knife catching in his eyes before it found him.

Something was knocked over inside the room, a chaotic crashing sound punching out of the doorway and shattering the silence.

Ali was up on her feet in a flash.

'I see him!' Ronnie boomed from the top floor. 'He's gone over the railings on the first floor! Hurry!'

Ali swayed along the landing, finding her feet as if on the deck of a ship. As she turned on to the stairs, Dave was there in front of her, trying to run the other way. Ali shoved him crudely out of her path.

'He's on the ground floor!' Ronnie shouted.

She took the stairs two at a time. Turning back into reception she saw the front door wide open. The familiar waft of dampness and turned earth crept through the empty space, and the mist beyond the door seemed to hang there motionless like fallen clouds. Watching her.

Ali ran outside.

The mist had become thicker; the cars were mere hints; the oak trees lining the road up to the building were now standing guard there without their trunks. The mist hovered in the graveyard in candyfloss whirls. Ali turned in a circle, listening for any noise, something to give away their visitor's location, but the night was still hiding its secrets. She took a wide arc around the cars, moving out alongside the church wall, then ran down to the oak trees and out on to the main road. The mist patches here did their slow swirling dance ahead of her, the only movement in a deserted road. Somewhere, far away, a car horn tooted and a small crowd of people cheered, and then silence rolled back over the scene.

'A squatter, I should imagine. Wouldn't you?'

Ronnie's torch beam was directed at an office desk in one corner of the first floor. There was a scattering of food wrappers inside an open drawer.

'What did you see?' Ali asked.

'Saw a man hanging off the railings there,' Ronnie flashed the torch beam between two cubbyhole shells and across to the barriers at the edge of the floor. 'He was hanging off it by one hand, and then he dropped. Pretty nimble, he was. For a dosser.'

'What did he look like?'

'Long straggly hair, saw that much. Might have had a beard. Beyond that, I couldn't say.'

Her mind reached back to her conversation with Mickey. *Long hair, beard, scruffy-looking,* Mickey had told her too. *Bob? Bobby? Think that was his name.*

Ali pulled the drawer open further with the handle of her own torch. A few mouldy crusts of bread sat amongst sweet wrappers and plastic sandwich boxes.

'You need to go now. All of you.'

'Yes. I quite agree.' Ronnie turned to Will, and a very pale-looking Dave in the doorway. 'Come on, boys, grab your things, and thank Ms Davenport for her hospitality.'

Ali ignored the mumbled thank you from Dave and instead started pulling the other drawers out of the desk, poking inside at the dusty emptiness. She flashed the torch around the floor, swiping the beam into the corners and then back across to the railings. Looking for something that wasn't there.

'Do you think he's right? Do you think it was a homeless person?' Will stood alone in the doorway, his video camera under one arm.

'I thought you'd gone?'

'I thought I might stay with you.'

'Why would you do that? If that guy comes back…'

'Exactly. I can't leave you here all on your own.'

Ali suppressed a smile. 'You really should get home, get some sleep.'

'Nah, I'm all right.'

'Don't you have college?'

'No.'

'What do you mean no? Are you bunking off?'

'No, of course I'm not!' Will joined her at the desk. 'What are you looking for?'

'I don't know. Something. Anything…'

'But it's just someone looking for a place to sleep for the night. What does it matter? Why is this one so special?'

'Because after Gage left, I locked the front door and put the key in my pocket.' She watched the realisation dawn on his face. 'Whoever it was had a key to the front door.'

She stood facing the front door, the knife in one hand, and her mobile in the other. Will sat opposite, just under the boarded-up window next to the door, fighting sleep.

From time to time the boy's eyes would close and he

would slump sideways slightly, then a second or two later he would jerk up and gawp at her. Each time it happened, Ali would smile back and tell him it was OK, and that he should sleep. And he would shake his head, cross his arms and attempt small talk before repeating the process all over again.

The fifth time, sleep won.

Disconnected thoughts blew through Ali's mind. Nothing held. Nothing wanted to stay. She always felt she had spent her life on the periphery, and now here she was again, walking wide circles around her own story with no idea what to do. She felt stupid. She felt a fraud. There had been a moment just after Will had asked to stay with her, as the mystery of the front door key, their anonymous guest and the legend of Chillman Grove had swirled around them, that she had acted as though she had a plan, that she was in control.

Will had gobbled all that up with such excitement that Ali had felt utterly wretched and quickly changed the subject. That was an easy thing to do with Will Kamen. As he had sat there nibbling on a sandwich and prattling on about college, horror films and repeating the story of William Gamble, Ali had wondered what he would think if she told him she had no idea what she was doing. That as far as plans went she was currently pinning her hopes on waiting, working on the assumption that eventually the bad guys always showed themselves.

'Talk to me, Ern,' she whispered.

She stared at the boarded-up windows either side of the front door. A recent addition, Will had told her.

If they looked at him, their fate was sealed. He would infest their lives. He would take their soul.

'Tell me none of this is real, Ern.'

As Will slept, Ali waited.

The building was silent.

Chapter 18

They stepped out into the car park. A crisp, autumn morning was building under a glass sky. The mist had cleared, pushed away by a gathering, insistent wind. Ali gave Will the car keys and as he trudged off with his camera bag and two tripods, she lingered at the front door, her key in the lock.

'You don't get to hide it all from me,' she whispered into the door, and then yanked the key out. 'Not for ever.'

'Hey, Ali? Come look at this!'

Will lifted a large hardback book from the boot of Ernie's car and handed it to her. The dust jacket was tatty, the once glossy shine dulled by finger smears and stains. The title, in a large gothic font that screamed at her, was *The Bumper Book of Spooky Stories & Twisted Tales of True-Life*.

'Jesus, Ernie. Seriously?'

'Chillman Grove?'

Ali flipped the book open and saw a library sticker on the first page. The book was a week overdue. 'Ernie didn't believe in ghosts. I don't either.' She was about to toss the book back into the boot when Will held his hand out for it.

'Do you mind if I keep hold of this? I can drop it back later.'

'Knock yourself out.'

She dropped him at the start of his road, just as he'd asked, and watched him traipse up to his house with his equipment and Ernie's book tucked under his arms. She took a slightly longer route back to her hotel, cutting around the rush hour traffic and coming into town on the main road parallel to the train station. She moved the car into the long tree-lined road behind the mini cab office and followed the curve around towards the intersection.

She had pulled in to the kerb to let a van pass her when she first saw it, and as soon as she did an icy hand ran up through her body and fumbled with her heart, turning it, trying to yank it free. The traces of flashing blue light grabbed her vision away from the road and pulled it momentarily across the intersection. A police van was parked up on the pavement opposite.

Ali turned the Volvo back out into the road, cutting in front of a car coming up behind her. She ignored the blast of its horn and the shouts of the driver, and drove slowly to the intersection. The view revealed itself in stages. Past the police van, she saw a young female PC standing in the road putting out a ROAD CLOSED sign, and then beyond her a police car was parked at the edge of Mickey's road stopping cars from turning in. A thin trail of black smoke rose up past the first house in the road and coiled up into the sky. As she inched past the turning, she saw the rear of a fire engine, the bustle of fire-fighters, the snake of the hose, and then finally the charred hole where Mickey's house had once been.

Her feet were working the clutch and accelerator without her feeling it, without her brain telling them to, and the car continued trundling along in the line of impatient early morning workers and curious rubberneckers. Her hands turned the wheel at the end of the road without her knowing it, and now she was in another residential street she had never seen before, and then another and another, and she was picking up speed, moving into second, then to third, desperate to get away from wherever she was. She gazed at people on the pavements, everyone a stranger, a killer, a ghost, and the hand inside her was now a fist, punching at her bones in perfect time with her heartbeat.

Chapter 19

She had no recollection of how she got there. Or even if she were really there at all. She was staring up at that ugly light fixture in her hotel bedroom, and those little black insects were doing their death dance again. She could taste blood, and her tongue pushed against a loose tooth. For a moment she told her delirium that she was having that dream where all your teeth fell out, that was all. Yet there was another taste burning her throat beyond the tang of blood. Vodka. Was she dream-drinking too? The idea amused her.

That would have saved a lot of trouble if you could dream-drink, wouldn't it? She was aware of wetness on her jeans. *I suppose pissing yourself is a natural by-product of dream-drinking. Oh well. You stink enough as it is, what difference does it make?*

That thought turned her mind back. The out-of-order sign on the shower door. She remembered that. That hadn't been a dream. Hadn't she come into her room, soaked one end of a towel and started washing herself at the sink? Then there had been a knock at the door.

Knock. Knock.

She reached down and felt the wet towel at her side. Then her other hand stretched out and pushed at the bottle of vodka she'd taken from the bar downstairs. Random moments connected and coloured in the previous hour. A familiar face swam into view above her. A voice she wasn't familiar with called her a bitch. Then a hand was at her throat and lifting her up. Choking her.

Ali slammed against the wall next to the window and then crumpled to the floor, her legs buckling underneath her as a shrill buzzing sound erupted and ran through her head. She coughed and spat out her loose tooth.

Now he was closing her bedroom door and standing in front of it. There was a St George's flag tattooed on his right bicep, the crest of a football team on his left. There were letters on his knuckles too. Left and right, perhaps. A limited man's obvious art.

'I'm gonna make you pay for what you done to me,' he said, an index finger escaping a clenched fist, and jabbing at her. 'Fucking pig bitch.'

Ali lifted the towel to her face, spat blood on to it then ran her tongue around her mouth to find the gap in her teeth.

'Am I supposed to know who you are?'

'Really? That the tactic you're gonna use now? You gonna play dumb, you ignorant rat pig?'

'Sure, I've seen you following me. Staring at me. I've seen you driving around and tailgating me. If you wanted me to be scared of you, you should have picked a different day.'

'Nah, it's your lot that picked the day. It's your lot that raided the clubs last night, your lot that fucked my business. Your lot that's gonna have to answer for it. If I'm going down then it means you're a free pass.'

'I don't want to sound like I'm unimpressed by your

grandstanding, but I really have no idea what you're talking about, or who you are.'

'Cocky little bitch, ain't ya?' He swaggered forward. 'All this shit started when you rolled in to town. Stupid cow, leaving your name on my answer machine, you think I wouldn't check up on you? Or maybe that was the idea? Is that all part of the plan? Double bluff me?'

'Oh, you're the bloke, the other bloke that worked the night shift. Morton? You work the door at a nightclub? OK, seriously, you've got all this upside down.'

'Have I now? Just a coincidence is it that you stick your face into my life just before the club gets turned over. You're a narc, aren't you? You're an undercover narc. Look at you, even look like a smackhead. Skanky bitch.'

'Rather a skank than a copy-and-paste patriot, sweetheart.'

'The fuck you call me?'

Ali moved away from the wall and stood facing Morton. 'Listen, this is all a big misunderstanding, and I think we've got off on the wrong foot. Really, you've got me all wrong.'

The wet end of her towel struck Morton flush across the bridge of his nose with a satisfying whipping sound. Then Ali launched herself at him, jumping on to his back and yanking the towel over his face.

Morton roared and spun on the spot, his arms flailing around, trying to grab her. Ali ducked and swung her head and missed the first few strikes and then he caught her hair and tugged. Ali responded by pulling the ends of the towel tighter, turning her grip. He was shouting garbled abuse at her, the words sounding clumsy and stupid through the thick material.

Morton turned once more, his free arm now up behind

him, the hand turning to a fist and thumping Ali just above her hip. Ali gritted her teeth against the pain and then slammed her left boot down on to his calf. Morton buckled in front of the door and Ali took a hand to the back of his neck and shoved him forward, hard.

The door handle struck Morton in his right eye and he gave a muffled scream. Ali shoved him forward again and this time she saw blood ooze out into the towel. She followed up by slamming her fist into the side of his head. Morton released his hold on her and instead his hands went to the towel in two balled fists, fingers digging in to the material, slowly tearing it. He stood with a strained wheeze and lifted Ali with him, this time charging backwards until Ali struck the door. Ali felt her grip loosen on the towel, and then fall away completely with a long ripping sound.

She hit the floor and her head struck the door as Morton shrugged himself free and turned on her. He announced himself with another nasally roar and swung a boot towards her face.

Ali was ready.

She ducked the swing and then came up between his legs, hard and fast with a clenched fist. The roar collapsed into a squeal, and then Ali came up again, this time with an open hand, gripping, squeezing and turning with a sharp yank. The sound Morton made was something she'd never heard before. He collapsed to his knees, and now they were face to face.

Ali threw her head forward with all the strength she could muster and head-butted him. He swayed, looked confused, and tried to blink his bloody mush of a right eye. Ali butted him again and a pain flared inside her, a red-hot corkscrew turning into her face, burrowing up into her head.

Morton collapsed on to his back, his chest rising and falling quickly as he fumbled at the edge of consciousness.

Ali lay curled up on the back seat of Ernie's car in the hotel car park, too tired to cry, her body too pained for her to think. She listened to people leaving the hotel, the idle chatter of mums and dads and children, of work colleagues and illicit lovers, as they all climbed into their cars and set off for their day. Her phone lay in the footwell, just under her trailing hand, and was vibrating for the tenth time as another call came in unanswered. This time it was Maggie. She was losing eight to two with Gage.

She picked at a loose thread in her jeans and saw that the bruises on her knuckles were already starting to turn. She flexed her hands, working the feeling back and then tried to rise. But no sooner had she moved up on to her elbows than the corkscrew pain returned, working its way through her body. Her right hand gently started to trace the bumps on her head and then the bruises on her face. She hadn't looked at herself in a mirror yet. She didn't want to. The horrified look of the hotel receptionist as they met at the front door had told her more than enough.

She had no idea what to do or where to go. She was a failure. Surely now she'd finally become the punchline to the joke that everyone thought she was. Ali Davenport, the naïve police constable with the chip on her shoulder and the daddy issues. Ali Davenport, now the great gumshoe, London's newest hotshot private investigator! *Invetigator*, don't forget. That's what you actually are. Not an investigator. If you can't even investigate a typo…

She'd wait. It was as good a plan as any other. He would come to her. He had to. *Good and bad*. They found each other eventually. It was what happened. You couldn't have one without the other. Also, she was the last link in the chain, the last thread in the rope that could hang him. Yeah. The Knock-Knock Man would have to show himself sooner or later. She just had to wait.

Her phone vibrated again in the footwell. This time she answered.

'Hey, you should be asleep,' she said.

'Can you come get me?' Will was breathless, excited. 'I have to talk to you.'

'OK. I could come along at...'

'Ali! It's happened before. Someone else has seen The Knock-Knock Man!'

Chapter 20

He was standing on the corner of his cul-de-sac, dancing from foot to foot against the cold, when she pulled up. Will bundled himself into the passenger seat, the library book clamped protectively in his hands. He recoiled on seeing her face.

'What the hell?' he said, leaning closer for a better look.

Ali gently pushed him back. 'I'm OK.'

Will furrowed his brow. 'Someone hurt you?'

'I'm fine. A misunderstanding. We got things straightened out.' Ali jabbed a thumb at the book. 'Go on then. Tell me a story.'

Will continued staring at her face. 'Was it the guy we caught in the building?'

'It was no one, it was nothing. What you got?'

Will rested the spine of the book across an open palm, balancing it in front of him as if it were the start of a magic trick. The book slowly opened out at a page about three-quarters of the way through. Will repeated the action twice more. Both times the book fell open at the same page.

'I've done that ten times in a row. Same page each time.

Seems Ernie might have been very interested in this story…'

'It's a library book, Will. Doesn't mean anything.'

Will pointed at the open page. Ali only needed to offer it a cursory glance. The LEGEND OF CHILLMAN GROVE shouted at her from the book in bold, unavoidable block letters.

'Chillman Grove,' Will said, simply. 'William Gamble. The Brotherhood Under the Moon.' He gave a little shrug as if to question why Ali couldn't see the obvious.

'Will…' She was going to tell him that it was merely an obscure little ghost story, that the whole thing was nonsense, and that not only did she baulk at the idea, Ernie would have done too. But that argument was getting thin. Ali couldn't find the conviction to draw the words out.

'There was something else.' Will slipped a folded newspaper cutting from between the last two pages of the book. 'I found this.'

As Will opened out the newspaper page, he was almost bouncing up and down in the seat. A photo of a rundown farmhouse next to a field of wheat dissected the meagre copy. To one side of the farmhouse a tractor stood rusting away, one giant back wheel resting against the side, and behind it was a large outbuilding, its roof bashed in. Further down the page there was a photo of a window and one of a small copse. The headline didn't shout at her this time, it didn't need to: CHILLMAN GROVE CURSE BLAMED FOR FARMER'S DEATH.

'Don't know how many pages were in the article, there's not much here, but listen to this.' Will started reading, his voice hushed and full of a reverence Ali couldn't grasp. 'The daughter of beloved farmer, Mary Boedecker, 51, has spoken publicly for the first time about her mother's death. Abigail Boedecker, 15, who was with Mary when she collapsed in the field behind their property, has told exclusively of how the local legend of infamous Satanist, William Gamble, may have played a part in her mother's…'

Ali waggled her hand around between them, urging Will to get to the point.

'She says that the night before her mother died, she had told Abigail that she'd been woken by two knocks on the living room window, and that when she turned around there was a ghost looking in at her.' Will held the newspaper cutting up before him and read again. '"She told me she knew it was a ghost because no one alive could have skin that pale."'

The excitement coming from the passenger seat was almost palpable. In that moment Will reminded Ali of her old dog Obi when he would fetch his lead and then sit in front of her with it in his mouth whenever he felt it was time for his walk.

Will pointed at the date at the top of the clipping. 'This was two years ago. I've done a search for her on Facebook. She still lives there. Abigail. She's a teaching assistant at an infant school…'

Ali moved the car into gear, a small twitch of a smile threatening her face.

Ali drove them back through New Salstone and then out on to the ring road, heading east towards Chillman Grove, and whatever slender thread Will had found them.

Will barely stopped talking for the entire journey. 'I'm surprised I've not come across this book myself to be honest. Ronnie always has us searching through these sorts of books looking for nearby places where we could investigate. Stories in these kinds of books tend to be more obscure, not your classic, famous hauntings. Ronnie doesn't like places that have been overinvestigated. That's crazy, if you ask me. I mean they are investigated for a reason, right? There's no Pendle Hill or Hampton Court in these books. Ronnie was never interested in the famous ones. Reckon that even if Borley Rectory was still standing he wouldn't want to check that place out either. Mad. But then, that's Ronnie. He was born to be contrary. He's your typical Lazenby-was-the-best-Bond kind of guy. You can't do anything with people like that.'

'You've never been to Chillman Grove to investigate?'

'Chillman Grove was always a no-no, the locals there get a bit funny about their past. Ronnie's never been one to care too much about annoying people, but that's just a little too close to home. We always wanted to though. There's a lot of history down there in Chillman Grove. Satanic rituals. Black masses, all sorts were supposed to have gone on out in those woods.'

'Fun for all the family.'

'Sir Joseph Gamble, that was William Gamble's grandfather, was said to be up to his neck in all that business. The story is he sold his soul to the devil in exchange for his wealth and all the land he ended up owning, and then after he died there was a curse on the land, things wouldn't grow, the soil would never be fertile, that sort of thing. Chillman Grove belonged to the devil and to prosper there you had to offer him your soul.' Will picked up the open book and started reading from it. '"Chillman Grove, a village in a picturesque part of Wiltshire, has a long history of the macabre, most notably the cotton merchant Sir Joseph Gamble upon whose wealth the local area flourished. Gamble, who legend purports was in league with the devil, is said to have sold his soul in exchange for his riches, and that since that time the residents of Chillman Grove will face hardship and misfortune unless they do the same. The murder of Gamble's grandson, William, in the 1970s, is another famous tale that local residents have long since wished to forget."'

'Famous?'

'Well, if you're in to that sort of thing.'

'What a sheltered life I've led.'

'"The darkness in the Gamble family ran through the generations,"' Will continued, his big bug eyes gobbling up the text. '"Sir Joseph, his son Bertrand, and then his grandson, William, all prospered while Chillman Grove suffered, its businesses closing, its residents relocating, or in some cases simply disappearing altogether. In 1914 alone, twelve people vanished from Chillman Grove, never to be seen again. By far the most notorious member of the family, William Gamble, it is said, was a man who would derive great pleasure from the chaos and torment caused to the residents in Chillman Grove and was determined to drive them all from the devil's land, one by one. As one former resident is quoted as saying: 'William Gamble got drunk on chaos. If he wanted us gone, he could easily have just killed us, like people say his ancestors did, but I don't think that would have been enough for him. He got off on our fear. He'd rather drive a man insane than stick a knife through his heart.' Stories abound that William Gamble would make his mark known by appearing at his victim's window and knocking twice. If he were seen, he would then insinuate himself into their lives, gradually destroying it from within. 'He fed on people's unhappiness. Their madness. It seemed to keep him strong,' another former resident has said. 'He infests your life, it only ends one way. He was as pure an evil as I ever did see.' The Gamble bloodline was finally severed in 1978 with the discovery of parts of William Gamble's dismembered body in three shallow graves outside Chillman Grove. Although no one was ever charged with the crime, many people believe that members of The Brotherhood Under the Moon lured Gamble into a trap and murdered him before he could sire an heir. Officially a gentleman's club for local dignitaries, now long since disbanded, some stories suggest that The Brotherhood was in fact created as a direct response to the wild stories circling about the Gamble family. Their sole purpose being to keep the Gamble family's activities in check and protect the local people from any further malevolence. But legend has it that the Gambles haven't yet released their hold on Chillman Grove..."'

The casualness of Will's storytelling was both endearing and horrifying to her. The childish wonder with which he viewed these stories, originally so fascinating to Ali, now seemed diluted with utter naivety. Ali wanted to shake him. She also wanted to hug him. She also had nothing else to go on.

'Do you really think it's him, Ali? The Knock-Knock Man? The man you saw that night. Jake Tooley. Ernie...the face I caught on film...Abigail...'

'The ghost of William Gamble turns up knocking on people's windows trying to take their souls?'

'Well...yeah.'

A weary-looking wooden sign leaning drunkenly from a hedgerow informed them that Chillman Grove was now five miles away and Ali gently pushed her foot down on the accelerator. It was the only reply she had.

Chapter 21

The turning to Chillman Grove appeared as if from nowhere. The world around them shifted instantly, the bland and sterile A-roads being replaced by a winding lane that snaked up through woodland decimated by the season, and then dropped down sharply under a railway bridge, before coming out on to a wide village green. Ali pulled the car into the side of the road just behind a shuttered cricket pavilion. Ahead of them a once cutesy, perfect English village scene sat dying, drained of any colour and seemingly devoid of any life.

'This place isn't real,' Ali said.

Will looked around the bleak picture postcard they had somehow fallen into, then back over his shoulder to the way they had come as if he'd forgotten something.

A neglected village shop was situated on the edge of the green, flimsy boards across the windows, its façade peeling and worn, a brittle embrace of weeds growing up around the doorway. Further along the street, houses peeped through thick tangles of bushes and past skeletal-looking trees, as if ashamed of their appearance. Even from inside the car, Ali felt the oppressive atmosphere that hung over the place. It made her think of a rain cloud in a cartoon that followed you around, hovering over your head.

A little old lady, seemingly drawn from thin air, now stood on the steps to the shop, sweeping the same patch of pavement back and forth with a broom. She did very little to hide the furtive glances towards the car.

'Time to meet the locals.'

The lady disappeared back into the shop as soon as Ali opened the car door. Outside the car the feeling of oppression strengthened perceptibly. It was a heavy blanket draped over everything, and Ali felt her footsteps grow thicker as though an invisible hand was holding on to her belt and trying to tug her backwards. The idea that she was being watched was strong too, even more so than at the building. Here, eyes judged her from those hidden places just at the edge of her vision. People hid in the bushes and up the trees and directly behind her, mimicking her movements perfectly so she could never see them.

A bell above the shop door announced their arrival. The shop was no more than a small box, a freezer at one end, a counter at the other, and sparsely stacked shelves between. A musty gloom hung over the space, a spotlight next to the counter providing a meagre spill, a poor substitute for the boarded-up windows. The old lady stood behind the counter, her back to them, fussing with a dusty jar of sweets. She didn't even turn at Ali's greeting.

'Yes?' the lady said, placing the sweet jar delicately on a shelf.

'Something wrong with your windows?' Ali asked, taking the direct approach. 'They broken, or something?'

'Broken,' the lady parroted. 'Something like that, yes.'

'Doesn't look broken from the outside.' Ali walked to

the window next to the front door; an ice cream price board was placed across it, held in position by masking tape. 'You should get them fixed. You need people to be able to look in…don't you?'

To that comment, the old lady turned and wandered out from behind the counter, her hands clasped against her chest.

Will stepped forward. 'My name is Will, and this is my friend, Ali. How long have you been in Chillman Grove?'

'Long enough.'

'Long enough for what?' Ali chipped in.

'Were you wanting to buy something? I have many things to do, if you are not.' The old lady's hands unclasped and spread themselves down her blouse, straightening the material. 'We sell maps, if that is what you wish?'

'Why would we want a map?'

A smile eased on to the old lady's face, but found no entry to her eyes. 'To find your way out again?'

'We were rather hoping we could ask you some questions,' Will said. 'We're interested in the local area. It's history. I was wondering if…'

'You know what happened up at the Boedecker farm?' Ali said, cutting Will off. 'The woman who died up there said she saw a ghost at her window. You know anything about ghosts appearing at windows here?'

The woman's smile shrivelled to a pout. 'I'm sure I don't.'

'Do you know anything about the Gamble family?' Will asked.

'They were pretty big around these parts once upon a time,' Ali said.

The lady shrugged.

'We just wanted to talk about the local area,' Will said. 'Nothing more.'

'This is a shop, young man. But I'm not for sale. I have nothing to say to you. Either of you.'

'The Gamble family, are you aware of the legend of…'

'Why have you got your windows boarded up?' Ali snapped.

'I told you…'

Ali gripped the top of the ice cream price board. With one hefty yank, she pulled it clean away from the window and tossed it on the floor. 'And you were lying, weren't you?'

The old lady drew in her breath sharply, her right hand rising to her heart, fingers gripping at her blouse as those tired eyes awoke and sparked into life. For several seconds, seconds that seemed unreal, a moment held in time, she glared at the window as her chest rose and her fingers clawed into a fist. Then, with a speed that seemed impossible, she ran at Ali, pushing her to one side as she fumbled the board back up and over the window, leaning into it to hold it in place.

'Get out of my shop. You don't belong here.'

They drove further through the village, the only traffic on the road. Each house they passed, the few with signs of life within, and the many that seemed abandoned, all hid from the road behind unkempt gardens. Most noticeably, all of them also either had their curtains drawn, or boards or shutters up across the downstairs windows. Neither Ali nor Will mentioned it. They didn't need to.

The road rose slightly as the houses ended and the fields began, and soon it narrowed to no more than a concession, taking them past worn patchworks of green and brown and beige, where birds circled high above their prey, moving in a well-rehearsed dance against the bleached-out sky, and further on a scarecrow was stuck on its side, tethered to a post snapped off at the base. They passed a giant mound of rotten pumpkins at the end of someone's drive, and an old rusted car with branches growing out of its sunroof. Deer watched them from the hedgerows, waiting for them to pass before bolting off.

The turning was so overgrown that they missed it and had to reverse back down the lane. The foliage was like a curtain, teasing what was beyond it. Ali could see an edge of the outbuilding and the abandoned wheel next to the tractor, the scene frozen in time just as the photo in the newspaper clipping was. She imagined Ernie here. Had he been too?

Stray branches, so much like arms and fingers, scraped and tapped at the windows, as they drove in to the edge of the photo and parked. Will was already out of the car before Ali cut the engine, his face alight with wonder and curiosity, a tourist wanting to soak up everything their eyes could find.

The smile didn't last. The rabbit sliced in two just beyond the tractor put paid to that. It was fresh, the oozing insides still covered in a feverish cloud of flies.

They approached the house slowly, as if it might suddenly come alive and grab them, feeding them into one of the broken windows, and chewing them up with jagged glass teeth.

'What do you think?' Ali said.

Will stood by the front door, staring out over the barren field, once so alive with wheat, towards the small copse in the distance. 'Got a feeling, this place. Feels…' He opened his hands out, palms up, and waggled his fingers as if he could somehow pluck the right word out of the air.

'Yeah.'

The front door was loose, a heavy push could probably

topple it inwards, but Ali moved on past it and stared in through the first window she came to. She could see a kitchen through the broken glass, everything of value stripped out, nothing but memories left behind. The linoleum floor was stained and curled up at each corner. The unhappy smell of age trickled out through the hole in the window and passed under her nose.

Ali carried on around. 'Safe to say she doesn't live here any more.'

'Who would want to? Even without what happened, this place isn't right.'

'Chillman Grove isn't right.' Ali felt coldness pass through her as she looked around her surroundings and started to entertain irrational thoughts she couldn't comprehend. 'How many of those houses we passed looked occupied to you? Five, six? This place is a ghost town.' Will's childish smirk at that comment made her respond in kind, against her better judgement. 'Those sightings of William Gamble, all those years ago, the people all died?'

'Uh-huh, yeah, I guess.'

'I'm at the point where I need more than guesswork.'

'They all died soon after, yeah. A few days, few weeks. He came for their soul, that's the way the story goes. A harbinger of death, come for the devil's dues.'

'And people really believed that?' Their ride through the village suddenly came to her mind, the boarded-up windows, the neglect, the decay and the defeat. 'OK, you don't need to answer that.'

A wooden fence ran around the property, broken by a kissing gate. Will wandered over and hopped up on to the gate, balanced on one foot and then jumped down. 'Hey, Ali! There are some markings here!'

'What?'

Will peered closely at the wood and then shook his head. 'No. Just initials. Love hearts.' He returned to the house and his macabre tourist trail.

Ali's mobile began vibrating in her back pocket. She didn't need to look at it to know who it was. There even seemed to be a little bit of Frank Gage in the tone of the phone when he rang. *Rip the plaster off!* she heard her father telling her, and as she answered the phone, she had a sudden image of ripping a giant plaster from Gage's mouth and taking off half his beard with it.

'Frank.'

'Oh, you better have some good answers for me, Davenport.' There was no smile in his words, no promise of laughter in his singsong voice.

'What's the question?'

'Don't get smart. Let's get that set right off the bat, you damn well ditch the attitude and the sarky gob because I am in no mood. You're only getting this call because we've a history, and because of Ernie; you turn your claws on me and we are going to fall out fast. I'm the only friend you've got left. You understand that?'

Ali turned away from the farmhouse and sat on the kissing gate. She took a deep breath and then plunged right in: 'Morton?'

'That fucking moron? Oh, he's quite far down on the list of things we need to chat about. So is the ABH charge that's going to come down the pipe at you. And you better bet he will push for it. Right now, though, I don't really give a damn about him.'

'It was self-defence.'

'I told you, I don't care.' Gage gave another of his long

and overly-dramatic sighs, and when he spoke again the bark had gone, replaced by a calm, patient teacher's voice, the anger there at the edges, ready to bite her. 'I'm a lot more interested, Ali, in why we found your mobile phone number written on the arm of a dead body tonight.'

Ali dropped her head and rested her chin against her chest, closing her eyes. 'I didn't do anything to him,' she whispered.

'Pardon me?'

'I had nothing to do with whatever happened to Mickey.'

'First name terms, is it?'

'I saw the…I drove past and…he didn't die in the fire?'

'Didn't he? You tell me. You tell me all about your pal Mickey, and you can also tell me why the woman on the switchboard at his mini cab office told me all about the young lady with the big scar over her left eye who came in asking about him yesterday, and his holiday, and the earring she dropped in his cab.'

'It's not what you think.'

'Where are you, Ali? Let me come get you.'

'And arrest me?'

'Talk to you.'

'How do I know I can trust you?'

'Shouldn't I be asking you that? You know, I'm really not comfortable that I've got three corpses under my watch in this past month, and all of them now seem to be connected to you.'

Ali jumped up from the kissing gate, her voice rising with rage. 'What the fuck is that supposed to mean?'

'Calm down.'

'I'm calm, I'm totally calm, I just want to know what that accusation is supposed to mean? Huh? Ernie and Lyman were suicides, you said. Or were they? Is there something you aren't telling me, Frank? It's Lyman, isn't it? He didn't top himself. I saw it in your face last night. I knew it.'

'Where are you, Ali? Let's do this in person.'

'Where do you think I am? I'm trying to find whoever killed Ernie.' Ali started pacing back and forth in front of the gate, kicking loose stones towards the house. 'It's happened before. Ernie...what happened at the building. Jake. All of it. Everything that's happened...this whole fucking nightmare... he's done this before. I'm on to him.'

'Ali...'

'It's fine, Frank, I don't mind doing your job for you. I will get all this sorted, don't you trouble yourself.'

'Look, I can't protect you from whatever you're involved in unless you come and talk to me.'

'I don't need you to protect me.'

'OK, then I can't protect everyone else from you. Either way, talk to me!'

She looked back at the house as another stone left her boot and pinged off the front door. Will stood further along, lost in his own world, admiring the building like it were a piece of art.

'This evening,' Ali said flatly. 'The Gravy Boat café, I will meet you there before I start the shift. When I'm satisfied you're alone.'

'The shift? You want to go back there? Why? That job is done.'

'No, it isn't. I haven't finished what I came here to do yet. Two more things, Frank. A Salstone mini cab made a drop off at the building the night Ernie was killed. Mickey was going to find out who was driving, and who they were dropping off. I need you to find out for me. Do that for me and I will tell you everything I know. You do that and I will trust you. Deal?'

'OK. Deal. And?'

'And what?'

'You said there were two things.'

'You were wrong.' Ali watched Will disappear around the side of the house. 'You're not the only friend I've got left.'

Ali hung up the call.

Will was at the living room window, his hands either side of the frame. He didn't blink, he barely moved, entranced by the gloominess inside the house, the stories it held. Ali stood to his side.

'You OK?' Will asked.

'Think I'm in trouble.'

'Cool,' he whispered, still distracted. He let his hands drop to his side with a hearty slap and moved further on around the building.

She looked down at her feet, at the mud and the tiny clumps of grass, at the spot where her Knock-Knock Man might once have stood, two years ago, and she felt a tingling inside her chest, a feeling like electricity. She drew her eyes back up to the window. A thin, lightning bolt-shaped crack in the glass cut through her reflection. She let her focus shift into the emptiness inside. She saw Jake in there, she saw Ernie and she saw Mickey too. Finally, she saw herself sat inside, staring at the window. Waiting.

Waiting...

Good and bad.

'I'm going to find you, you fucker.'

Three pathways led across the field from the farmhouse to the copse, trampled down over the years. Ali and Will took the centre, most direct, path. The Chillman Grove woods started about a hundred yards south of the copse, and seemed to be watching their every move. There the trees huddled close, almost like they were interlinked, forged together, and the scattershot gaps between the trunks were filled with an impenetrable gloom. It was a fairy tale wood, with a beauty and a danger that could surely only come from a child's mind.

The copse itself was much larger than Ali had assumed from the farmhouse and the slender tree trunks seemed to move apart as they approached, more pathways opening up around them, beckoning them further in. Ali saw the first bone less than ten yards into the copse. Part of a ribcage, she thought, as she kicked it from her path. It was the first of dozens that she saw; small and large, old and new, animal and...

'You OK?' she asked Will.

'Yeah.'

She saw rotting meat on some of the bones, others positioned into shapes and small mounds on the ground, several jammed into the earth. 'These are all animal bones, right?'

'I'm sure they are. Yes. Of course they are.'

Ali was convinced again that they were being watched. Her eyes darted back and forth between the trees, looking for one of the shadows that hung there to suddenly move, for one of the indistinct shapes in the distance to come alive and charge at them, for a nightmare face to gradually reveal itself and smile at her.

'Ali?' Will was further on, standing just before a wide, grey boulder in the middle of the pathway. It was nearly as tall as him. Moss and lichen grew in ragged patches along the sides, but the top was clear, almost smooth. It also seemed to be completely flat.

The same images came to Ali and Will at the same time. They almost said the word in unison. As it was, another voice said it for them instead.

'Sacrifice. Up there on that boulder.' The man stood behind them, a grey-muzzled Labrador at his heels. If it's true that dogs end up looking like their owners, Ali was currently stood in front of exhibit A. The man drew a gnarly index finger across his neck. 'At least that's what they say. They say a lot of things though. They. Them. People have a lot of things to say about Chillman Grove – it's not always necessarily true.'

Ali took one step to her side, blocking Will from the man.

The man seemed oblivious. He nodded once to Ali and then tilted to his side to offer the same to Will. 'Harold. Pleased to meet you.' He pointed to his dog. 'Thelma. My girl. Unlikely she feels the same. Developed a bit of an attitude in her dotage.'

'What are you doing here?'

'Walking my dog. Why? What are you doing here?' Harold moved around Ali and ambled up to the boulder. Thelma looked on, unimpressed. 'You and your boy taking in the sights?'

'My what?'

'They should charge, might kick this village back to life, amount of people we get out here gawking at us. Ought to charge a pretty penny, if you ask me, not that anyone does. Why would they? Eh, Thelma?' Harold patted the boulder. 'Yep, this was supposed to be some sort of sacrificial altar or some such. Satanists. Something about this place. Chillman Grove. You know our history, of course?'

'Why do you say that?'

'No other godly reason you'd be down here. They say this boulder just appeared one night as if by magic, just rolled itself here from who the heck knows where? Load of horseshit, most likely, but we all like a campfire story, don't we?'

'How long have you lived here?' Will asked.

'All my long and wretched life, fella.'

'This village is dying,' Ali said.

'It is that. Lot of people scared to live here, what could I tell you? We got a reputation down this part of the world.'

'A curse.'

'Call it what you want.'

'The Gamble family?'

'Aye, they might the cause, they might just be a symptom. Couldn't rightly tell you. Not that it really matters, does it? Devil's village, people call us. Maybe the Gambles brought the devil to our doorstep, or maybe the devil brought us the Gambles. It doesn't matter a piss in a stiff breeze, to me. A legend sticks. Could be that we might have moved past it were it not for that business couple years back,' Harold motioned his head in the direction of the farmhouse, 'but can't see it happening now, not after that. And if it does, I will be long in the furnace by then, so couldn't really give that much of a mind.'

'You're not scared living here?'

Harold chuckled to himself. 'If William Gamble really wants my rotten old soul, then there's no hope for any of us. As long as he lets me see my old Thelma into the ground, then I'm not losing any shuteye over it.' Harold nodded down to his dog. Thelma offered a feeble tail wag and a low grumble in reply. 'Best get the old girl home. You got more questions, feel free to walk with us.'

'Thanks.'

Walk was something of an overstatement. As Thelma meandered back and forth between the trees, snuffling half-heartedly at the ground, Ali and Will edged forward slowly either side of Harold, who seemed in no hurry to get anywhere soon.

'What can you tell us about the incident at the Boedecker farm?' Ali said. 'Did you know Mary Boedecker?'

'Of course, a fine lady. As for what happened, I know only what the newspaper said. Mary took over the farm back when the girl was still a baby. Place had been empty for a long time. This was Gamble land. Everyone told her that there was something wrong with this place, that she'd get nothing to grow here. But she picked it up for a bargain, said she'd make it work. She didn't. Livestock kept her going, I guess.'

'The Gambles owned this land?'

'Course, they pretty much owned everything, but yeah, back in the sixties, this place flourished under William Gamble. When he died, land died with him.'

'You believe all those stories? That this place won't prosper unless you sell your soul to the devil?'

'Enough people do. I believe in people. Someone tells me that the ghost of William Gamble comes a-knocking on their lounge window wanting their soul, well, that's their tale and I've no right to shoot that down. Course, that legend did for us. Once, twice, maybe people forget, but we had five die with that tale on their tongues. Spooked enough people out. Place got left behind. But the curious thing with a legend is the effect time takes on it. Goes one of two ways: time either cements the legend or it breaks it apart. I'm inclined to think we'd have been fine had whatever happened at the

Boedecker farm not happened. People had started to let it go. People were moving back. There were children here. Life. A point. You've seen boards up in people's downstairs windows, I'm guessing?'

'We have.'

'Saw the first one day after the Boedecker girl blabbed to the paper. Started seeing these here bones not long after too. What other conclusion you going to come to other than it were happening all over again?'

'It didn't scare you, Harold?' Will said. 'When you heard what had happened to Mary Boedecker?'

'I'm too old to be scared.' Harold gave a light laugh and rolled his shoulders until something clicked. 'But I do always sleep with my windows locked.'

They reached the edge of the copse and Thelma waddled ahead of them, taking a different pathway through the field. Harold gave a reedy whistle and Thelma stopped, lumbered around and stared at him, unamused.

'Hold your horses there, girl.' Harold inclined his head to Ali and Will. 'Well, looks like I'm going this way. Guess I will be saying my goodbyes. Hope you find whatever you're looking for. What are you looking for?'

'I don't know,' Ali said.

'No. Well there's something to be said for that.'

'The Brotherhood,' Will suddenly blurted out. 'Do you know anything about The Brotherhood Under the Moon?'

'Guess I know no more than you do, fella. A secret society, they say. People of power. Always has been a secret club, hasn't it?'

'They were blamed for William Gamble's death. I read that they vowed to end the Gambles' bloodline, to try to stop everything that was happening.'

'Heard the same thing. Self-appointed protectors. They lured William Gamble into a trap and did for him. Stop him spreading his seed. My mother always said they were pious men. That they came from the church. Founded with the sole purpose of protecting us from what the Gambles were doing. Good and bad, you know? That old chestnut. I guess there's mileage in that. God and the devil? I don't know about them guys, but good and bad is our daily battle. We're all dancing on puppet strings, down to you which hand you favour.' Thelma, increasingly unimpressed with the conversation, wandered off. Harold turned to follow his dog.

'Wait!' Ali called out. Harold half-turned back. Thelma didn't bother. 'The Brotherhood...you talked about them as though they still exist. But they don't though, surely?'

'Power, piousness and wealth? I doubt anyone gives that up easily.'

Chapter 22

The bird-like school receptionist stared at Ali's cuts and bruises over her bifocals, and raised a suspicious eyebrow.

'A friend of Abigail?'

Ali stepped forward, giving the fake limp another airing. 'Yes, and I feel so bad about bothering her at work, but I've got to wait an hour for them to come and help me get my car out of the ditch, and I'm very late for an appointment, so I was really hoping that...Abbey...would give us a lift.' She tried a smile out for size too. Will remained in the doorway, standing at the edge of the charade.

Was Abigail an Abbey to her friends? Surely, she was. Did she drive yet? Was she there today? Did she even still work there?

Ali waited for something in the act to trip her up and in that moment regretted letting Will talk her in to it, even if she knew that he was right. Walking in to a school and playing the police card with no ID to back her up and looking and smelling the way she did wasn't exactly the greatest idea.

'Oh, you poor dear, please take a seat. I will go and give Abigail a knock. She's only in 2B. I'm sure Mr Parsons can spare her for a while.' The receptionist ushered Ali to a chair. 'Would you care for something to drink? We have a medical kit, if you would...'

'Oh, you are a sweetheart, thank you. But I think if I sit right now, I might not get up again! If you don't mind, I think I will wait outside – the fresh air helps.' Ali was convinced she could hear Will gulping back a laugh across the room.

The receptionist followed Ali and Will out, scuttling off down the corridor while they walked out of the front doors and into the playground.

'Very impressive,' Will said.

'Now for the hard part.'

Will gestured covertly at the school block behind them. Three windows ran along the wall, and they all had metal shutters closed across them, fastened in place by a padlock. Abigail Boedecker tumbled out of the doors a minute later, her coat half on, looking decidedly harassed.

'Abigail?'

'What's happened? Who are you?' She looked between them and then out across the playground. 'My friend...'

'Yeah, that was us. Sorry for the deception,' Will said.

'I don't understand?'

'I need to talk to you.' Ali offered her hand. 'I'm Ali Davenport.'

Abigail pulled her coat on and walked past Ali's outstretched hand. 'They told me that a friend of mine was hurt...'

'We need to talk to you about what happened two years ago,' Will said. Abigail stopped and glared at him. 'About what happened to your mother. Sorry for lying to you. We weren't sure whether they would let us in... I mean... Would that be OK? To talk to you about it?'

'You're friends of the other guy, I suppose?' Abigail said.

'Sorry?'

'The guy that phoned me a couple of months back.'

Ali drew up to her. 'Ernie?'

'Yeah, that was his name. Has he found Amery?'

'Who?'

'Robert Amery. Hasn't he told you about this?'

'Ernie's dead.' Ali breathed the words into Abigail's shocked face. 'I think he was murdered. And I think it might have been by this same man. The man your mother saw at her window. The…y'know…'

'Ghost,' Will finished.

'I need you to tell me what you told Ernie.'

Abigail's face drained of colour. 'My mother died of a heart attack. But the man she saw. I don't think he was any ghost.' Abigail beckoned them to follow her. 'Not here. These walls have eyes.'

'Just as well, seeing as no one round here uses a window.'

Abigail led them around the side of the building to a small concrete bike shed. Perching herself on the rear rack of the nearest bike, she took a packet of cigarettes from her coat and lit one up.

'Bit of cliché, smoking in the bike shed. I'm sorry about your friend. Ernie. He sounded like a nice man.' Abigail took a drag on the cigarette and then nibbled absently at a loose bit of skin on her thumb. 'Go on then.'

'I think Ernie opened a can of worms that someone was trying to keep closed.'

'This same guy?'

'I think so, yes. Help me find him. Help me stop him. Tell me what you know about him. Please.'

'You first.'

Abigail listened as Ali gave her the condensed version of

what had led them to this point; Deveraux, Jake Tooley, The Knock-Knock Man, and then finally Ernie and Maggie, and the camera footage.

'Ghost hunter, eh?' she said to Will, once Ali had finished. 'Cool.' Abigail put the cigarette out and flicked the butt into a nearby bin. 'Well, I hate to burst your bubble, but the man my mother saw, it wasn't Gamble's ghost. It wasn't a ghost at all. I'm sure of it.'

'But you told people your mother saw a ghost?'

'Did I? Because you read it in a newspaper? I told the newspapers nothing. I wouldn't sell my mother out like that, despite what people may think. You know, people round here think I did it on purpose, that I raked up the old William Gamble story again to try to get some attention. Or maybe I was playing a prank. That they think I had so little love for Mum that I would make up stories about her death. Well, fuck them. Fuck that. They sicken me. You've seen the village, I guess? Seen the boards and the shutters and the empty houses? Maybe you've even seen my old house that no one will touch?'

'Yeah.'

'Yeah, well I did that. Me telling the truth about what happened to Mum did that. Everyone hates me for reviving that story. Kids here, some of them look at me funny. Heaven knows what their parents are feeding them about me. Suppose it's just as well class numbers are dropping off. If they didn't take kids from The Oaks here, they'd pretty much close this place too, I reckon. Fucking sad, if you ask me.'

The more Abigail talked, the more she reminded Ali of Will. Find her passion, wind her up and watch this girl go – she had a lot to say and didn't hold back. Ali also saw a girl with a story she needed to release who had clearly never been listened to before. A person desperate for someone else to indulge her outlandish tale and not ridicule her. Ali could sympathise.

'Friend of mine at the time,' Abigail continued, 'her brother ran a blog on the history of Chillman Grove, anything spooky, anything weird. He loved all that. Well, he took what I told my friend and ran with it, twisted it and turned me into persona non…thingy. I spoke to no one, except my mate and the police. Told them what happened, no one else. She should have kept her trap shut. I didn't want this. Whatever you will have read, most of it will have probably come from that blog.'

'The newspaper quotes you.'

'Not me.'

'Who is Robert Amery?'

'Amery worked on the farm, he was a…kind of a drifter, you know? A junkie. My uncle had met him in rehab, and he knew that Mum liked a charity case, so he figured she could put him to work, keep him straight. She needed the help at the farm, with her condition and that.' Abigail saw the question on Ali's face. 'Her ticker. She hadn't been well for years. Kept trying to get her to slow down, sell the place and retire – she'd never listen though. Even with all the shit that was going on around the farm, she refused to consider it. "They'll not drive me out!" she kept on telling me. She was belligerent. But I loved her for it.'

'What was going on at the farm?' Will asked.

'Over the years we've always had odd little periods where rumours surface about crazies out in the woods. A lot of people pass through here because of our past. And sometimes they stick around. Living where we did, we'd sometimes hear things down in the copse. Chanting. Shouting. Noises.

Weird stuff. You ever hear a pig scream? Most horrible noise in the world. Sometimes there'd be a dead animal turn up, hanging from a tree. Things carved in the bark. Symbols. Stuff like that. Police never seemed to care about all that. "We legitimise lunatics round these parts." That's what my mum always said. Well, I think she always thought Robert Amery was just that, because he turned up during one of those times. There was a lot of weird things going on round the farm, things we couldn't quite explain, and we'd had a few animals go missing too, only for them to turn up down in the woods. Dead. All that business really set Mum on edge. She was so scared during that time. Whether she would have warmed to Amery if he hadn't turned up during silly season, who knows? I would doubt it though. There was always something a little off about him. I never really considered it at the time, I guess I was still in shock, still grieving, but the more I think about it now, I think Amery was in on it. I think he was meant to push her to the edge. Guy at the window, he came to push her over. I think they planned to scare her to death. Daft as that sounds.'

'For what purpose?'

Abigail gave an elaborate shrug as she sparked up another cigarette. 'No idea. You tell me.'

Ali leaned down to Abigail until they were almost face-to-face. Her body was tensed, her eyes unblinking and greedy. 'Tell me about the man at the window.'

'Walter.'

Heat bloomed inside Ali's head. Her heartbeat skipped and fluttered, just for a moment. 'Tell me about Walter, Abigail.'

'I got to thinking of him as Walter Noon. In the weeks before Mum died, Amery would meet this Walter on his lunch hour. Every day. Twelve on the dot. Mum even made a joke of it, asked who it was he was going off to meet all the time and did he have himself a nice young lady in the village. He just told her, blankly, that he was meeting Walter, and he said it as though she were the biggest idiot in the world. As if it were impossible he could be meeting anyone else.' Abigail took a long drag on her cigarette before dropping it, half smoked, and scrunching it out under the heel of her boot. 'Amery started to change. Small things at first, like he would get very quiet, looked like he had things on his mind. Then he started to look ill, figured perhaps he was back on his vices, he was all twitchy and fidgety, ants in his pants kind of thing. Then all that just stopped and the guy was totally withdrawn, like he was there but he also wasn't there. He changed during those weeks he was meeting Walter. He became something else. I followed him one time. Amery. He went down to the copse to meet this Walter and I saw them together.'

Ali dropped to her haunches in front of Abigail. The girl seemed to see Ali's face for the first time then, the cuts and bruises and that scar over her eye, her branding. She looked momentarily repulsed, then concerned, and finally curious.

Ali felt the question marching unbidden towards her and stopped it before it came. 'Go on, Abigail.'

'Amery was down on his knees before him. Head bowed. Weeping. He looked broken. That place is creepy enough at the best of times without whatever all that was about, so I didn't linger. It freaked me out. It was wrong, all of it, just felt all wrong down there. Not least Walter. This guy was all kinds of wrong. His face...'

'What about it? Tell me what he looked like, Abigail.'

'His skin was so pale. He looked ill. Yet he also looked

powerful too, if that makes any sense to you? Like he could reach down and split Amery in two if he wanted.'

'What else?'

'I don't remember.'

'Short? Tall? What was he wearing?'

'I don't know. I'm sorry. I just remember his skin.'

'And you think it was Walter that your mum saw at her window?'

'I do now. Yeah. I'm sure of it. When she told me that she'd seen that face at the window, I actually laughed. You live around here, you know all about the Gamble legend. When I was at school, sometimes kids would try to scare each other by knocking on classroom windows and shining a torch under their chin. May have done it myself a few times. It is what it is. You live here, and it's part of the fabric of the place. So, yeah, I told her she was nuts. That it was someone playing a joke on her. It didn't occur to me that it could have been Walter Noon. Not then. And I feel so dumb about that. Not that it would have made much of a difference to her. She was so scared. I think that night she was actually prepared to go. Just up sticks and get out. Put the place on the market and let Chillman Grove win. Maybe she would have done. Maybe she would have been OK if she'd got out. But next night, he came back.'

Abigail absently lit another cigarette, and took several quick drags, her free hand playing with her lighter, her right foot tapping nervously on the concrete of the playground.

'I came home around dusk. Walking up the lane I just had the strangest feeling. Call it a sixth sense, maybe, I don't know, but something felt out of place. I walked past the turning to the house. There was this nagging feeling that there was something I'd forgotten, something I had missed that I needed to see, so I walked on past the house to the field, jumped the fence and just stood there, looking out across to the copse. At first it didn't look like her. Didn't really look like anyone. No one human, anyway. Then, bit-by-bit, I pieced her together. She was staggering through the field like she was drunk, wavering around all over the place. Then she just dropped. I ran to her, but I didn't feel like I was there. It was like I was running alongside my body, and I couldn't feel myself, like I was just made up of air. It was the strangest thing.' Abigail stood from the bike and pulled her coat tight around her body. 'I got to her just before she died. She looked peaceful. That was the thing that really stayed with me, her calm expression. It totally didn't fit with her last words. Of all the things that stopped making sense since that day, that is the thing that confuses me the most.'

'What did she say, Abigail?'

'She told me not to go into the house because the devil had come back. And he was smiling.' Abigail leaned against the wall just as a bell sounded three times inside the building. 'Never saw him again, of course. Walter. Never saw Amery again either. It's like they were never there at all. My uncle cleared the house two weeks later. I never stepped foot inside again.'

'You told the police about Walter?'

'Of course, I did. Robert Amery was in New Salstone when it happened, sobering up in a police cell. He said he didn't know anyone called Walter. No one else round here seemed to either. As soon as I mentioned Mum seeing someone knocking at her window, I pretty much screwed any legitimacy they might have given me anyway. I was just a kid with a vivid imagination and a little too eager to believe ghost stories. I'd be surprised if the police lifted that many rocks. Mum wasn't a well woman, you know? Doctors said they were surprised her heart had held out for as long as it had. That it finally gave out wasn't exactly some great mystery. They weren't going to pull up trees. Not for a fifteen-year-old girl claiming her mother had seen a ghost.'

'I'm sorry,' Will said.

'Why?'

Will blushed and stared at his trainers.

'He wasn't a ghost, Will. I'm sorry to disappoint you. He was just a man.'

'And now he's come back,' Ali said. 'You should be careful. Is there somewhere you can go?'

'Yeah. Right here. My mum ran from him. I'm not going to. But if you find him, let me know. Let everyone know. Tell people my mum wasn't mad. Tell people I'm not a liar. I might sleep better.' The school bell buzzed again. 'I have to go.'

'You asked if Ernie had found Robert Amery,' Ali said. 'Why?'

'When I spoke to him, he said he'd heard about a Bob Amery in New Salstone. A vagrant. He said he was going to try to track him down at one of the local homeless shelters.'

Bob? Bobby? Think that was his name.

'What did Robert Amery look like, Abigail?'

'Long hair…'

Long hair, beard, scruffy-looking, she heard Mickey repeating in her mind.

Ali felt Will shift next to her, heard a sharp intake of breath.

'Do you think he found him?' Abigail asked.

'Yes,' Ali and Will said in unison.

Chapter 23

Ali parked up at the end of the road, leaving Will in the back seat of the car, and walked amongst the lengthening shadows. The large rectangular window of The Gravy Boat café shone brightly against the gloom outside and Gage sat alone at the table nearest the window, framed like a lonely figure in an Edward Hopper painting. She saw impatience writ large on his face, even without the frequent glances at his watch, and the looks up and down the road.

In the faint background, she could see the waitress washing up, stacking dishes, and throwing her own glances at the clock on the wall. She watched the traffic coming and going and then walked further up the road and peered casually into the cars parked there, before looking up at the darkened windows above the café. She returned to her original position and watched him for another minute before returning to the car and dialling his number.

'Where the hell are you?' he barked.

'Meet me outside.'

Ali swung the car to the curb just past the café, and then pulled away before Gage had even shut the passenger door.

She took a sharp left at the end of the road, followed the road to the right and then double backed and drove past the café in the opposite direction.

'You're not being followed,' Gage seethed, before jabbing a thumb over his shoulder. 'And what the hell is he doing here?'

'He's my friend. Leave him alone.'

Gage fumbled his seatbelt into the lock and clocked Ali's face. 'Jesus!'

'Oh, you sure know how to make a girl feel good about herself.'

'Morton?'

'Of course, Morton, who else?'

'Never know with you, you could get in a fight with your own reflection.'

'Frequently have, Frank.'

'You know I should be arresting you?'

'For Morton?'

'Fuck, yes, for Morton! That sorry sack of shit is going to have a field day with us. What the hell were you thinking?'

'It was self-defence, I told you.'

'Self-defence? You broke his nose and almost put his eye out!'

'You're right. I should have killed him. That would have been better.'

Gage swivelled in his seat and glared at her, unable to tell if she was joking.

'You should arrest me, Frank. If anyone makes a connection between you and me, that might be used in court.'

'You think?' Gage said sarcastically. He rubbed a hand through his beard and then up to his hair before giving another of his dramatic sighs. 'Ali…where do I even begin with you?'

'I haven't done anything.' Ali took a turning off the main road into town, and slowed the car as they came out into a large residential area. 'Anything else, I mean.' She pulled over next to a wide patch of grass where children were playing on swings and kicking footballs, using up every last drop of the light. 'Right. OK.'

'OK. Where do you want to begin?'

'The cab office, did you find out about that night?'

'I did. That was the deal. I told you I would.'

'And?'

'Ernie and his bleeding heart had set up an account with the cab company for some homeless guy to charge. He visited Ernie at the building sometimes.'

'His name is Robert Amery, right?'

Gage looked stunned. 'Quite the detective, aren't you?'

'Hardly. I'm just picking at the case Ernie built, trying not to constantly be two paces behind. So, Amery was there that night too? Interesting.'

'Well, no, not so much. See, the cab driver wasn't dropping him off. He was picking him up. Got him back just before one. He's in a squat out towards Heroes Ridge. So, that's my side of the deal. Now give me yours.'

She started with Morton and then worked back to Mickey before jumping forward to Abigail Boedecker, Robert Amery and Walter Noon. The story tumbled out of her mouth in a machine gun blitz of words – the connections, the coincidences and the guesswork. As the story headed to Chillman Grove, Will fired in a few asides of his own.

Gage stared silently from the passenger window as they spoke, watching the children at play; he made no interruption and barely even moved. With the facts and the supposition finally laid before him, he folded his arms, his stony face impossible to read.

'I've heard the Chillman Grove story before.'

'And?'

'And it's bollocks. All this ghost nonsense has messed with your mind. You and Ernie were coppers, why are you swallowing this fantasy? You deal in what you can see. In evidence.'

'How do you know it's fantasy?' Will asked, quietly.

'I don't need input from you, thank you very much,' Gage snapped.

'Don't speak to him like that.'

Gage turned back to face Ali. 'Well The Brotherhood certainly doesn't exist any more. That's a load of rubbish. I'd know.'

'You'd know all about that secret society, would you, Frank? I suppose they can't exist because you never got an invite, is that it?'

'Don't be ridiculous. If they still existed, I'd know. People would talk.'

'Would they? Seems to me one thing that the people round here are good at doing is keeping secrets. I was shut down when I told people who I saw at Deveraux's that night. Abigail's story was ignored too. I thought the police just didn't care, didn't believe me. Now I'm inclined to think it might be the exact opposite. Superintendent Moss took over the Deveraux case and held it close. Who is to say that the same didn't happen with Abigail?'

'What are you saying? That Moss is a member of The Brotherhood?'

'Why not?'

'Because it doesn't exist any more!'

'But if it did, you don't think the super wouldn't be a prime candidate? Taylor told me that he knew Deveraux too. Self-declared important men controlling everything because of overstretched opinions of their entitlement? You don't think such a group could thrive in these enlightened times we're living in? Easier to believe in than ghosts, I would suggest. This whole thing stinks of some sort of cover up.'

'For what purpose?'

'Garrett Lyman didn't kill himself, did he, Frank? What about Mickey? If you saw that I had written my number on his arm, then he probably didn't die in the fire. What happened?'

Gage jabbed his thumb towards Will in the back seat again. 'He needs to go. He can't be here.'

'No. He's OK,' Ali said. 'He's with me.'

'No.' The tone of Gage's voice left little room for argument. 'The building has been sold, did I say? They sign the contract tomorrow. Dalton is delighted. Of course, that's no comfort to Maggie. I wonder whether you've rather forgotten her in all of this?' Gage turned to Will and offered a tired smile. 'Perhaps you would like to call in and see her now, young man? I'm sure you would like to offer some comfort to a grieving woman, wouldn't you? Maybe you could put her mind at rest that there was nothing untoward in Ernie's unfortunate passing. Nothing supernatural. Nothing at all. Suicide or accident. I really don't care which she believes. You understand me?'

Ali swivelled around, reached over and squeezed Will's hand. 'It's OK. I'll call you.'

He looked exhausted, his hair sticking up in places, his eyes heavy-lidded, and now he looked hurt too. For a moment it seemed as if he were about to speak, to argue the point or plead with them to let him stay. Instead, he simply squeezed Ali's hand back and slipped out of the car.

'Nothing untoward?' Ali asked, with a Frank Gage-style laugh behind the words. 'You don't still believe that, do you, Frank?'

Gage had returned his attention to the passenger window. He was watching the football players launching the ball to each other as if shooting hoops in basketball as they made their way home across the green.

When he spoke again, he sounded crestfallen. 'We haven't had a murder here for two and a half years. Did you know that? It's like the world just rolled on by and forgot us. Let us do our own thing.'

'Garrett Lyman?'

'There was minor trauma to the back of his skull. They think perhaps something metallic. The fire at Mickey's was arson, they aren't saying it officially yet, but there are clear traces of an accelerant. He jumped from his bedroom window into a glass patio table. And then there's Ernie...'

'Yeah. Then there's Ernie.'

'Let's go find out what happened to him, shall we?'

'So, you believe me?'

'I'm open to the possibility of believing you. That might be the best you get though.'

Ali turned the keys in the ignition. 'I'll take that.'

Chapter 24

As they drove out to Heroes Ridge, another great piece of wisdom from her father came to mind, one that always amused her. *The sweeter the name, the shitter the place*, he would say. He had been convinced that any area, in any town, given a cutesy moniker would invariably mean it would be the exact opposite. This was the man who counted Blueberry Tower, Puffin Avenue and Mint Gardens amongst his watch, and three more undesirable places you couldn't wish to find. In Ali's experience, none of those locations came close to Heroes Ridge. She'd lost count of the amount of call-outs she'd attended here over the years.

Beyond the heavily graffitied welcome sign, a parade of abandoned shops stood on each side of the road. The road led them over a small hill where scattershot groups of identikit children in hoodies stood huddled together, as others cruised aimlessly up and down on bikes, throwing accusing glances at them.

'Used to be the most exclusive part of town, you'd never believe it now,' Ali said. She pointed across Gage, to a derelict building over to her right. 'The old inn, used to be a nice haunt, that place.' The inn was a gloomy, sorry-looking structure, set in front of a wide concreted surface, where yet more children were congregated; little black shapes moving in and out of the falling dusk. 'Tell me about Amery then.'

'Minor rap sheet, dealing, breaking and entering. He was nicked five years ago after spending a weekend pulling the pigeon drop up and down The Oaks with a woman he was seeing. Got a few hundred. We're not talking about a master criminal here. He's been in and out of hostels for years, few odd jobs here and there. Rehab. Fallen off the radar these last few years. I don't think we're looking at a murderer there. I just don't see it.'

'I don't either. What about acquaintances, anything come up?'

'Usual deadbeats and dope heads. No Walter.' Gage pointed to a narrow road on their right and Ali took the turning.

'Smack alley. Didn't think I'd have the pleasure of being back here. Thanks, Frank.'

'Well, you've been away a while. Thought you'd want to reacquaint yourself with the sights.' He signalled for her to stop about halfway down.

On first glance the road always seemed achingly suburban and seemed to stick out from everything else in Heroes Ridge. Edwardian semis, for the most part, the houses were snuggled together within spitting distance of their identical counterparts across the road. Looking closer, however, the buildings weren't that dissimilar from the houses in Chillman Grove. Not in their style, in their despair.

The house directly next to where they had parked, a red brick semi with giant bay windows and balcony, seemed to be trying to hide from sight. Empty windows like doleful eyes peered out around peeling paintwork and rotting wood, as a fat crack worked its way up through the brickwork from the front door. The house looked embarrassed. Ali saw variations of the same sad sight either side. The whole street, save for a few houses here and there, was covered in darkness. And it seemed to prefer it that way.

'Regeneration,' Gage said, casting his own eye across the opposite side of the road. 'So they keep saying.'

'So they've always been saying.'

'They leave it much longer, they're going to be better off burning the whole place to the ground and starting again.' He raised a gloved hand to the window and tapped an index finger against the glass. 'Four houses up, I think.'

The house was one of the few that showed any signs of life. A hazy orange light shone from several windows across its three floors, and the muffled beat of monotonous music found Ali and Gage and counted them across the road. Just before the front gate, Gage pulled up and turned to his right. Directly opposite the first house, an almost identical one, this one cast in darkness, stared back at them. Gage looked between them both.

'You don't know which house it is, do you, Frank?'

'Just as easily be either. Want to flick a coin?'

'I'll take right, you take left?'

'I don't think so. You stay with me. And keep your claws in check.' Gage carried on across the road to the first house. 'We find Amery, you let me handle it. OK? You're a citizen now, don't forget.'

Ali strode past him and into the front garden.

Walking through the front door, they were met by a lazy, slow-moving cloud of smoke in the hallway, threaded with the pungent smell of weed. The steady thump of music was coming from a room at the back of the house and was broken sporadically by the unconsciously loud voices of the inebriated and the dreamy ramblings of the stoned. A man in cut-off jeans and no top wandered past them in the hallway, not seeing them and not caring to. A woman sat on the top step of the staircase rolling a joint, nodding along to her own music pumping out of a pair of headphones.

To the right of the hall was a living room, before a narrow corridor fed off to the rest of the ground floor. They peered in and saw a woman lighting a makeshift bong, fashioned from a large mineral water bottle. She was sitting on a long, threadbare sofa just about holding on against age and an excess of blim marks. A man was asleep on his side on the floor, resting his head on a bunched-up coat, and between them a large table was covered in half-drunk drinks and overflowing ashtrays.

'I'll catch you up,' Ali said, lingering in the doorway.

'You'll catch me up? What does that mean? What are you doing?'

'Going undercover?' Ali slipped into the room, giving Gage no say in the matter. 'Hey, how are you?' she said to the woman on the sofa before picking up a glass from the table. She sniffed it, recognised the old familiar aroma of vodka and knocked back the dregs. She found a larger mouthful in another glass and threw that back too.

The woman held out the bong to Ali, her eyes pinched together, cheeks puffed out as she held the smoke in. Ali shook her head and instead licked her index finger and dabbed at a small mound of white powder on the edge of the table before rubbing it into her gums. The woman closed her eyes and tilted her head back as the smoke trailed slowly from her nostrils and her mouth, and then gave a satisfied sigh.

'You scoring?' the woman with the bong asked, and then waved a limp finger above her head as if to indicate where to go, before letting her hand drop into her lap, tired with the effort.

'Looking for Bob. Bobby? Robert Amery?' Ali crossed to the man sleeping on the floor, rested a boot on his arm and gently rolled him on to his back. The stranger stirred and began snoring. 'He around?'

The woman fell back on the sofa, letting the hit have her. A huge grin reached her face before the lazy finger was back up in front of her and waggling towards the front window.

'What does that mean?' Ali said. 'He's outside?'

'Over the street. Keep your voice…' She held the finger to her lips. 'You got anger in your voice.'

Ali swiped another glass from the table and knocked back an inch of whisky. She could hear Gage further on in the house, heard the singsong tone and the ingratiating lightness. She strode down the hallway, out of the house, and within three steps was in another front garden, standing before another open door. There were no voices in this house, no music and no sign of life. Darkness seemed to smother every inch of the place. Instinctively she reached behind her, searching for the knife she knew she'd left in the building, her hands curling momentarily into fists instead.

Ali considered knocking, but instead she wandered in and gently closed the door behind her. She could just make out the staircase ahead of her, and to her right, just like the house opposite, there was a living room feeding off the hall. Ali slipped her mobile from her pocket and turned on its torch.

Her free hand stroked the wall looking for the light switch, and her fingers caught on tatty tangles of cobwebs and pushed against brittle curls of peeling wallpaper. The room smelled of dust and age, and something else too, something wet, and sharp. She crossed to the living room and let her hand roam the wall just next to the doorjamb. Her fingers found the light switch straight away this time, but nothing happened when she pressed it.

'Right.'

The ghostly white light from the phone's torch swept the living room floor, instantly picking up a large doll sitting on the carpet. Its arms were held out before it as if it were asking for a hug. It was missing an eye, and a large clump of its thick mousey hair lay by its feet. Scattered around it were some beer cans and food wrappers, and in one corner a small bloodstain. Next to the blood was the mangled body of a bird.

Ali raised the light up to the living room window and saw three thin cracks running through the glass, meeting at a small, jagged hole near the middle. Two large patches of damp bloomed out on the far wall, evenly positioned either side of a framed painting. Just for a moment they were eyes, the blackened and dead eyes of the house itself, watching this intruder.

Ali took one tentative step inside the room and held the torchlight at the painting. She saw a large ballroom in a mansion, couples from centuries gone by dancing and drinking and laughing together. A silhouette stood in one of the ballroom windows, looking in.

The kitchen at the back of the house was narrow, and rubbish was piled high along the work surface. One end of the work surface had been prised away by a crowbar, which remained wedged between the wood; a little army of ants wandered in and out of the gap, some skittering up the handle of the crowbar. Washing up was piled high in the sink and mouldy food squished and broke under her boots. Ali pulled the crowbar free and then backed out of the room, heading to the staircase.

The carpeting on the stairs was wafer-thin and worn, and each footstep was announced by a weary creak. The light probed the landing as it dropped slowly into sight, and for a split second the carpet seemed to move, to shift in her eyeline, as though it was being pulled into one of the bedrooms. She didn't realise it was rats until she trod on one's tail and heard the screeching objection. They scattered from her path, parting around her boots and heading to the stairs, or ducking away into the two bedrooms along the landing.

At the end of the landing Ali could see a very faint orange glow on the wall. It was coming down the next set of stairs from the top floor. She pushed herself against the wall and moved slowly towards it.

The door to the first bedroom stood ajar. As Ali pushed it open with her foot, two rats ran over her boot and beat her inside. The two rats became five, and then the five became ten, twelve, fifteen. They swarmed across the room to a bed in the far corner, and then they ran up the nearest leg of the bed and joined a huge, heaving mass of their brothers and sisters on top of the duvet cover.

At first, when something moved under the duvet, Ali assumed it was simply yet more rats. Then slowly, unimaginably, she realised there was a body in the bed, and it was rising up to a seated position, rats clinging to almost every inch of its torso. It stopped and then it turned, a blank face watching Ali as rats ran over its head and down its face.

Ali backed away in disgust and hit the door, her

elbow slamming into the handle, the phone toppling out of her grasp and falling to the floor. She was on her knees instantly, scooping it up and shining it back at the bed, as she shuffled on her backside, out of the room. A mannequin was sitting upright in the bed, its head turned to the door, its expressionless face showing no interest in its wriggling bedfellows or the terrified intruder in the doorway.

Ali took a second to calm herself, releasing a torrent of whispered swearing, and then she was back on her feet, leaning into the wall and moving to the second bedroom.

The door was wide open. Ali approached slowly, turning into the doorway with delicate steps. The room was a stark contrast to the first, yet somehow the scene unnerved her a whole lot more. There were a few rats here, huddled together in the far corner, but the rest of the room was bare, except for a single, rickety-looking chair positioned in the middle of the floor.

She let the torchlight roam the walls, search the corners and the floor, sure that there must be something else there. As she turned the light back to that solitary chair, she was convinced it had moved, shifted around ever so slightly so it seemed to now be facing her. But, of course, it couldn't have done.

The staircase to the third floor was shorn of any carpeting and was splintering at the edge of the first few steps. At the top of the stairs a beaded door curtain hung over the entrance to the landing and tinkled gently as she pushed it apart. The soft, amber glow of candlelight caressed the walls. The light was coming from a bedroom to her left. Further along, on the other side of the landing, she could just make out a sink and the edge of a filthy-looking bath. She pocketed her phone and turned towards the bedroom, the crowbar up in front of her.

She just had time to see the candles – ten, maybe even more – on a table in the corner, and the single, dead rat, eviscerated in the middle of the floor. And then she saw him. The tall, emaciated-looking man standing just before the single window in the room now took all of her attention. She saw him through hazy eyes, the candlelight softness edging at everything and denying any immediate definition. He wore tatty jeans and a short-sleeved collared shirt that was open. There was a messy grouping of scars across his chest and down his arms, and two long rows of stiches along his left side. His face came to her last, the dirty, sallow skin, the unkempt beard and the long, greasy hair framing it all.

'Hello.'

Robert Amery's greeting seemed to come from somewhere behind her. Ali felt her step falter. Cold fingers started tickling at her insides. It wasn't the dislocated voice that scared her, and it wasn't even the horrid, leering smile he offered. It was the unshakeable feeling that he had been standing here waiting for her. For a long time.

Chapter 25

A gentle breeze blew through the open window behind Robert Amery, ruffling his shirt. The candlelight gave his scars a dark, bruised look and lit the simple madness in his face. He stood as erect as his bony frame would permit, his arms down by his side, gnarled yellow fingers stretched flat against his trousers.

Ali held the crowbar before her, trying to feel the heft of her weapon, but she found no comfort. No protection. Whatever Robert Amery used to be had long since left the pathetic shell that stood across the room from her.

'Robert? My name is...'

'I know who you are.' Amery's wild eyes found her scar. 'What you are. Don't worry. We're all orphans here. There are other mothers, other fathers. Better people. Different paths.'

Ali's throat felt clogged up with cotton wool. Her mouth moved feebly and her eyes began to water with the effort to speak. She managed just one word, one name, and as soon as it had left her lips, the crowbar slipped out of her sweaty hands.

'Walter.'

Amery closed his eyes and nodded his head. When he opened them again, for a split second the pupils weren't there, and then, as he spoke, they slowly rolled back into the sockets. 'Soon.'

'Where...' Ali spluttered.

'He is everywhere.' Amery raised an index finger to each eye in turn, and then took the finger to each ear and finally his head, tapping twice on his skull. 'He is in front of you, and right behind you. Ernie learned this. You will learn this. You will understand that when you ask so many questions, sometimes you won't like the answers. Ernie didn't like the answers. Ernie died.'

Ali felt the strength drain from her legs and, before she realised it, she was down on her knees before him. 'Walter... killed...my friend.'

'It was sad that Ernie had to die. Ernie used to like to see me. He gave me a key so I could stay there if I wished.'

'A key...you gave...to...Walter.'

'No.' Amery slipped a hand into his back pocket. A second later a key landed on the floor by Ali's knees. 'I liked Ernie. Ernie was my friend.'

'He wasn't...your friend. He used...you.'

'No. I used him.'

Suddenly greasy fingers were in Ali's hair and trailing across her face.

Amery was down on the floor, holding her and she couldn't find the strength to fight him. 'I am his eyes and I am his ears. I was entrusted to hear your questions and smell your lies. That was my calling. Walter wanted me for that. He needed me. Me. Me!' Amery's emotionless voice broke, just for a second, as he screamed the last word into

Ali's face. Acrid breath smothered her nostrils and made her gag. The anger abated almost as soon as it came, and that horrid detached voice was talking to her again, from behind, in front and above. 'You think it's any coincidence you are here? No. It is no coincidence you are here. You are exactly where Walter wants you to be. You always have been. Ernie, Garrett, Mickey, these deaths were all for you.'

'I...I...don't...'

Amery pulled her to his chest and Ali felt the cluster of scars rub against her forehead. 'You could never have run from him. You should know that. You will find comfort one day in that fact. I know you will. This was always inevitable. This has been inevitable for so long. Decades. The slow twist of a lost life, always meandering on its aimless course. This is the point that was chosen for you from so long ago. This is your destination.'

'Tell me...what...' She tried to pull back from his hold but had no strength, weak hands pushing at his marked skin and finding no purchase. 'I need to know...please...'

Amery shook his head, seemingly disappointed in her. 'I asked no questions. I asked nothing of him. Look what he granted me! Look what he gave me. He's in me. He's on me. He's a great man and he's allowed me to see great, impossible things. Right here, in this house.' Amery licked at her scar and then carried on up to her hairline. 'The devil talked through him. In this very room.' His fingers were back, combing through her hair again, fingernails digging at the scalp. 'We've all been abandoned. But there are other homes. You don't have to fear them.'

'No...I...'

Amery's lips pressed to her ear, his voice dropping to a putrid whisper. 'Madness nourishes him. Fear feeds him. You can choose not to give that to him. That is the only victory you have left.' His left hand cupped her cheek. Humour, pity and indifference were all there, somewhere, swirling around his ink-spill eyes. He chewed at his bottom lip as he considered the pleading expression on Ali's face. 'I was lost too, when he found me. Then he showed me what was truly possible.' Part of Amery's lip flapped free as he spoke, and blood dribbled down his chin.

'Chillman Grove...'

'Chillman Grove is the devil's land.' Amery's left hand now slithered down to her throat and gently started applying pressure. 'People were long overdue a reminder of that.'

As his fingers pressed down and his brittle nails began to prick at her skin, the cotton wool sensation began to abate, the restriction loosening, her words coming easier. 'Mary Boedecker... she was nobody.'

'We are all nobody.'

'Why kill Mary? Why spare Abigail?'

'Of course, you believe Walter to be a monster, so you can't see any other way, can you? You are still limited. Impeded. Walter had no desire for her demise. Just her fear. And dear Mary did give him so much fear to feed on. His return needed to be announced. Where better, more symbolic, than the land of his father? It made little difference who delivered the message. Mother or daughter. He only needed one of them to remind people who it was that watched over them. People had forgotten who built their homes and allowed them their lives. We needed to remember his name, his family, his bloodline.'

'His family? No that isn't...'

'Possible? You still question what is possible?' Amery's fingers slowly released their hold, a hot and clammy smear now staining her skin. He stood and in one fluid movement was back at the open window, sitting on the windowsill. 'Certain pious preachers in these quarters needed to know that the sins of their fathers bore them no victory.' He offered her a pitying, bloodied smile. 'You want to know what is possible? Could it be possible that Walter could will an affliction on Deveraux's wife that would drive her to the edge of her sanity? It is. Could it be possible that a deeply religious man such as Deveraux could find himself so desperate, so hopeless, that he lets a man like Walter across his doorstep, knowing his bloodline and his history? It was. Is it even possible that Deveraux could fear for his wife so much that he turns to Walter and offers his very soul in return for his wife's life? That he agrees to shed everything he believed himself to be to spare her? It's remarkable to see what fear and desperation will do to a human. All that we hold, all that we are, we can discard everything so easily. We should be condemned for it. Some of us will be. Deveraux was.'

'Jake…'

'Yes. Surely it couldn't be possible that Deveraux could allow Walter to convince him that the sacrifice of a child would cure all his ills? That a man like Deveraux could ever find himself swiping a child off the street and chaining him up like livestock, ready to be butchered?' Amery licked the blood from his lips, though more soon replaced it. 'It was. Deveraux would always commit unspeakable acts, just like his father did. And so would you, given the chance. We become our parents in ways grand and small. We can't avoid it. Walter was always destined to continue his family's legacy.'

Ali pushed herself to her knees, a rage that that couldn't be released coursing through her. She needed to shout, to scream. Instead, she merely spluttered random words and slumped back to the floor.

Amery didn't even seem aware that she had spoken. 'William Gamble was pulled apart, desecrated. His heart removed and shoved in a shallow grave. His killers had the hypocrisy to call it God's work. Their god would allow no such thing.' Amery punched at his own chest to enforce the point and Ali saw that the scars on his chest were beginning to weep thin trails of blood. 'But The Brotherhood Under the Moon killed the wrong Gamble. William Gamble's wife was already carrying a child inside of her. Now that child has returned home. Debts are owed.'

Ali fumbled for the crowbar and used it to push herself up. The floor felt as though it were made of rubber, the wall built from paper as she leaned against it for support. She took three deep, struggling breaths, summoning the strength to speak. 'He murdered a fifteen-year-old boy! He's a...sick fucking murdering bastard.'

'Walter killed no one that night.'

'He did. I saw...'

'What did you see?'

'Walter was there...Jake...'

'What did you see that night?'

Ali watched in mounting horror as the old wounds on Amery's chest suddenly began to open, parting like small mouths all wanting to tell their stories at once.

'I...I...saw...'

'You saw what you wanted to see, believed what you wanted to believe. Deveraux's wife spared the boy. She released him. You brought him back.'

A gust of wind swirled into the room but it was devoid of freshness and provided no relief.

'I know Walter killed him!'

The candles on the table blew out, one by one. Moonlight etched at the window, and the blood drenching Amery made him glisten in his final moments.

'No. That was you. That was always you.'

Robert Amery blinked once over pure white eyes and then tipped himself forward and slipped smoothly out of the window. His body didn't even touch the sides.

For a moment the room shifted around her, and then that too was tipping forward, the ceiling falling down as the floor rose up and swapped places with it. Then everything suddenly settled. The sensation in her throat disappeared, her strength returned, and now her mobile was up before her, her thumb swiping across the screen and finding Gage's number. She gawped at the open window as if expecting to see Amery still sitting there, then turned in a small circle taking in the moonlit room, looking for something that would convince her that the last few minutes had been some sort of waking dream.

If it were a dream, she was still wholly submerged within it.

It didn't sound like Gage's voice. There was no humour, no song, and he sounded far away, his mechanical voice echoing out of the phone.

'Ali? Listen to me. I need you to…'

'I'm in the building across the road. Get an ambulance.'

'Ali, I need you to go to the window. Please. Do it now.'

Ali was there in a single stride. She could just make out Robert Amery directly below her, his body splayed out face down in a perfect star shape. 'I think Amery's dead, he just took a dive, and I couldn't stop him…where are you?'

The question was almost immediately redundant. When Ali pulled her head back in and straightened, she saw Frank Gage instantly. He was standing in the top floor window of the house directly opposite her, his left hand out to his side holding his mobile. She questioned why she was on speakerphone until she saw the fear in his face. She even had time to consider that his compact little frame seemed to have shrunk, the famous white linen jacket dwarfing him now, before she registered that Gage looked more terrified than she'd ever seen him. Even then, it still took the large hunting knife to appear at his throat and the slither of that nightmare face to peep out from behind him, for the full picture in that window frame to be complete.

Ali's heart seemed to stop for a moment. When it started again it felt as if it was vibrating rather than beating. The cold chill that had so far swamped her insides was gone, burned away by the heat of an implacable, burgeoning rage.

'Hello, Walter.'

That slither of face now disappeared behind Gage's skull. The hunting knife twitched, the blade tilting up, pushing gently into Gage's beard.

'You want me,' Ali told him. 'Let him walk away.'

'Want you?' It was a bland and empty voice with no accent and no emotion, much like Amery's. 'I've already got you.'

'You want to kill me? Let him go and I'll be right over.'

Gage was suddenly thrust forward, his head slamming into the glass and causing it to crack. Walter yanked him back into position and returned the knife to his throat. 'No. I don't want to kill you.'

'Then what the fuck do you want? You've killed everyone else connected to that night – why let me walk away?'

Gage's groans were high pitched and childlike. Walter responded with a gentle 'ssh' directly into his ear.

Ali leaned her forehead against the glass in her window. 'You know what I think?' Blood was now trickling from Gage's nose, running into his beard and dripping on to the blade of the knife. His terrified saucer-shaped eyes were locked on Ali. She raised a hand up to the window, meaning to try to calm him, but it looked more like a wave. 'Walter?'

That slither of face returned from behind Gage's head. She could see now that his hair was cut close to his scalp and it accentuated the pale skin. Even at this distance, Ali could see the edge of his mouth turning up. He looked like he was enjoying himself.

'What I think, Walter, is that you want me alive because if you kill me then no one is talking about you. Your family will be forgotten once again, you'll be that little itch in the back of the mind. You don't exist if no one is talking about you. If no one is afraid of you. That's what I think. Tell me I'm wrong.'

For a few moments that horrid glimpse of face remained still, then bony white fingers were wrapping themselves around Gage's outstretched left hand, and Gage's phone was being brought closer to that upturned, smirking mouth.

'Death is not nearly enough, for you. You have more suffering to do, there is much more left to break. I want you on your knees before me, begging for me to put you out of your misery. I want you to plead with me to leave your life. Only then will your debt be paid.'

'Debt? I don't want to dent your hubris, but until today you were supposed to be a ghost.'

'A ghost?' Walter gave a small, empty laugh.

'Have a look in the mirror.'

'My affliction is genetic. Yours though? We both know how you got that scar.'

'You know nothing about me.'

'I know everything about you. Since the day I found out who you were, I've followed every part of your sorry, pitiful little life. I've watched you fall so far already. But it's not enough. It's not nearly enough. I've often dwelled on the irony of you being there that night at Deveraux's estate. That it would be you that came.'

'A lot of people died that night because of you.'

Walter gently pushed the phone back away from him and placed his hand on top of Gage's head. The knife turned in his other hand, the blade now pointing up, resting just under Gage's chin. 'I killed no one that night.'

'You drove Deveraux to it.'

'I did *not* put the gun in his hands, nor the knife in his wife's. I saved your life that night, perhaps you don't remember? I pushed you out of the way of a shot that would have taken your head off. I shoved you down into the cellar, out of harm's way. I saved you.'

'And why would you do that?'

'I told you. Death, for you, is too easy.'

'Was death easy for Jake?'

'You tell me.'

'You killed him.'

'No. The boy fell.'

'You killed him!'

'His death is your responsibility. Your nightmare to live with.'

Ali pulled back and thumped the window frame in a flash of rage. 'I've killed no one!'

'But you have. And you want to kill more. I can see the

rage within you, desperately wanting to be released. I can see you becoming the person you are meant to be.'

'You, I would kill. I'd consider that a pleasure.'

'And that makes you a good person? Would it be worth it? Would my death be worth the price you'd pay?' The first flash of emotion threaded through Walter's words. Enjoyment. 'You should kill me. Become the person your rotten soul demands you to be. I was there the day your mother died. I watched you break. I watched you get your scar too. Your branding. I was there. I've always been there.'

Ali thumped the window frame again and wood splintered free as the glass rattled precariously. 'Don't talk about my mother!'

'Why ever not? My parentage was fractured too. My father slain at the hands of godly men, my mother forced into hiding with me, finding herself in squalor and destitution. Denied her husband's wealth. You can't begin to imagine the things she did to keep me alive. Or maybe you can? Maybe you will. She took her own life to spare mine. Should you ever fall pregnant, this would be better for your child too. What sort of life would they have with you?'

Ali stood stock-still, a hostage in the window, the unwelcome salty sting back in her eyes, as rage and helplessness battled for her focus. 'What do you want from me?'

'Can you comprehend how long it took me to piece my life together? To find out who I was, what I was meant to be?'

'William Gamble was a murderer!' Ali spat, saliva speckling the glass. 'So was your entire, worthless family.'

'My father was a great man.'

'He was a killer!'

'So was yours.'

For a moment the glass in the window seemed to shimmer. She saw her own distorted reflection staring back at her, saw it sway and then rock forward, as the two figures in the window directly opposite pulled away. She heard Walter's ghastly, hollow laugh again, and now the tears bubbled up unbidden and began to stream down her cheeks.

Ali thumped the window frame for a third time, an easier expression than trying to find the correct words. The hungry look on Walter's hideous face as she found it again told her it was the reaction he had wanted. Needed.

Ali tilted forward, her hands either side of the window, holding her up. 'No. My father was...'

'A member of The Brotherhood Under the Moon. One of my father's killers. Yes. Deveraux became quite garrulous at the end. People often do.'

'You're lying to me. I get it. I know what you want. I know what you're trying to do. I won't let you.'

'Were you his princess? Were you his little angel?'

Ali felt bile rise in her throat. 'Shut up!'

'You never understood why it was so easy for him to walk out on you, did you? Daddy was a murderer. Daddy couldn't align his actions with his faith. Daddy was going to hell. Maybe he thought his absence would make you safe? You never looked for him, did you? All those questions, and you never looked for the answers. Your mother, perhaps? Too much hurt. Yes. Easier to cut that little piece of history out than to relive it, again and again.'

'Stop it!' Ali screamed. 'None of this is true!'

'Now look where we are. You've become your father.'

In one swift move, Walter pulled the knife down and then forced it up into Gage's chest, just under his heart. Walter's left hand casually moved from Gage's head, opened at his side and caught Gage's mobile phone as it slipped from his hand.

In Ali's mind she was already leaving the room, charging down the stairs and across the road, but her legs kept her where she stood, rooted in the window, watching in mounting horror as Walter slowly forced the knife up, twisting the searching blade. Blood belched from Gage's mouth and splattered his white linen jacket.

'There's so much more left to break,' Walter whispered into Gage's phone. 'You're going to lose another one tonight. One, I think, that will really hurt. Another teenage boy that you dragged into my path. How many will be enough?' Walter yanked the knife free with a dramatic flourish and let Gage crumple to the floor.

Ali turned from the window and ran.

This time her mind and her body were in perfect agreement.

Chapter 26

By the time Ali got to the front door of the house opposite, Frank Gage's lifeless body had taken the direct route to the front garden and now lay in a messy heap just next to the doorstep. People were gathering at the open front door, huddling together, unable to prise their horrified eyes off the scene.

Ali scattered the onlookers like bowling pins. She took the stairs two at a time, the crowbar feeling deathly strong in her hand. The layout on the first floor matched the house she had just been in, but instead of rats, all she found here were people asleep on mattresses or slumped on the floor, lost in clouds of smoke or their own drugged-up paradise. She kept on moving.

Deep down, she knew he wouldn't still be there. That he would never make it that easy for her. But her rage carried her there regardless. The empty room, a near identical match to the room where Robert Amery had taken his own dive, held the sharp November breeze filtering through the shattered window like an exhibit.

She saw the bloodstain on the floor from the corner of

her eye but refused to acknowledge it; just like the impossible questions and the horrific possibilities that Walter had pushed into her mind. If she were lucky there would be time for all of them later. She saw only one person as she tore back through the house and vaulted over the corpse on the doorstep, sprinting back to her car: Will Kamen.

She drove one-handed, dialling Will's number on her mobile phone with the other as the car sped through Heroes Ridge and back towards New Salstone, swerving in and out of traffic that wasn't moving at her requisite speed. After three rings, Will's answerphone kicked in.

'Will. Call me back. If you're still at Maggie's, stay there. Stay out of sight. I'm on my way. Call me back.'

He hadn't called back by the time she reached the outskirts of New Salstone. He still hadn't called as she returned to the housing estate and pulled back in again next to the wide patch of grass where they had watched children playing football in what felt like another lifetime.

Ali dialled again, got his answer machine message again. 'Will? Where are you? This isn't funny. Call me back!'

She swung the car into Maggie's driveway ten minutes later, a sense of dread building inside of her. The lights were off in the house. She peered along the side alley and saw that the small slither of garden visible there was also in darkness. She pounded on the front door and held her finger down on the doorbell, then pressed her face against the living room window, trying to peep between the slender gaps in the curtains. She saw nothing, and nothing stirred within the house.

She tried Will's mobile again as she climbed back into the car and reversed into the road. This time she didn't even leave a message.

Five minutes later she became convinced that she was being followed. A car, its headlights on full, swerved in behind her and tailgated for two roads, only falling back when Ali flashed her hazard lights. As it dropped off her tail, Ali sped up and then swerved across the road, blocking the other car off and forcing it to brake. Ali was out of her car in a flash, storming over to her pursuer and yanking the driver's door open, a raised crowbar ready to greet them.

He looked about fifteen, bound up in a thick coat with a baseball cap at a slant on his head. As Ali reached out and grabbed him around the neck, the cap slipped off and landed between his legs.

'Who are you?' she shouted, moving him from side to side in his seat and making his head wobble. The terror in his face was enough to convince her he wasn't a threat, but she asked him again anyway while forcing his face into the steering wheel.

'I'm…I'm nobody,' he spluttered.

'Learn how to drive, nobody.' Ali released her hold and strode back to her car.

She didn't park at the end of Will's cul-de-sac this time; she drove straight up to his house and parked next to the car in the drive, half on the lawn. There were lights in the upstairs windows and a small lamp on in the hall, shining through the glass in the door. She walked in and called out his name, then crossed the hall and opened the door to his room. There was no sign of him anywhere.

'Will!'

She turned back to the front door to see Will's mother, bound up in a dressing gown, her hair wrapped in a teetering mound of towel, standing at the bottom of the stairs, holding a hairbrush as though it were a weapon.

'Who the hell are you?' Ali asked.

The theft of her own question made Will's mother's response stumble out in gibberish. She waved the hairbrush at Ali and backed up against the wall.

'Oh, you're the mother,' Ali said, the words dripping with contempt.

'Get out!'

'Where is your son?'

Will's mother jabbed the hairbrush towards Ali's face. 'Get out or I will call the police!'

Ali snatched the hairbrush from her and tossed it over her shoulder. 'I *am* the police.'

'Wh…what's the matter? Is he in trouble?'

'Well, you just wouldn't know, would you?' Ali took two quick steps across the hall and then suddenly they were face to face, Will's mother flat against the wall. Her eyes found Ali's scar, the cuts and the bruises, and then her nose joined in and found Ali's rancid aroma. 'Why don't you have any pictures up of your son?' Ali punched the wall, just above the woman's head. 'What's the matter with you?'

Ali didn't wait for an answer.

She drove through the centre of town and saw Will in every pedestrian, and Walter at the wheel of every car. There was only one more place to try, and the car seemed to take her there on instinct.

As New Salstone fell away, the sky above darkened by the second. When the ghost town of the industrial estate appeared, Ali flicked the lights on full and slowed the car. The felled beast sat there in hiding, its charred carcass lost against the inky sky, its probing tongue of rubbish now somehow edging into the road. She passed the dilapidated warehouses, the burned-out cars and the white-goods graveyard and saw shapes, shadows and suggestions all along that grim parade of decay. But that was all they were now. There was nothing real here and nothing for her to fear.

And then, just as the giant oak trees came into view, she saw him. She knew his shape, she knew his walk, and as he heard her approaching, he turned and then she saw his face too. Will Kamen beamed at her as she got out and pulled him roughly into a hug.

'Where the hell have you been?' she whispered. 'I've been calling.'

He tried to move out of the hug, but she held him there a little longer.

'Sorry, I've no juice left on my phone. Maggie wasn't in. You OK?'

Ali broke the hug, but held him firm by the shoulders.

'You've found him, haven't you?' Will asked.

'Yes.'

'And?'

And I've put you in danger. You shouldn't be here. It isn't safe.

'You'll always be safe as long as you're with me,' Ali said. 'I promise.'

Chapter 27

The final shift

The stray cat slinked out of the night and padded up to greet Will at the front door of the building, purring loudly as it weaved itself around his legs. Will smoothed its coat and ran a finger under its chin.

'Hello there, you.'

Ali parked next to the church wall. St Augustine's was nothing more than a dark block tonight, a shape pushed out of the blanket of the night. Her eyes roamed the rising ground of the graveyard all the way back down to the giant oak trees standing sentry. The feeling of being watched was there again, as it always had been. But now it was more acute, more tangible.

They were not alone.

Ali turned back to the graveyard, the crowbar swinging loosely in her hand. An invitation and a threat. She peered into the darkness, looked for shapes or movement, anything that the night wanted to offer forth. So far, the night was keeping its counsel.

The night can move around you. You can make it alive if you have a mind to.

'Ali?'

'Coming.'

As Ali approached the building, the cat darted to the side and walked in a wide semicircle, eyeing her up.

'I don't think he likes you,' Will offered, with a chuckle.

'He's in good company.'

The cat bolted back into the night as Ali slid Amery's key out of her pocket, opened the door and guided Will quickly inside the building. She gave one final glance out into the car park, one last scan of the graveyard and the church, and then pulled the door to, locked it and slipped the key back into her pocket alongside her own.

Will silently set to work with the halogen lamps. When they were in place, he wandered into the room at the back of reception and started filling the kettle.

Ali retrieved Mickey's knife from the desk and slipped it into place against her belt. 'You haven't asked me any questions.'

'I figured you'd tell me,' Will said, raising his voice over the boiling kettle.

'Yeah. OK.'

'Mr Gage arrested him?'

'Walter got away.'

Will nodded his understanding. 'OK. But he won't get far though, will he? Police are on to him. Doubt he will even get out of town. They'll flush him out.'

'Yeah. I'm sure someone will.'

'Tea?'

'You feel safe with me, don't you?'

He faced her in the doorway, a teabag pinched between his fingers, an adorably confused expression on his face. 'Of course, I do.'

A single tear trickled down Ali's cheek, breaking at her broad smile. 'Thank you.' Still the confused expression remained. Ali gestured to the teabag. 'For the tea.'

She hadn't given any thought as to whatever story to tell him, what would be the most convincing and least frightening tale to keep him with her. As it was, Will already had his own story, and all she had to do was nod in the right places and offer the odd grunt. He didn't mention Robert Amery. Will even spared her that.

He shouldn't be here. You need to get him out of this place.

No. Where could I take him where I know he would be safe?

Not here. Anywhere else but here.

He's with me. There is nowhere safer for him.

'Can I ask you a question, Will?'

Will handed her a mug of tea and took his own to the desk. 'Yeah.'

'What are you doing here? No ghosts in this building, after all.'

'I dunno. Just...Y'know?' he mumbled in teenage boy, before slumping down on the chair and gazing at his trainers. 'Oh, sorry.' Will quickly stood and backed from the chair.

'Don't apologise to me, Will.'

'Yes.'

'Sit down.'

Will sat again and nursed his mug of tea.

The dirty linoleum flooring made ripping sounds under her boots as Ali walked into the open space at the back of the building. The great empty nothingness sat above her, and for a second she imagined herself floating up there, rising up and up until she was at one with the emptiness, stripped of all weight and burden. Free to drift away for ever.

'Ali.'

Her name brought her back to earth. 'Yes, Will?'

'Can I ask you a question too?'

'Sure.'

'Haven't you finished your job now? Why are you here?'

Ali stepped out of the light spill and into the surrounding gloom, hiding her face and the lie she knew it would reveal.

'I agreed to work until the end of the week. Plus, I'm still owed money.'

'Oh. OK.'

Ali sat on the edge of the fountain sipping at the dregs of her tea, watching Will swivel around on the chair at reception as he thumbed through one of Ernie's trashy old thrillers. From time to time she would stare at the front door and imagine Walter standing there on the other side. She thought about the feel of her knife opening his skin and skewering his heart, or maybe the crowbar connecting with his skull until it cracked open and spilt his brains all over the floor. It felt good. But more than that, it felt easy.

'*You've got a code, Ali-cat. Never lose that,*' Ernie's voice reminded her. '*People will try and take it from you, but make sure you keep it. It's worth more than anything anyone could tempt you with.*'

But this is the man who killed you, Ern. This is the man who ruined my life. Those things don't apply here. Fuck codes. Where has that ever got me?

An idle breeze was slithering in from somewhere behind her and wrapping itself around her shoulders and stroking up her legs. Suddenly she was back in that hideous, childish dress again. The dress her father had bought for her and told her she would look so pretty in. She could recall the itchy material so easily, the distaste at having her legs and arms exposed, the goosebumps. The feeling of looking like a stupid little girl.

She remembered so vividly the disappointment, the realisation – so strong and defined in her young mind – that her father just didn't know her in that moment. Their conversations, their special Sundays at the café and the cinema, none of it really meant much in the end because he still didn't understand her. But more than that, even when she put that dress on to try to make him happy, and to try to convince him not to walk out that day, he hadn't even looked at her standing there on the front lawn. He hadn't acknowledged her tears or her pleading screams. He had just gone and never come back.

Daddy was a murderer. Daddy was going to hell. Maybe he thought his absence would make you safe?

It was a possibility too awful to consider.

That he killed the father of the man you so desperately want to kill?

It's different.

Why?

Because he was her father. That was the simple truth of it. He was her father, her best friend and hero. She had idolised him. The wound he left behind inside of her never got dressed, and never healed. She had just slowly let it poison her. It was inconceivable that anything could ever make him walk out on her. Even murder.

Sparkleville.

Waves rolled high somewhere, far away, reaching a perfect sandy beach before breaking. High above, in a clichéd blue sky, gulls sounded warning cries. The walls of a beach house sighed, the wooden signpost bearing its name swinging back and forth on rusted chains.

'Hmm?'

'I asked if you were OK?' Will was standing next to one of the lamps, watching her. 'You go somewhere?'

'Nearly.'

'You all right?'

'Will?'

'Yeah?'

'The devil lies, doesn't he?'

'I don't know. Yeah. I guess. There was something in the Bible about that, I think. RE was never my strongest subject.'

'The father of lies? Was that it?'

Will shrugged. 'Yeah. I dunno.'

'Not as interesting as ghosts then?'

'Humans don't worship ghosts. What's to be scared of there, except your own mind? Humans have always scared me more than ghosts.'

'Me too.'

'Yeah, well, you were in the police, so that doesn't surprise me. You must have seen human nature at its lowest. Oh…I'm sorry. Of course, you have. Can't believe I said that.'

'That's OK, Will.'

Will returned to Ernie's chair. Ali joined him at the desk.

'People can be horrible,' Will said. 'I've always known that. Even from a really young age. I think it's probably good that I've always known that. You build defences to it.'

Ali pushed herself up and sat on the desk.

'I've known how cruel people can be since infant school,' Will continued. 'It's human nature, I suppose, to mock people who look a bit different, who stick out. Crooked nose, big ears, fat belly.' Will flashed a furtive glance at the scar around Ali's eye. 'I actually think children are worse when it comes to cruelty. They're more relentless. At least, they were to me.

Adults, I reckon, just take the piss out of relief. Like, they're just happy they aren't the ones with the affliction. I think that's why I became friends with Dave. Not sure it was films or ghosts that brought us together as much as it was being the butt of other kids' jokes. Odd people always gravitate together.'

'Who wants to be normal? Take it from an adult – normality is overrated.' Ali charged her empty mug and then Will duplicated the action. 'You can ask me, if you want. About the scar.'

Will shook his head. 'That's OK. I bet everyone asks you. You must be tired of talking about it. I don't want to be like everyone else.'

'People ask me. Yes. Some people know already, because people gossip. Difference is I don't tell anyone. I honestly don't think I've ever sat down and talked about it with anyone through choice. So, you see, you aren't like everyone else at all. You'd be kind of unique.'

'S'OK, Ali. I don't want to pry.'

'I did a bad thing. When I got the scar. I'm not a good person.'

'I think you are.'

'You don't know me. What I've done.'

What are you doing? He isn't safe here. Get him out of here.

I can protect him.

'It's not my business.'

Ali slipped off the desk. 'I did it to myself. The scar. Everything.' She walked to the window and peered through the bent corner of the corrugated sheet, out into the car park. It was so dark out there that she could barely even make out Ernie's car next to the church wall. The night was a smothering heaviness pressing in all around their little scene, removing all definition and clarity. Nothing moved out there. Perhaps nothing could.

Where are you, Walter?

'You don't have to tell me, Ali. Not if you don't—'

'A little over a year ago, my mother died.' Ali pulled the knife out and held it reassuringly in her right hand. She remained at the window, her back to Will, her eyes to the car park and her mind somewhere else entirely. 'Have you ever met anyone with dementia, Will?'

'No. No, I don't think so.'

'It's the cruellest thing. My mother used to be so sharp. So utterly in the moment. She never forgot a name, or a face, or a birthday. Crosswords, quizzes and puzzles. She loved all that. She could dredge up obscure facts that she had learned years ago. She was amazing. My mother was incredible. And it was so slow, when she started to go, so damn slow. Her mind just started to slip. Bit by bit. Good days and bad days, but every day she knew what was happening, she knew what was at the bottom once it all gathered pace. Until one day, when she didn't know. When she didn't know anything much at all. Then the good days only came once in a while, and the definition of good started to shrink. Sometimes she looked so desperate. Those were supposed to be the good days, because it meant that a part of her knew where she was, and what was happening to her. I'm not sure you should call those days good. I think sometimes she still recognised me. Sometimes. But it was recognition like you would have for an old school friend, someone you knew you knew but couldn't quite place. And then when the nurses would tell her who I was, she wouldn't believe them. She would look at me and look hurt, as though I were playing a trick on her.'

Ali tapped the knife blade against her leg, and then let the tip pick at the plaster on her leg through the slit in her jeans.

'My father walked out on us when I was a child.' Ali rested her forehead against the window, watching the condensation building on the glass. 'She was never proud of me being a police officer. I know she wasn't. My father took that. I never had the education, the degrees, or the model professional husband. The expensive house, or the social standing. All I was was a police officer and it was the best thing in the world. I was one of the good guys, but that was never going to be enough. Because I was like my father. And my father broke her heart. Parents, you see, Will, they spend their lives providing for you, and then, when you are an adult, you have to provide for them. You have to provide them with something to be proud about. It's not enough to be a good person. You can't measure that. You can't quantify that, or show it off, or crow about it. It's not tangible. I never gave her a grandchild. Maybe that would have been enough.'

Ali pulled sharply from the window and slammed the knife into the front door. She waited for the echo of the thud to dissipate and then turned to the desk.

'I held her hand as she died. She went in her sleep, which was something, I suppose. Took me a few minutes to even realise.' Ali's hands curled into loose fists in front of her chest. 'Then a carer came in. Ben. A lovely guy. Really, a lovely, sweet man. He used to sit and talk to her all the time. Listen to her mad, rambling stories. He had the patience of a saint. All he did was touch my shoulder and try to move me away.' Ali looked to her hands. The tears came in a painful trickle. 'I hit him, Will. I broke two of his ribs. I mashed his nose to a bloody pulp. Again and again and again, I hit him, and I can still feel every single blow. I can feel my hands on him. I can feel his blood.' The painful trickle broke and the tears came on strong. 'I got away with it too. Circumstances, I suppose. But no one wanted to press charges, and I never deserved that kindness. I'm not a good person because that moment made me feel…alive? No. No, that's not right. It made me feel safe. Yes. Safe. Does that make sense? Will, since that night…that night at the Deveraux place, I've been numb. Lost. Can you understand? That night stripped me down, and what I found revolted me. I've been on the outside of my own life, circling around it with no way to get back in. And I've been frightened…terrified…that I never would. I've been drowning. It feels like I've been submerged in a great bottomless ocean and people have just been waiting for me to let go and drop.' She wiped at her tears with a fist but it made no mark, barely breaking the flow. 'But then suddenly I felt safe. I felt safe. And I heard…

The sound of breaking waves on a shoreline.

'…things, I heard things in my head. I could get there. Where I wanted to be. I could get to…

Sparkleville.

'…safety. No one could touch me. No one could get to me. It was my world, and I controlled the walls.' Ali pressed her back against the door and slid slowly down to her haunches. 'I've lied to myself for as long as I can remember. I'm not one of the good guys. Maybe I never was.'

'Yes, you are,' he said, his voice floating to her from miles away, causing a pain in her heart.

'When I sat there waiting for the police to arrive, I felt no revulsion or shame, I didn't even feel scared. I saw a glass bottle of my mother's perfume smashed on the floor. But I couldn't smell the perfume. I remember that. Couldn't smell it at all. In that moment I didn't feel as if I was even there. I just wanted to feel something. Anything. So, I jammed the end of the smashed bottle into my head.' She held one closed fist to the top of her scar and slowly ran it along the semicircle around her left eye, as if Will needed the picture completing. 'I felt nothing then either. Nothing at all.' Ali sunk to the floor. 'What am I, Will? What the hell am I?'

He was no longer on the desk. He was right there, crouched down in front of her and his hands were on her shoulders, his gentle voice in her ear. 'You're my friend, Ali.'

Will held her and, inside his gentle hug, Ali broke. 'What the hell have I done?' It was no longer Will who held her now. It was Jake Tooley. 'Why did I do this? What's wrong with me?' Ali began to fight his hold, pushing away from him. 'It's not safe here.'

'It's OK, Ali.'

Ali forced Will away and struggled to her feet. 'God, what have I done? You shouldn't be here.' In the split second she stared down at Will's face, she felt her heart break. Now it was Jake Tooley's face, his mouth forming the word, his voice repeating it. *Safe?* 'You can't be here. I'm so sorry. I shouldn't have done this. I'm so sorry, Will.'

'Done what?'

'Get out. Get away from here. Please. It's not safe.' Ali pulled her mobile from her pocket. With her free hand, she yanked Will up to his feet. 'Please!'

'OK, but I don't need you to call me a taxi. It's cool.'

'I'm not calling a taxi.'

'Ali, what the hell are you—'

'I'm calling the police.'

'Huh? But why?'

The answer came with two loud knocks on the window, directly behind them.

They stood like musical statues watching the window, waiting for the knocks to come again. Ali heard Will whisper her name. She couldn't bring herself to look at him. She held her phone out behind her and felt his twitching fingers take it.

'Police. Do it now, Will.'

As Will's breathy, frantic voice gabbled into the phone, Ali tiptoed to the door and slowly worked the knife free. It felt hot in her grasp. She turned side-on and rested her ear to the wood. She could hear nothing beyond a weighty silence that seemed intent on pressing against the building. She turned the door handle and pushed, needing to feel the lock. Two wavering steps took her to the other window and there she bent down and peered past the bent corrugated iron.

Still the darkness ate through any definition, Ernie's car now seemingly swallowed whole. The oak tree sentries just about held on, standing impassively along the pathway, and here, between them, the night seemed to shift momentarily.

Ali watched the scene, not daring to blink. 'There's someone out there. By the trees. On the pathway.' Another shape joined with the first, becoming one, and then becoming nothing but night again. 'Two? I think there's someone else there. There can't be.'

'Him?'

Ali faced Will. She could feel the sweat on his hands as he handed back her phone. Revulsion and self-disgust swilled around inside her gut. It would have been easier to bear had he shown her the same emotions. His anger would have hurt, but the look of innocent helplessness was a hundred times worse.

'There's only one way in, Will. He's not getting over the doorstep. You're safe. I promise.'

'You're not going out there.' It didn't sound like a question. She hoped it was a statement of fact. 'Ali, please?'

'I won't let him hurt you. I promise.'

'The police are on their way. I called them.'

Memories. All those nightmare memories that played their charade in her mind; unchecked and unwelcome, they were never far away. Another impenetrable night, another child she put in harm's way.

She could smell the air of that country lane that lead to Deveraux's estate, and could feel the uneven ground beneath her feet as she walked to Jake Tooley hunched down like some wild animal in the road. She could feel him as he flopped into her arms. More than anything she could hear his voice. *Safe*. And she could hear the lies she told him back.

'Don't, Ali. Please don't.'

She ran a hand into her pocket for the key. 'I need to protect you.'

He rested a hand on her arm. 'Don't do this.' Will moved between her and the door, making her acknowledge him. 'You're not the person you think you are.'

'Will…' Ali wasn't sure whether she was about to thank him or admonish him. The scared expression on his face as he looked back over her shoulder made her words stall too. 'What?'

'I saw something there. Lights. Two small lights.'

Ali spun around and followed his gaze towards the dark space at the back of the building.

'I don't see anything.'

'I saw them. Two of them, low down, and then they clicked off, they…look! There…'

The lights came again, two tiny ghostly orbs that seemed to be moving across the floor, getting nearer to them.

'Will…' Ali grabbed the nearest halogen lamp and moved the beam into the darkness at the back of the building. 'They're cat's eyes.'

The stray cat strutted across the beam and ambled out into the reception area with an air of regal aloofness. He was carrying a dead rat between his jaws. The rat's belly was split open: its insides outside, a trail of gooey, stringy parcels left in their wake. The cat leapt up on to the chair and then on to the desk, dropping the rat and gently swiping and prodding it with a paw.

Ali gave a nervous laugh. 'Lovely.'

The cat turned to Ali and hissed.

'Ali?'

'What?'

Will didn't seem reassured by the presence of the cat. If anything, he looked even more frightened. 'How did the cat get in?'

They both stared at the slice of light running across the floor. Thin streaks of blood and the odd lump of rat gut marked the path the cat had taken.

Ali took the crowbar from the desk and passed it to Will. 'Stay here.'

She picked up the torch and walked into the darkness behind her, cutting a wonky path between the light and the trail made by the rat blood. The sticky slap of her boots on the grotty linoleum echoed in the open space, somehow louder the slower she walked.

Droplets became smears at the fountain; the source of the kill, perhaps. The fallen cherub had an ugly splat of some bloody mush on its face, and then further on, towards the back wall, the droplets started again in a neat line like a bloody ellipsis. She took the torch beam up the back wall to the windows, too high for the cat to get to, and then back down to the linoleum.

Between two old sofas pushed slightly apart, a small scattering of rubble trailed out from the base of the wall. Ali noticed something else too: the linoleum in that gap was curled up slightly in a patch about three feet across. She approached in slow, deliberate steps.

She was less than a foot from the wall when her left boot suddenly sunk down through the linoleum and brought her to a staggering halt. She put a steadying hand against a sofa and then bent down to the curled linoleum and yanked it up. It rose about a foot in the air. Slashing the knife into the rotting flooring, she sliced the loose part clean off and tossed it away. She could feel the chill winter air drifting up at her instantly from the floor, snaking over her body, a nightmare caress. Ali tilted the torch beam back down to the floor.

Her heart froze in her chest.

The torch had illuminated a jagged hole in the wall, just below the level of the floor. Through the hole, a deep channel dug down through the muddy bank outside at the rear of the building and into the crumbling floor. This too was at least three feet across. More than big enough for a cat. Big enough even for a...

Ali pivoted on the spot and almost put her foot back into the hole. Her legs suddenly felt hollow and were beginning to buckle. Her throat was tightening, wedged to the brim with wads of invisible cotton wool.

'Oh...God,' she spluttered. The torchlight swept through the back of the building in a haphazard dance. 'Will!' Ali dropped the torch and ran her free hand into her pocket, scrabbling for the key. 'Get...'

The blow was hard and fast and took her legs from under her. A second later she was on the floor, her face against the linoleum, and the knife was skittering out of her hand, sliding all the way back to the fountain. Will was shouting something incomprehensible, and then he was at the front door desperately turning the handle, and trying to shoulder-charge the door.

Ali flopped over on to her back and stared up into the great nothingness above her. Walter Gamble's face floated there now, upside down, drifting down towards her slowly. Those ink eyes swirled, that deathly pale skin was threaded with bulging veins, and that wide, self-satisfied smile looked ready to open and gobble her up. He gently rested his forehead against hers, and those horrid fingers splayed out and then closed around either side of her skull.

'Witness your demise,' that emotionless voice said. 'I'm going to butcher your friend. You will watch. Then you will beg me to leave your life.' Walter pulled her head up into his lap and then forced it around until she was facing the front door. He put his lips to her ear and spoke softly. 'Look what you've done. Again, children seem to have to suffer through your actions. Look at that fear. When I slice him open, how strong do you think that fear will be? It will be thick, and stinking and pungent. It will be alive. Can you imagine it?'

Ali slapped weakly at the side of his head, her fingers trailing pathetically along that horrid skin, then her hand was back on the ground, searching the floor for the knife. Will had given up on the door and now turned to the windows, smashing the glass in each with the crowbar and then striking the corrugated iron, trying in vain to loosen it.

She could hear him screaming for help, over and over, calling out into the night for someone to save them.

'Jake Tooley had so much fear at the end,' that dead voice continued, breathing into her ear. 'He was nearly insane with it. Possessed by it. Immersed in it. Why did you bring him back? Why did you bring him back to die?'

'I...didn't...'

Walter yanked her head back and forced her face into his. His fingers slithered into her mouth and stretched it open, and as he spoke again, the words came threaded with a putrid, decaying breath that floated straight into her mouth.

'Yes, you killed him. You are your father's daughter. You think you can kill with impunity because of the badge you carried or the God you worship. No. There are always consequences, always ruined lives to be pieced back together. Jail is not punishment enough, not when you cling so tightly to your virtuousness. Then you're just a martyr. And martyrs never learn.'

Will was trying to squeeze himself through the window now, pushing out past corrugated iron that wouldn't yield to his strength. Splintered glass was cutting into his jeans, jabbing at his legs. As a longer piece took a slice out of a finger, he flopped back into the reception area with a pitiful wail.

'The sins of the father need to be answered for,' Walter continued. 'Your torment must be unimaginable. Your fall, never ending. I want your entire...worthless...soul.'

Walter seemed to unfold as he stood. Will was back on his feet now too, gathering the crowbar and turning to the staircase. Ali just had time to see Walter's knife unsheathed at his side, the blade still smeared in Gage's blood, barely an inch from her face, and then Walter's other hand was in her hair and he was dragging her limp body across the floor.

Rubble crunched under her back, and as her hands meekly swept at the floor, she felt fingers push through the blood trail of the eviscerated rat. Past the fountain the back of her hand slapped against the fallen nymph and her fingers grabbed for it, managing to drag it a few feet before letting go. The darkness above was now replaced by the brightly lit ceiling of the reception, as Walter hauled her roughly around the desk. She could feel the cool night air slipping inside through the smashed windows. No sooner had she dared to imagine an escape than she felt the glass shards under her back, tearing into her shirt and nicking her skin.

Walter's grip tightened in her hair as he took the first two steps and turned around into the stairwell. The steps slammed against her shoulders and yet more detritus turned and broke under her weight. Ali raised her hand to the bannister and gripped her fingers around the peeling paint, and as she did, her heels dug into the stairs. With all her might she fought Walter's hold. The resistance proved fleeting, her returning strength merely a tease.

Ali resumed her bumpy journey up the staircase. But just as the light of the reception area was slowly drawn away she was afforded a quick glimpse of the nearest window. What she saw was brief enough to be a trick of the eye, the last drop of wishful thinking in her hopeless situation, perhaps. It took the wood splintering thud on the front door, just as they reached the top of the stairs, to confirm it; an arm was snaking in through the window, past the corrugated iron. There were people outside.

Walter turned on the top step, just as the thud came again and reverberated through the building. Ali felt the hold on her hair slacken and tilting her head up she saw his momentary distraction. Her hand slipped behind her and returned holding a small jagged rock that had been pressing against her spine. She squeezed her hand around it and let the sharp points jab into her palm and break the skin. The pain pushed her from Walter and whatever miasma he had infected her with, just far enough for her to slip past.

The rock exploded across his kneecap with one sickening crunch. Ali felt him sway and as his leg reacted to the impact, she took her other hand to his ankle and forced it up and off the step. Walter tipped forward, fell into the wall and then smashed his head down on to the bannister, the force of the impact pulling it out of the wall. The knife slashed out behind him in one last desperate action and then he hit the stairs and tumbled to the bottom, coming to rest in a clumsy heap.

'Will!'

Ali scrabbled up the last step and fell on to the first-floor landing. A dull metallic echo punched up through the stairwell behind her, as someone hammered at the corrugated iron board over the window. There was another almighty thud on the front door and she heard voices now, giant muffled barks, nothing distinct.

She considered calling out to them, but Will had already beaten her to it. She heard his shouts coming from an upper floor. Somehow, she knew which floor it would be. A small line of blood from Will's slashed finger led her to the next set of stairs. She shouted his name once, twice. Then as she stumbled out on to the third floor, swaying like a drunkard as her body wrestled back control, she screamed it.

Will shouted back then. The relief was all too evident in his voice.

Ali began to climb to the fourth floor. Again, just as they had the first time she climbed them, the steps felt uneven, or twice the height of the ones below. She had a sudden recollection of an amusement park she had visited with her father, so many years ago, and the Crooked House attraction that she had enjoyed so much. That was what this felt like. Something designed to disorientate you. Yet it couldn't be. The steps here were no different from the ones on the other staircases, she could see that with her own eyes. It was merely her mind doing this.

Yes. *Merely your mind.*

Will stood at the top of the stairs, the crowbar at his side. His cheeks were flushed with fear, anger and, Ali considered, a good dose of confusion too. *Humans have always scared me more than ghosts*, she heard him saying again. A smile fell on to her face, and for just a moment Will returned it, big and bright. But then it started to freeze, and bit-by-bit, his beautiful smile began to curdle. The whole building seemed to hold its breath, even down below the banging and the shouting had stopped, the very air around Ali was alive, imbued with electricity that made it hum.

'Will?'

The crowbar was rising up now in slow motion. Higher and higher it went until it was arching behind him, ready to take a swing.

'Get out of the way!' Will bellowed.

Ali turned on the step as the knife slipped into the side of her belly. She felt nothing in that moment except the blood trickling down her side and running into her jeans. Even as Walter began to turn the blade inside her, the sensation was little more than a tepid numbness. She was face to face with him again, that horrible pale skin now marked with its own injuries. A deep gash cut across his forehead, his nose was misshapen and one eye was beginning to puff out, promising a meaty violet bruise.

'Leave her alone!' Ali could feel Will behind her, heard his trainers on the stairs. 'Don't touch her!' The crowbar struck the wall to their right, causing nothing but a small dust cloud to bloom and then break in front of their faces.

Ali held her arms out to her side and rested her palms against the wall. 'Keep back, Will. Don't come nearer.' Walter moved the knife out of her belly a few inches and then returned it, harder, faster, moving the blade up. Her body spasmed in response, and now the pain came in a wave.

'Are you really going to make me go through you?' Even now Walter's voice could find no emotion beyond dull confidence.

'Please! Leave her alone!'

'Get away, Will! Get back!' She heard his footsteps retreat up the stairs, squeak across the landing, and then a second later his shouts came again, from the fourth floor, screaming down at whoever was outside, pleading with them to hurry. Another thud echoed up the staircase as if in response, but Ali barely heard it. It meant very little to her now. 'You can't have him.' She seethed the words into Walter's face as another jolt of pain zigzagged through her, and the blood running down her leg seemed to flame and burn. 'I won't allow it.'

'Do you still not understand?'

'They're coming for you. The police, they will…they are coming…'

'Even here. At the end. You decide to put your faith in the police? You, of all people? I don't know if that is comical or tragic.' Walter slowly started to draw the knife out again, his grin widening at each shudder and jerk of Ali's body in response. 'I will kill them all. Every last one. And you will watch. Because every one of them will be for you. You never had any choice. Maybe that fact helps you. You never had a say. This was always your destination. I've been in you this whole time.'

Ali's hands left the wall and formed a loose grip around Walter's throat. For the first time since he had infested her life, Ali saw his eyes betray emotion. Pity. The sight enraged her. 'Time you got the fuck out then.'

Summoning the last of her waning strength, Ali jerked her forehead down as hard and fast as she could. She felt Walter's misshapen nose break again and snort warm blood on to her face. She moved quickly without giving him time to react. Shoving as hard as she could at his throat, she forced him off the step, and then they were both colliding with the wall at the bottom of the staircase and falling out into a heap on the third-floor landing. She heard the knife clatter against the railings, saw a flash of bloody blade and then heard a clank on the next staircase as it fell out of Walter's reach.

Now Ali was leaving the ground and rising upwards. She felt as if she'd been pulled out of her body, and that now she was little more than clothes and air, everything solid left behind on the floor. Except the blood.

Walter hauled her into the third-floor room, one hand at her throat, the other playing at the wound in her belly. She felt dizzy and sick. The room was tipping up at a slant, as the chessboard ceiling and the dangling light cords seemed intent on swapping places with the rubbish-strewn floor.

'Watch them come to save you,' Walter whispered. 'Watch them all die.'

Ali heard voices directly below them, footsteps pounding

up the staircase, and then, as she felt the great emptiness behind her, and the cool of the railing beneath her backside, she saw dark figures gathering in the doorway. She heard her name, yet it sounded strange to her.

Alison? No one calls me that.

And then she saw the recognisable shape of Will Kamen amongst them, the crowbar still up behind him. He was getting nearer, jumping between the ragged holes in the floor, and coming their way, ignoring the shouts from the doorway and the reaching hands.

'Walter?' She spoke his name calmly, wrapping her arms around his waist and lacing her fingers together behind his back. 'I'm not frightened of you.' By the time her legs had done the same and her boots had crossed each other tightly behind his legs, Walter began trying to prise her from him. Ali didn't see the look of surprise on his face, as she had already closed her eyes, but she liked to believe it was there. Maybe a simple look of resignation too. 'Get out of my life.'

Ali rocked back on the railings, gripping Walter tight with everything she had left. She felt the air change around her, she heard voices shouting words she didn't care to listen to, and then she gave herself to the great empty nothingness.

Still Ali fell.

The deep and bottomless ocean was as dark as the night she had just left, and things hid there, she was sure of that. All the monsters she had ever made swam in lonely circles, turning in on themselves, just as faces floated past at the edge of her view, sinking like stones. And everything incidental became flotsam on some far away surface that couldn't pull away from her any more.

Time ceased to exist in that moment. She resigned herself

to the fact that she would likely fall for ever and never reach the bottom. She tried to tell the faces that loomed over her, the strangers and those she thought she recognised. She tried to tell them to leave her, that she would only drag them with her if they didn't let go.

But she had no voice. Just a scream trapped in her mind.

Their hands were on her, in her, putting her back together again and soothing whatever was left. She tried to tell them that it was hopeless, that she was already broken, but still those faces came and still those hands carried on their work. The machines kept bleeping. And time bled away.

And still Ali fell.

Chapter 28

One month later

The room was small and sparsely decorated, painted an inoffensive eggshell colour. Ali still found plenty to be offended by. The framed painting opposite her bed was hideous – a watercolour depicting a trio of spruce trees in a snowy landscape. It was so weak and anaemic, Ali thought it looked like the painting was crying.

The plant on the windowsill was fake and waxy and looked like it had dust on it. But worst of all was the timid concession of Christmas decorations – two burgundy paper chains were strung up from each corner of the room, meeting at a point in the middle that was now sagging. The small Christmas tree on her bedside table had flickering optic lights, which gave her a headache whenever they were turned on. The two Christmas cards next to it had fallen over.

She shouted at Taylor as soon as he tried to pick them up and set them right. 'Sorry,' she said on seeing the stupid embarrassed expression on that ridiculously young face.

Taylor shrugged and took a seat next to her bed. For an uncomfortable moment they stared at each other, unsure of where to steer the conversation.

‘Good to see you looking…’ Taylor let the words trail off, his gaze leaving her face and pretending to find fascination in the cast around her arm. ‘Alive.’

Ali had no need of a mirror, the expressions on her visitors’ faces told her everything. It would heal though, that’s what everyone said. Yeah. Everything would heal. Sometimes she even allowed a moment to believe them.

‘Well?’ Ali asked, the fingers poking out of the end of the plaster waggling at Taylor, urging him on. ‘Was it him?’

‘From your description, and what your little friend said…’

‘His name’s Will.’

‘Will. Yes. From what you both said, it sounds like it’s him. Walter. They’ve scaled back the search for the rest of him. I guess the head is enough.’ Taylor sat forward, shuffling his backside to the edge of the chair. ‘That’s the official line, is it? You fell. It was an accident. He was never there?’

‘Will came calling and found me. Saved me.’ She stared at the pot plant’s waxy sheen and felt her eyes growing heavy.

‘But the police that came that night?’

‘There were no police. It was them. They made it all go away.’

‘Ali, The Brotherhood Under the Moon folded up years ago.’

Ali shook her head, the plant’s leaves blurring in her vision. ‘There’s a thousand pounds in my bedside drawer. Have a look.’

Taylor pulled open the drawer and plucked out a wedge of fifty-pound notes, held together by a silver money clip. He swore lightly under his breath and then whistled. ‘This is the rest of what you were owed? Well, that’s great. Isn’t it?’

Ali said nothing, just offered him a half-nod.

Taylor sat back in the chair.

'I think they used me,' Ali said eventually. 'I think that's all it ever was. The job was a sham. I was bait. They knew he would come for me.'

'I wish I knew more, but the whole Gamble case has been taken over by top brass. Locked down tighter than a nun's chastity belt. I'll ask around. I'll find out what I can.'

'No.' Ali turned her battered face to Taylor, and this time he held her gaze. 'Don't do that. The narrative has been created. Stick to it. I am, and so is Will. They don't like questions. You know too much as it is. Don't make them see you.'

'OK.'

'Promise me?'

'I promise, Ali.' Taylor mimed zipping his mouth shut.

'What about Frank?'

'Frank Gage, acting on a tipoff connected to the drugs raids at the clubs, entered a known drug den in Heroes Ridge where he was murdered. DNA is pointing at your old friend, Morton.'

'Fancy that.'

'Small world, isn't it? They like Morton for Ernie's murder too. Just a case of forensics joining the dots. They're confident they will. Ernie's partner is following developments with interest.' Taylor stretched his legs out and then stood. 'Will I be seeing you at Ernie's funeral?'

Ali let out a ragged breath and winced at the pain. 'I've already said goodbye.'

'You be OK?'

'Yeah.'

Taylor crossed to the doorway. 'Are you sure?'

'I didn't want it like this. This feels dirty.'

'So, it isn't perfect.'

'No. It really isn't.'

'Good and bad. They don't always mean what they should. Take your victories where you can find them.'

'And now a twenty-three-year-old is giving me pearls of wisdom. What a messed-up world.'

Taylor laughed and left the room.

She sat in the chair in the corner of the small room. Her rucksack was by her feet, her crutch leaning against the wall by the door. One end of the paper chain had come loose and hung down just over her head. The thick and cloying scent of flowers had been wafting through the open door for the last five minutes from somewhere out in the corridor and she was close to calling for a nurse and asking her to do something about it.

She thought she could see a shape out there, a figure reflected in the window of the room opposite hers. They looked like they were holding a large bouquet, but she wasn't sure. She had called out to them, given an inquisitive hello, and then when she'd looked back, they were no longer there. Only the smell remained.

Five minutes later, Will Kamen was standing in her doorway holding up a set of car keys. 'Need a lift?' He tried to casually swing them around on his index finger but they slipped off and fell on the ground. He quickly gathered them up, his cheeks turning a light red. 'Sorry I'm late.'

'You passed then?'

Will beamed at her. 'When they said intensive, they really meant intensive. But she said I was good. I think she really meant that. Said I was a natural. That she knew I'd pass first time.'

'Quite right. I knew you would too. Well done, Will. I'm ashamed to say it took me the best part of a year and five tests before I passed.'

'Really? What happened?'

'They said they didn't like my road rage.' Ali handed Will her rucksack and then hobbled across the room to her crutch. 'Right. Let's go.'

The corridor stretched before them like a tunnel, a small square of light at the far end. The rays of a sunny December morning were edging against the glass, and it was promised to be a glorious day. All the pains inside of her had coalesced and now, dulled by drugs and pushed aside by sheer willpower, Ali felt nothing beyond a soft throb. She walked with difficulty, sometimes leaning on Will as well as the crutch, and her friend walked calmly and stoically beside her, chatting away as they inched slowly along.

'Are you sure you don't mind me having Ernie's car?'

'I don't mind. I don't drive in London. I've no need for it.'

'That's cool. Thank you. I had it valeted. I hope you don't mind.'

'Well, I hope you haven't broken it. I always assumed it was the dirt that was holding it together.'

'I meant to ask, where am I taking you? I don't think I could handle a drive to London just yet. Is that OK? Where would you like to go?'

'Ms Davenport?'

The cloying smell of flowers announced the nurse before Ali saw her. Ali pulled up and leaned on her crutch as the nurse strode up to them, cradling the ostentatious bouquet like it were a baby.

‘I’m so glad I caught you. A gentleman asked me if I could give you these. Aren’t they beautiful?’

‘Aren’t they?’ Ali stared at the small white card nestled amongst the rainbow of colours. *Alison* was written across the front. ‘Thank you.’

‘The gentleman asked me to say that he’s in the waiting room, just along the corridor here. Just take your first left.’

Ali delicately picked the card out and pocketed it. ‘Could you do me a favour?’

‘Certainly.’

‘Give those flowers to someone else? Someone you think would like them, please. Would you do that?’

The nurse nodded her understanding.

‘Thank you.’ Ali gripped Will’s shoulder and they began to walk again.

‘They looked expensive,’ Will said. ‘Who were they from?’

They inched slowly past the turning to the left. ‘Nobody.’

‘So?’

‘So what?’

‘So, any idea where you want me to drive you?’

Ali considered it for a moment. ‘I fancy seeing a film. Want to go to the cinema with me?’

Epilogue

The church stood in silent contemplation behind her. Ahead of her, across the car park and past the security fences with their warning signs hanging from them, the Portakabins and the machinery, the building sat in a giant mound of rubble under the impassive, silent watch of a crane.

The stone bench inside the doorway of St Augustine's church was cold and firm beneath her, and Ali considered that just as well. Tiredness could easily wrap its heavy tendrils around her if she were comfortable here. Sleep could wait until she was somewhere she belonged. She looked back to the higgledy-piggledy line of gravestones that stretched away up the hill to see if the girl was still there.

She was.

She hadn't vanished as Ali assumed she would the moment she blinked or looked away. Will was frozen in a crouch, about fifty yards away, his video camera rock steady, recording the scene.

The girl was still walking between the gravestones, a skip in her step. They could see her clearly, despite the darkness. From time to time she would be carrying a small bunch of flowers and she would stop, bend down and place them at a spot where there was no grave. Then she would weave between the old, grey stones, gazing at the names carved there.

Ali closed her eyes.

The deep and bottomless ocean was as dark as the night she had just left, and things hid there, she was sure of that. All the monsters she had ever made sank slowly past her as she floated gently to the surface.

Now she was on dry land, leaving the ocean behind and crossing the sand. Her wet clothes stuck to her body, and water squelched in her boots and ran to tiny little droplets at the end of her hair. She kicked off her boots and then slowly started to disrobe as she walked, letting her soaked skin warm under the high, noon sun. She was dry by the time she reached the house at the edge of the beach.

She wasn't surprised to see that the ginger tomcat had returned and was now on her window ledge, meowing at the glass, waiting to be let in. She pulled on some clean clothes, fresh from the hanger, and yanked the window up for the cat. She considered that he probably deserved a name by now. She'd have to think of a good one.

She sat and put her feet up on the windowsill, a hand stroking the cat at her side. The view through the open window was beautiful; the ocean and the sky both a child's painting blue, broken only by the spit, reaching out in a protective hug. She could stay in this position for the whole day, she thought.

Maybe she would.

This was her place, after all. And she was safe. She controlled the walls and the doors, and she controlled the sky and the earth too. Nothing changed here, because she didn't let it.

Acknowledgements

My thanks to everyone that had to put up with me during the writing of this novel, encouraged me to keep going, and made sure I didn't acknowledge those knocks on the window.

For their advice, my thanks to Dan Coxon, Christine Nielsen-Craig, Kirsty Applebaum, Sean Memory, 'Hammers' Steve, Will Dean, Caroline Smailes, Tarn Richardson, Julia Silk and Judith Long.

A huge thank you to the wonderful RedDoor team: Heather Boisseau, Lizzie Lewis, and in particular my publisher, Clare Christian, for her faith in my story.

I originally began this novel while studying with Curtis Brown Creative and would like to thank the staff and my fellow students for their advice and support, especially the endlessly patient superstar, Jack Hadley.

Special thanks to Tom Bromley for a lot of calm wisdom and coffee; Jo Boyles and the simply awesome, Rocketship Bookshop; Suzannah Dunn and Cathi Unsworth for being great teachers, lovely people, and supremely funny; and most of all, for pretty much everything, love and thanks to the Millies.

About the Author

Russell is a novelist, playwright, and producer based in the South West of England.

He is the author of the novels, *Stone Bleeding*, *Bleeker Hill*, *Darkshines Seven* and *Cold Calling*, and the short story collection, *Silent Bombs Falling on Green Grass*.

Having studied film production in London he has also worked on various short films and is an associate producer on the award-winning documentary, *Rise: The Story of Augustines*.

He works at The Rocketship Bookshop in Salisbury, an independent bookshop for children and young people, and is also one of the founders of The Salisbury Literary Festival.

Also by Russell Mardell

BLEEKER
HILL
RUSSELL MARDELL

Prologue

Arrival

They arrived just after dawn, the two old army utility trucks slowing and sliding on the icy road that cut through the forest and then broke on to the top of the hill. They came to rest neatly together whilst the small quad bike snowplough carried on down, cutting them a slithering path towards the house. To call it a house seemed an understatement of magnificent proportions. It was grander and more opulent than any of them had ever seen before – a great, sprawling mansion, a monument to a forgotten time. To see such a building in such a time as they were living in was almost unheard of and none of them could tear their eyes away. The house seemed to be all there was for miles; a forgotten life picked up and dumped down where nothing else could see it or touch it. It was the perfect place to disappear, the ideal place to start again, and it didn't take a genius to see why it had been chosen.

As the weak sun gave its token gesture above them, contemplating its position amongst the greying clouds, they saw the balloons in the sky that they had been looking for ever since cresting the hill. It was the sure sign that they were close. The balloons bloomed together in clusters as they rose up from beyond the great house, before breaking apart in the sky and then drifting away on the sharp breeze; red, and white and blue shapes, the only colour in the tired and washed-out skyline.

Everyone rechecked their weaponry for what felt like the hundredth time. Now, though, there was a finality and threat in every click of every gun as their nervous fingers and hands set to work. Their journey had been arduous. The many miles of travelling along the valleys treacherous, narrow roads had been bad enough, but the oncoming snow had caused long delays and improvised detours. The three-day trip had become a five-day expedition and now, finally at their destination, they felt spent and ruined. But the real work hadn't even begun.

Lucas Hennessey held Mia in his arms in the cab of the lead truck, stroking her hair and gently rocking her from side to side, pulling the rug tighter over her shoulders and folding the ends over her bare neck. Her fever appeared to be getting worse, her face seemed to glow in the darkness of the cab and the tacky, sweaty skin he could feel whenever he mopped her brow worried him. His daughter had been fine when they set out; she'd even taken turns at the wheel of the truck, her eighteen years seeming impossible, her boundless energy and enthusiasm an infectious encouragement. But by the end of the second day Mia had started to change, to seemingly age under his gaze and slowly shrivel in his arms.

Wallace had been a medic in the army back in the old country, many years before everything that had happened and he would tend to her as best he could, but medical supplies were pretty scarce and what was there seemed to be ineffective. By the third day he had all but given up on her, and by the fourth no one spoke about her any more and everyone stared.

As Finn hopped off the snowplough and waved back up the hill to the two trucks, Hennessey looked down at his daughter to see her asleep against his chest. Wallace turned the engine over and shifted the lead truck forward as gently as he could, pumping the brake in short blasts. Behind them, Connor fired up the other truck and delicately edged forward in their tracks. With his free hand, Hennessey pulled out his mobile phone from his jacket and clumsily thumbed a number. The signal was weak and the voice that answered the call faint, but between the rasp of the truck's engine and the angry crackle of the phone line he just about recognised Kendrick's voice.

'This is point team,' Hennessey shouted into the phone. 'The king has his castle. Repeat, the king has his castle.'

'Huh?'

'The king has...'

'Who is this?'

'This is Hennessey, you dickhead. We've arrived. Out.'

They cut the truck's engines before reaching the house and rolled the last few yards, coming to a stop in the snow-covered courtyard; the ploughed walls along the freshly cut pathway a gentle buffer against the tyres. Connor jumped down from the second truck and, with Finn, rounded the south side of the building, their machine guns primed in front of them, beckoning on whatever they were about to face. Wallace turned to Hennessey in the lead truck and Hennessey waved absently in the air between them, urging Wallace on.

'Take position, I will be right behind you.'

'We go in pairs, Lucas. That was the deal. That was what you said.'

'Whose safety are you concerned about, Wallace? Mine or yours?'

'He's a madman.'

'We've got a job to do.'

'You've heard the stories about this place, I know you have.'

'After everything you've seen, now you're scared of stories?'

'What about Grennaught?'

'He's dead. What about the living?'

'People disappeared here.'

'Take position, Wallace.'

Wallace seemed to be trying to gulp down air in his throat. His right hand instinctively went to the side of his neck and seemed to hover there, the index finger tapping against the skin. 'I had this dream,' he started, before stopping abruptly and pulling his hand away, seemingly surprised by his own voice.

'Dream?' The word knocked Hennessey's calm demeanour momentarily and shook the authority from his voice. 'What dream?'

Wallace narrowed his eyes and seemed to be scrutinising Hennessey's face.

'What dream, Wallace?'

'I dreamed how I was going to die. I saw it. Felt it.'

Hennessey moved to speak but could offer nothing more than a grunt.

'You have too, haven't you, Lucas?'

For the longest of seconds they said nothing, though their eyes were quick to betray their silence. It was enough for Wallace and he answered his own question of his boss with a slow, purposeful nod of the head.

'Dreams and tall tales,' Hennessey snapped, stealing back his command and jerking a finger to the house beyond the windscreen. 'Do you really want this conversation, Wallace?'

'The way the country is, it's easy to believe in fate, right?'

'Take position.'

'I mean, it's normal isn't it? It doesn't make me a madman, does it?'

'Take position, Wallace. Now.'

Hennessey waved Wallace on again and turned back to Mia. Decision made, conversation over. Wallace shifted slowly around in the driver's seat, his hand pausing at the door, and then gently slipped out of the cab, landing with a soft crunch on the snow.

Staring at his daughter's sleeping face, Hennessey found Wallace's words echoing through his mind, trying to distort his vision and his control. He had dreamed deep and long these last few weeks. Ever since he was tasked with the mission, he had remembered his dreams vividly. He had seen things in his dreams, had felt them encroaching over his waking hours, and now, as so many times before, he took a hand to his heart and felt the pain his sub-conscious mind had already revealed to him. He refused to give Wallace's words space in that moment, he wouldn't allow questions that made no sense; he had got this far by controlling facts and acting on whatever truth lay before him, he wasn't going to succumb to any sort of madness now. That was for the rest of the country. Not him. As the pain in his heart slowly abated to its usual nagging dullness, he took his hand away and gripped the certainty of his shotgun, and as he did, everything made sense.

Hennessey brushed away a knotted clump of hair from Mia's forehead and gazed at his daughter's face, aware already of the tears trickling down his own and hoping she wouldn't wake at that moment and see.

'I'm so sorry, Mia. This is my fault. I should have left you with your mother. But it wasn't safe there, you know that, don't you? Your mother is a very stubborn woman. But I will keep you safe here. I promise I will. When everyone else arrives we will get you seen to properly. Then sooner or later we will make this place home. We are going to start again. We are going to build everything from scratch. The Party will see that everything is okay. We will be happy here. Just you and me. I promise.'

Hennessey lowered his daughter down across the front seats of the truck's cab and readjusted the rug around her neck. For one brief moment he seemed to freeze, his hands clutching the end of the rug, not wanting to let go, wanting to hold on and pull it tighter. But, no sooner did the feeling come over him, than it went again and then Hennessey was sat upright, staring out at the house through the snow-splattered windscreen, distracted by something at the back of his mind that wanted to be heard, grabbing at a thought and a feeling that he wanted to understand. The icy winter breeze came into the cab, whistling like the devil's own theme tune, and slowly, uncomfortably, Hennessey took his shotgun back into hands that didn't feel like his own and climbed down from the cab.

He followed Wallace's footprints in the snow, across the courtyard and around to the north side of the building. A lifeless balloon hid in the snow under his feet and he jumped as it popped under him, fumbling the shotgun in his hands, his heart shooting through his body as if it had just been drop kicked. He stopped, waited, and breathed deeply, steadying his control. Pulling the shotgun back into his grasp he continued forward again, edging around the house and walking as lightly as he could in Wallace's path.

The north side was more exposed than the courtyard and the wind whipped up instantly and battered him, the heartless cold force probing every inch of exposed skin. He crouched down, gun in his lap, and tightened the toggle at the top of his coat. He looked forward towards Wallace's footprints and then craned around and stared back up the hill to the point where they had entered, between the trees. It seemed so far away at that moment, the forest on either side sucking the road out of sight. His eyes followed the snowplough's path down to the house and rested on the truck where his daughter slept. He had to keep Mia safe; somehow, amongst all that was happening, and all he had to do, nothing else would matter if he failed to protect her. Looking up, he saw the balloons floating over him and he suddenly wanted to take the machine gun from his back and blast them all out of the air, decimate them under a wave of brutal gunfire. Maybe he would, he thought. Once the mission is done, maybe he would do that very thing.

Hennessey pulled himself up and started walking in Wallace's footsteps again, the shotgun sweeping left to right in front of him, his painful eyes alert to everything, yet seeing nothing. He had gone no more than twenty feet when his left foot, instead of slipping neatly into Wallace's next footprint, crunched down through a patch of virgin snow and brought him to a staggering halt. Wallace's footprints had stopped and in front of him was nothing but untouched snow. Hennessey spun around on the spot, first behind him, then to the house. There was no trace of Wallace anywhere.

'Wallace?' Hennessey whispered into the air. 'Wallace? Get back in position, don't make me come find you!'

He moved on, crunching through new snow, his finger hovering over the trigger of the shotgun, and then he stopped again and was crouching down. In front of him, about ten feet ahead, a wide channel seemed to have been carved in the snow, running across his position and then away to the right, directly into the wall of the house. Looking back to the channel in the snow he followed it the other way and saw it break ahead, the smoothness becoming a large, body-shaped dent and giving way to a clumsy set of footprints scattering away into the distance. The first three footprints were splattered with blood, and after that they didn't look as if they were footprints at all.

It was just a phone call. Just meaningless words between two strangers. It didn't mean anything...

Still reeling from the break up with the love of his life, insurance firm cold caller, Ray English, has become a bit of a screw up. To put it mildly. Cynical, and withdrawn, Ray is aimlessly drifting through life in London alongside his long-suffering best mate, Danny. Asked to reform their college band for a friend's wedding, Ray is soon forced to face up to his old life, and the hometown he had tried so hard to turn his back on.

Anya Belmont is a woman with a secret, and a history that continues to shape her life. A coffee shop owner in Salisbury, Anya is successful, yet bored; married, yet lonely, and is also trying to avert a looming mid-life crisis, whilst struggling in vain to control her best friend, Eva Cunningham, a slightly unstable, child-hating children's author.

Fate, coincidence, or just bad timing, Ray and Anya's lives begin to change when Ray cold calls Anya and the two strike up a seemingly innocuous phone conversation. Against their better judgement, that conversation is soon the start of a phone relationship that grows in frequency and intimacy as the weeks and months pass, and a curious, almost dependent friendship is born. But can there be anything 'real' in a simple phone call?

As circumstances bring these two lonely souls to the same town at the same time, both are forced to question the truth of what they have started, and the realisation that if they are to move on in their lives, they will have to start by looking back and facing the ghosts of their past...

'A refreshingly modern take on romance and friendship, 'Cold Calling' spikes with warmth and wisdom. Genuinely funny, shrewdly observed and really rather brilliant'

Caroline Smailes,
author of *The Drowning of Arthur Braxton*

'A really funny, really clever and really entertaining read. A warm and wise, heart-felt romantic comedy'

Anne Cater, Random Things Through my Letterbox

'Cold Calling felt fresh and I thoroughly enjoyed it. the ending was perfectly done. Not trite, not ruthless, but real'

The Bookbag

'A smart, quick-witted take on love and friendship, perfect for readers with less starry-eyed views of romance'

Kirkus Reviews

'From speed-dating to tomato-gate this is an amusing tale that bites (with barbed fangs)'

LoveReading.co.uk

Find out more about RedDoor Press and sign up to our newsletter to hear about our **latest releases, author events,** exciting **competitions** and more at

reddoorpress.co.uk

YOU CAN ALSO FOLLOW US:

@RedDoorBooks

Facebook.com/RedDoorPress

@RedDoorBooks